The Last Voyage

The Last Voyage

The first of the
StarVista 4 Saga

A Science Fiction novel

By Paul Money

Cover artwork (2023):
Principal Designer ASP
Based on ideas by Paul Money

@ Mary McIntyre

Shutterstock.com
@ Catmando
@ Andreiuc88
@ Dave Wetzel

The Last Voyage of the StarVista 4

Copyright Notice

Astrospace Publications
18 College Park, Horncastle, Lincolnshire LN9 6RE
www.astrospace.co.uk

Copyright © Paul Money
November 2021/March 2023
All rights reserved.

The right of Paul Money to be identified as the author of this work has been asserted by him in accordance with the Copyright, Designs and Patents Act 1988 (UK).

All the characters in the story are fictional and any resemblance to real persons either living or dead is purely coincidental.

No part of this novel may be reproduced in any form other than that which it was purchased and without the written permission of the author.

This novel is licensed for your personal enjoyment only and may not be re-sold or given away to other people in either this or any other format.

Language: UK English

Acknowledgements

The author would like to acknowledge the support and help of his wife, Lorraine who patiently listened to the idea and subsequent development of this Sci Fi novel and gave invaluable advice, encouragement and editing ideas as the story evolved.

He would also like to thank the following for their advice, informed opinion and wisdom as this novel took shape.

Gill Hart
Julian Onions
Mary McIntyre
Peter Rea
Peter Williamson

The Last Voyage of the StarVista 4

Preface

The StarVista 4 luxury passenger space cruiser:

A Voyage of a lifetime.
　　The diary and adventures of an eight-year-old passenger.
　　Stunning encounters with fabulous interstellar destinations.
　　Sabotage.
An unexpected addition to the itinerary.
　　The mysterious ringed gas giant planet Tianca in the hardly explored Cantrara system.
　　A 100 year old mystery in the making…
　　　　and an old foe re-emerging from exile…

Prologue

2481 AC
The Hansone family home

Freckle faced, he lay there and casually flicked through the hundreds of vid channels, bored out of his mind. The holoscreen flashed through the choices in quick succession as the twelve-year-old sighed. Andrew J Hansone had been quarantined much to his chagrin, all down to Missy Smart Pants, his older sister Carla to be precise, contracting a rare and almost unheard of in their time, case of mumps.

You know, the sort of thing that medical science had eradicated centuries earlier yet every now and then somehow, someone thought better of the advised wisdom and didn't take precautions. Now one third of the group that had visited Saldayas Six on the school trip were down with the condition and all were under quarantine until the medication had cleared their systems and got them back to full health.

He sighed again. He felt a little drowsy but then one channel offered something that caught his eye, a docudrama about the mystery of the StarVista 4.

He paused play, then backed it up to the start as his interest was piqued. He had vague memories of something about a star ship full of passengers which vanished but the overwhelming consensus was that it had just been an awful accident and the ship had crashed with the loss of all aboard.

The Last Voyage of the StarVista 4

What the heck, he was bored and this, good grief, almost a two-hour, docudrama was the only thing that had caught his eye. He settled down to watch with the sinking feeling they would probably spin out some yarn about mysterious occurrences, sightings and then at the end conclude it had indeed crashed and there was no mystery. Well, he had plenty of time to waste so he flicked his finger at the holoscreen and it began to play ...

...the Last voyage of the StarVista 4...

The Last Voyage of the StarVista 4

Part I

2405 AC
Cherice's Voyage diary

Days are numbers... (Watch the Stars)

Messages and diary of my adventures on the StarVista Four voyage, to my brother Daniel

by Cherice Richmond
Aged 8 (and 1 month)

Day 1: Embarkation

They were the first to board, well ahead of the other passengers.

Put it down to privilege and an acknowledgement of their, soon to be confirmed, status. Cherice Richmond looked around with wide eyes as she and her parents, Natalie and Carl, stepped out through the docking port and the steward, a tall, pale sea green skinned, Atrician greeted them.

"Welcome ambassadors, the captain asked me to greet you and ensure things are in order for your voyage on the StarVista 4. May I just activate your biocoms so that the ships medical team can ensure you have a healthy and enjoyable stay whilst on board?"

"Indeed, go ahead, we knew the bio implants had not been activated and wondered how soon it would be. Now we know." replied Natalie as Carl took Cherice gently by the hand knowing his little girl was wary of this new, and possibly scary, aspect of her life. Cherice looked into his eyes with just a hint of trepidation. Carl smiled warmly at her and spoke in a warm and calming tone.

"Now my poppet, we discussed this and there is nothing to worry about, it's painless ..." He shot a quick glance at the Atrician who quickly realised his meaning and did the best, broadest smile she could, to reassure the little girl.

That was a big mistake for, as anyone who has met an Atrician will know, their so-called smile looked more like a terrifying apparition due to their oddly shaped chin and vertical slit eyes, all three of them.

So, there was no wonder that Cherice shrank back with a wild frightened look about her and Carl quickly changed tack.

"Guess what Cherice, this is their funny face, imagine what they must look like when they're serious?" Carl again shot a glance at the Atrician who picked up on what Carl was doing and carefully nodded her head in a slightly comical way, enough to make Cherice smile and chuckle at the sight. Before she knew it the Atrician waved a small gadget over her and Cherice felt nothing at all as the Atrician studied the display and smiled again.

"I thank you all, biocoms are now active. If any of you get into difficulty, clench your fists tightly and this will send an alert to security for them to be able to home in on you. Once you are settled in your cabin the ship's medical team will signal you to confirm all is in order. The captain has assigned a personal steward to you, I expect they will be along shortly to escort you to your cabin. If you follow the orange line illuminated on the far wall, it will guide you in the right direction if you wish to make your own way and meet them."

The Atrician turned to go back through the docking port but Natalie gently held her back.

"Are you not on the voyage then?"

"Oh no. We Atricians are quite happy to help at our star port, but for us long voyages are not good for our well-being. No one yet knows why we don't fare well on such voyages. For many of what I think you call centuries we didn't venture too far from our system.

It is said there are very few of us that have undertaken such a voyage as you are about to embark upon. I do hope you have an enjoyable cruise amongst the stars and I look forward to perhaps seeing you another time if you visit star port Atricia. Farewell."

She turned and seemingly slid away, not surprising as she only had a single leg-cum-foot and for a moment Carl wondered if the Atrician had ever seen a Terran snail or slug. He decided not to mention it to the departing alien for fear of upsetting her. Well, he and Natalie were now ambassadors, or rather they would be once the official confirmation came through. All had effectively been signed and sealed, otherwise they would not be on this family trip.

Family.

It was such a shame that their oldest child, Daniel, was unable to come with them due to his university studies. Natalie had done a sneaky check with the university just to make sure Danny wasn't just getting out of the trip so he could both study and party. They had indeed confirmed there was a rigorous policy in place which meant students could not skip out of their studies even under the best of excuses.

Something to do with ensuring their students were serious about their future and their studies. Suddenly Carl and Natalie noticed the Atrician had stopped and was coming back to them.

"I am very sorry that I failed to report that your eleven items of baggage are already on board and in your room. My apologies for the error."

Natalie smiled and thanked the Atrician who departed quite quickly, just as she realised none of them had asked for the Atricians name. She turned to Carl and was about to say something to that effect when she saw the puzzled look on his face.

She gave him a quizzical look tilting her head to the right, something which always caught his attention and was quite endearing, in Carl's opinion.

"What is it love?" she asked.

"I could have sworn there were twelve, not eleven." he said in a thoughtful manner. Natalie shrugged.

"We did seem to pack a lot of things... I'm sure we didn't leave anything behind. Someone would have the paperwork to scan and clear them; I bet we'll find all of them in our room and it's just a slip of, well whatever the Atrician has for a tongue." She turned to ask Cherice and her faced turned to horror. "CARL! Where is Cherice?"

They frantically looked around but there was no sign of their eight-year-old bundle of mischief...

#

She was bored already! Cherice had become fed up waiting whilst her parents were discussing things with the tall Atrician.

The Last Voyage of the StarVista 4

She realised she didn't know the Atricians name but it was too late now and she had decided to explore ahead of her parents. What could possibly go wrong? They were the first of the privileged passengers to board. To Cherice that surely meant she would be safe as there was no one else aboard. That was her logic and she was sticking to it.

So, undaunted, she had decided to head off in the direction the alien had suggested and follow the orange line on the wall.

It reminded her of a very, very, very old song her father had once chanced upon when she was younger and he was trying to find something to help soothe her after a nightmare. Something to do with a yellow road made out of bricks. Silly as no one used bricks anymore and she had to confess she had no idea what a brick was anyway!

She dismissed the memory, shook her head of mousy coloured curly hair and wandered round a bend in the corridor as she dutifully followed the orange line glowing gently on the wall. That made her feel safe and as she walked, she noticed the floor was quite smooth.

Very smooth indeed.

She couldn't help herself, but as the corridor seemed very long with no one in sight she ran as fast as she could, then turned sideways and slid on the floor for several metres. She giggled and ran a bit further along, turned and repeated the feat as she began to laugh.

She turned and began to run again looking up too late to stop herself crashing into an alien who towered above her.

It scooped her up and swung her round, effectively stopping her and gently set her down on the floor as she tried to hold down her fear.

Cherice guiltily looked slowly up at the alien and then lowered her head.

"S-sorry." Somehow the word slipped out of her in a hushed deferential tone.

She felt alone and a little frightened as she realised her parents had still not caught up with her. Then it struck her, she was alone, with an alien looking down at her.

It was almost as tall as the Atrician, but was definitely a different type of alien. She struggled to remember the major races that populated the Galactic Arm Association and which it might be standing before her.

It spoke.

"Ahh, you must be the little humarling I have been assigned to?"

"Humerwhataling?" she tentatively asked in a quiet and nervous voice.

"Cherice Richmond, femal youngest humarling of Natalie and Carl Richmond, soon to become the newest Terran ambassadors to Zianca.

Pleasure to meet you. I am your assigned steward for the voyage. I am Alteran and my human form name is Lariq. How doing do you?"

Cherice giggled a little. "I'm female not femal and it's, how do you do?" and she did a little curtsey at which Lariq appeared bemused.

"How do you do what?" Lariq asked whilst curtsying back and Cherice just shook her head then wondered as she looked at the Alteran.

"Are you a boy or girl Alteran?"

"CHERICE! What a question to ask of a stranger!" Natalie and Carl caught up with the odd pair and Cherice looked sheepishly into her mother's questioning eyes.

"But Lariq, well, I don't know, well, err, sorry Lariq."

"There is nothing to worry about humarling Cherice. Ambassadors, I am Lariq, your steward for the voyage ahead. For your, clarification, little humarling, Alterans begin life as, how shall we say, not boy or girl, but neutral.

Once we reach a mature age we become female. I am now in the third and last stage of my life and so I am now what you would call the male of the species." Lariq smiled down at her and Cherice knew in an instant they would be friends.

"Wow, that's, that's really neat!" Cherice exclaimed as she turned to her parents, who were by now quite amused and had recognised the lapel badge on Lariq's top left shoulder confirming his statement. Cherice wasn't quite finished.

"Daddy, will I turn male when I'm older and why hasn't Mummy done it yet!" She made out she didn't quite understand why, despite the fact she really knew the answer. Her parents, and indeed Lariq, began to laugh. Natalie, recovered her composure first.

"We're human, my dear Cherice, so we don't do that. We stay as one, er, gender, all our lives, but some do choose to change if they wish. It's complicated, and best left for another time."

The Last Voyage of the StarVista 4

She was reluctant to mention the word sex, even though she was aware that Cherice was pretty advanced in her knowledge for an eight-year-old and the topic had been broached a few times both through her studies and why Cherice was different to her brother!

Carl shook his head as he smiled at Lariq.

"Pleased to meet you Lariq, may we proceed to our cabin now before our little girl gets even more ideas into her head?" Lariq smiled, turned and led them away as he came to the conclusion, he would like this human grouping.

#

She stood in line waiting her turn, but finally Sicanrinka Tavaska presented her credentials to the boarding officer, an Alteran who checked them, then presented the biocomms implanter. Sicanrinka winced slightly as it was applied.

"Everything is in order Miss Sicanrinka, your biocomms is now active and will monitor your health and well-being whilst you are aboard the StarVista 4 and when you undertake any of the planned excursions. Your cabin is C2001 and if you follow the blinking red marker now showing ahead of you on the wall then you are free to board.

Enjoy your voyage with us on the StarVista 4. In your cabin you will find plenty of information at your disposal about the protocols for the voyage, especially as I see you are with the Haverian news guild.

The Last Voyage of the StarVista 4

May I assume you are on holiday, considering this is a standard cruise, to see many of the wonders of the GAA?

"Yes, indeed. I look forward to spending eight months aboard this metal hulk." she replied a little sarcastically.

The officer noted her attitude but declined to say anything. The passengers were always correct, or so they were trained to believe. The staff knew otherwise but always maintained the highest standard and never questioned their passengers when they were clearly wrong, or downright ignorant!

"Travelling light?" asked the Alteran as she noted only one item of luggage listed for the passenger.

"Always." came the curt reply as Sicanrinka strode away and began to follow the indicated red markers on the wall.

Almalcil cal-Letur shook her head as only an Alteran could and turned to the next set of passengers, a group of short stature humanoids knows as Traxz who were clearly excited about the voyage.

'Now this is more like the right attitude' thought Almalcil as she happily engaged with the group and all thoughts of the odd passenger evaporated as she busied herself with the scanning and checking the biocoms implants.

Finally reaching cabin C2001, Sicanrinka threw her one item of luggage on the bed and surveyed the room.

The Last Voyage of the StarVista 4

Her thoughts turned to the sheer hell of having to put up with her current form until they reached Viliak Spaceport Shalaiq, the last stop of the voyage. It was still the quickest way to get her back home, or at least to the star port where she would have to commandeer, or even steal, a ship to make the final journey in secret to the Cantrara system.

From there she would be able to rendezvous with the construction/support ship which was due to return to their home system via the gateway hidden amongst the so-called rings of the gas giant planet Tianca.

She carefully checked the room for surveillance systems but was satisfied that only the biocomms medical chip was active, so she opened up her luggage and prepped the duplicator. She'd have to wear it for at least a few weeks as it gathered data before she attempted to remove the biocomms implant and keep it safe, relaying a false set of data so that she could go about the ship unhindered.

It was going to be a long voyage but after years of undercover surveillance for her superiors in preparation for their eventual seizure of the ignorant and despised Galactic Arm Association, at last she was going home…

Ambassadors suite and departure

"Hi Danny, well we're here and this is my room." Cherice slowly panned the holovid recorder around to show off the suite her family had been allocated. *"Mummy and Daddy said I should send you these messages when something interesting happens although I know it will take several days to reach you, even with hyper messaging.*

I wish you could have taken time out from university to come with us, big brother. It sounds really, really, exciting and I've already found out I am the youngest ever to be allowed on board. Something to do with Mummy and Daddy and a promotion but I know they both wish you could be with us as well as it is so special." Cherice looked round and sure enough her mother, Natalie, stood behind her and smiled.

Cherice was quite mature for an eight year old human, with only the occasional slip to indicate her age. It was this quality that had convinced the powers in charge of the mighty StarVista fleet of luxury space liners to give her parents special permission, when they had been promoted to full time Earth Ambassadors to the Ziancan civilisation.

The promotions did mean however, that the family would have to relocate to the Ziancan home world for what was probably at least a decade in human terms. Hence the Richmond family had been given special status when her father had asked to take the family for one last major outing before taking up their duties.

Well, almost all the family.

The Last Voyage of the StarVista 4

Natalie was a little annoyed that the university Daniel was attending had not considered the unusual circumstances but neither she nor Carl had the clout to make them change their minds.

Cherice held up the fancy holosheet with details of the voyage and began to quote from it in a quirky, official like tone.

"The latest voyage of the StarVista 4 interstellar star liner will take in a minimum of eighteen magnificent destinations. Each having been chosen with something stunning to offer the curious space traveller. The journey of a lifetime will take eight months to complete." She stopped reading and looked directly into the holorecorder with disdain raising her eyebrows and pulling a face at the length of the upcoming voyage.

"We boarded, or rather Daddy called it 'embarked', at the Alteran Star Port Atricia which, according to this sheet, will take place smoothly, hah! Well as smoothly as it could with two thousand passengers and the ship's compliment of seven hundred highly dedicated crew, who will make it seem easy and relaxing." She finished off with a hint of sarcasm in her tone.

Natalie again smiled, nodded, winked at her then left Cherice's bedroom to give her daughter a bit of privacy whilst she recorded her message for her brother. As the door closed and Cherice was finally alone, her face changed.

"Oh good! Mummy's gone now, I'm already BORED! I've been told that I can't go anywhere on my own so have to always be with Mummy and Daddy. They promised me it would be fun! I want to explore everywhere! Instead I have to go with them to everything they want to see." She pouted her lips then continued.

"Oh well, sorry to sound like a meanie but once we were in our cabin and Mummy and Daddy had gone through the luggage, they found there was one case missing - it was my TOYS! They'd allowed me to bring some aboard as the voyage is so long, but it's been lost! Mummy is trying to find out what is being done about it but we will soon be leaving the star port so there is not much time.

I hope they manage to find my lost case of toys and games. That's why I feel like crying. It seems the baggage handlers mistook an add on pack as a separate item as it had come undone and that's why they thought they had all twelve bags. Huh!"

She paused as if listening. *"Oh, I can hear Mummy calling. Must be time to eat. I hope it's something good and not that Ziancan salad thingy that they tried to get me to eat two days ago. Yuk! I hope they have lasagne on this ship!*
Got to go but hope you are OK and I miss you already.
Byeeee"

She put the recorder down but left it uploading the message to the ship's core communications hub as she skipped out of the room to see what her mother wanted. As Cherice entered the living area, Natalie smiled and beckoned her to come over to where Carl stood checking the ship's manifest.

"There's about to be the official welcome announcement so sit here with me and watch and listen, OK my love?"

"Yes Mummy, it won't be long and boring, will it?"

The Last Voyage of the StarVista 4

Natalie shook her head, uncertain, as Carl came over to them just as a light pinging sound indicated everyone should pay attention to the holoscreen.

It was going to be a special announcement for one of them.

"Attention all passengers. I am First Officer Graylor zXanders and on behalf of Captain Xaoping Shoo and the StarVista corporation, welcome aboard the StarVista 4. We hope you find your accommodation to your satisfaction. Please contact your assigned steward for help and any enquiries regarding your stay with us on this voyage amongst the stars. Information is located on your consoles in each room for your convenience.

Details of the StarVista 4 passenger access areas including the various amenities, observation decks, pleasure activities, amphitheatre, nourishment and refreshment areas can also be accessed from the consoles and information booths throughout the ship.

Note that for your safety certain sections of the ship are off limits to passengers so that the crew can perform their duties to the highest efficiency. We are sure you will enjoy being with us for the duration of the voyage.

In one standard time interval please make your way to the observation decks on the docked side to view our departure from Star Port Atricia as we begin our voyage of discovery and adventure. Everyone on board is classed as a VIP, however we are honoured on this voyage to have as our guests the newly appointed Terran ambassadors to the Ziancan civilisation, Natalie and Carl Richmond.

We would also like you all to extend a very warm welcome to their eight year old daughter, Cherice, who is the youngest person ever to be allowed on such a long pleasure voyage. We hope you will all make her especially welcome and help her enjoy this amazing voyage of discovery."

At the mention of her name, Cherice was open mouthed and wide eyed, for once, lost for words as Natalie and Carl stifled their amusement at her reaction.

First officer Graylor zXanders continued.

"For our departure, our captain has decreed everyone is entitled to a free drink to celebrate the start of our journey and on behalf of the captain, myself and the crew, we hope you have a great stay with us on this magnificent Star Cruiser." Graylor zXanders holo image faded from view as Cherice looked at her parents in astonishment and wonder.

"Wow, they mentioned ME!!! Does that make me famous?"

Carl smiled at his daughter. "I guess so. We did have to jump through many hoops to get them to allow you on the voyage. For such a long trip it is usually thought too much for many youngsters of most of the GAA civilisations. But let us just say that your mother and I can be quite persuasive." He could see Cherice was thinking hard about something else and looked at her quizzically.

"I am not sure but is that person we just saw a Gu-Alt?" Cherice asked hesitantly. Natalie thought for a moment before replying.

"No, I think there are two species that look similar and share a common distant ancestor. I think they are actually a Krelti.

The Last Voyage of the StarVista 4

It also explains what I think you are about to ask. Yes, they do look like a Terran Octopus but are much stronger and must have evolved away from their oceans a very long time ago as they are equally at home on dry land."

"And indeed in space as I have heard both species are quite at ease in their own versions of a spacesuit and enjoy being outside in the vacuum of space." added Carl. "Anyway, we ought to head off to the nearest observation deck ready for departure," he indicated to the door and they set off for Observation Deck B.

#

She had been led by the hand back along the original walkway until they took a new turning where the corridor opened wider. On one side was a travelator, a moving walkway which had a section that, once you stood on it facing the direction you wished to travel, would be activated. In turn they merged with the main travelator joining the many other passengers that were now on board as they all headed to the observation deck.

Cherice was becoming a little unnerved, however, as some of the passengers had begun to point at her and in most cases wave with whatever appendage was the equivalent of a hand for their respective species.

"It's okay poppet, they know you are the very special guest so you will have to get used to it. I suspect you will be quite popular." Carl said as he felt Cherice's hand grip his harder.

She didn't reply but tried to relax and smiled at anyone who seemed to wave at her or do their version of a smile on seeing her.

A short while later, close to their destination, a group of relatively short stature humanoids joined the travelator and stood next to the family, smiling and nodding at Cherice. One of them spoke in a very broken form of terran.

"We like, hello you little. Stand holoscreen?" Cherice looked up at her mother then at the alien, perplexed.

They tweaked something behind their antenna like ears then tried again. "We are like you, little. You are famous passenger. Can we take holoscreen image of us together?" Cherice giggled and nodded; the group looked so ecstatic she wondered if they would fall off the travelator. They gathered round her as Carl and Natalie shrugged and stepped to one side as the leader of the group activated the holoscreen, struggling to get in the image.

Carl stepped closer and indicated he would take the image. The group broke out in excited chatter in their own language, which for some reason did not translate, but it was clear they were very happy for him to take their image with Cherice.

The deed done the group individually made little bows to Cherice, then to Natalie and Carl in turn, before again resuming their original place on the travelator, excitedly talking amongst themselves.

Natalie bent down and whispered into Cherice's ear.

"Best get used to that, you're a star now. Make sure however that we are always with you, OK?"

"Yes Mummy, but that was really odd. I hope there are not many like that."

"There could well be. At least the Traxz were friendly and quite civil about it." Natalie smiled at Cherice to reassure her.

"Traxz?" Cherice had not heard of this group before.

"They are from the far side of our part of the Galactic Arm. They've come a long way already for this trip. As our voyage gets underway we will be arranging schooling for you so you can research all the species that are on the voyage. When we get back and you begin school on Zianca you can give a good account of what you will have seen and experienced," said Carl as he noted they would soon be at their destination.

Little did Cherice know how important building such a rapport, and knowledge of, the other passengers would become in the not-too-distant future.

Two couples, one of them humans from Mars, had their pictures taken with Cherice before they all reached Observation Deck B ready for departure and she decided to keep close to her parents. The attention was still a little disturbing to her.

#

The Last Voyage of the StarVista 4

"Passengers of the StarVista 4, prepare for departure from Star Port Atricia." boomed Graylor zXanders voice that seemed to emanate from all around them. Another voice then filled the air.

"StarVista 4, Atricia Star Port Docking Authority here, docking ports and system support latchings retracting. You are cleared for departure. Safe voyage and we will see you back here in a little over a terran year from now."

"Thank you. Support structures and docking ports confirmed clean separation. StarVista 4 is clear and Helmspilot Delieezas is cleared to begin departure sequence. See you on the other side Atricia and thank you for your wonderful facilities. StarVista 4, out." replied xZanders.

Cherice looked up at her mother questioningly.

"What do they mean, see you on the other side? Other side of what?" she asked.

"It's a traditional saying, it means they will see them again after the voyage."

"Then why didn't they say that instead?"

"Tradition, it's tradition." replied Natalie as she smiled at the way her daughter always got straight to the heart of something.

Silently the docking port embarkation extensions slid away and into the side of the vast star port and for a short while nothing seemed to be happening. Then, slowly, majestically, the vast ship began to drift away from the star port, building momentum, making the huge star port appear to shrink away from them with increasing speed.

As it did so, the planet it was orbiting began to emerge from behind the star port; its multi-hued banded appearance showed it was a massive gas giant planet. Huge powerful storms raged in its northern hemisphere, whilst a string of alternating dark and light ovals marked a zone close to a large jet stream, with swirls of gas appearing to gently move across the view. Carl bent down and whispered into Cherice's ear.

"That's Auriliain, the largest planet in this system. Those ovals are almost the size of our Jupiter's famous great red spot, before it shrank to nothing. The Alterans and Atricians have special space stations that gather the energy up to power large parts of their primary worlds. Amazing don't you think?"

"Suppose so. I'm confused, why are there two species?"

"What? Alteran and Atrician you mean?"

"Yes, why two for one system? One is greenish, tall with one sort of leg, the other like Lariq, is pinkish and also tall with two legs."

"Ahh, they are called symbiotic. Neither can survive in the long term without the other species. They used to war between themselves many thousands of our years ago, until both sides were almost extinct. Then it finally dawned on them that they were effectively killing themselves.

The Atricians were under surface dwellers for a large part of their existence and so for them travelling out into space is one of the most terrifying things any of them can do. So they are happy to remain where they are and let the Alterans venture out to the stars instead.

Most Atricians only ever venture as far as the orbiting stations in their system and as far as I know there are only a handful that have travelled around the primary GAA systems." Carl said with a lowered voice, almost in deference to the two species, although there were no Atricians on board as far as he was aware and there were no Alterans anywhere near them. Lariq had told them he was busy, about his other duties.

"I think that it is sad the Atricians don't travel like we do, think of what they are missing …" ventured Natalie.

Cherice nodded thoughtfully as Star Port Atricia became little more than a bright 'star', almost lost against the bright gaseous planet, Auriliain. Three moons of varying size quickly came into view, but in turn became like stars as the ship drew further away and Auriliain began to shrink to nothing but a point of light as the voice of the first officer once again came to life.

"Passengers of the StarVista 4, you may have noticed from the almost full phase of the large gas giant Auriliain, that the Alteran home star was on the port side of our ship. As we follow our pre determined flight path out of the system we will be rotating to face towards Altaria, which is a G5 type star. We will be heading for a gravity assist by flying under the star at a safe distance of four million Terran kilometres to send us up out of the plane of the galactic arm.

Our initial course allows us to loop up, then back down to our first official destination in the Anchi system, so that we don't have to negotiate the busy interstellar highways which would slow us down.

The Last Voyage of the StarVista 4

During the first few days of our flight we will be undertaking the mandatory safety drills as the StarVista corporation takes your safety in our care very seriously. We ask you cooperate to your fullest in the coming days. In the next five hours we will be approaching Alteria and if you wish to view spectacular close-ups of this energetic star then please feel free to do so from the upper observation decks in complete safety as the ship is fully screened from all types of harmful radiation.

The Alteria solar monitors are showing moderate activity with several large prominences potentially viewable as we leave the star behind, so please do enjoy the view. Our own on-board monitors will also be tracking activity on the lookout for additional flare activity as an extra precaution. Information booths in your rooms and on the observation decks will provide advice on how to view in the full range of spectral frequencies for your additional enjoyment. First Officer xZanders, out."

The StarVista 4 continued to accelerate, gradually adjusting course, swooping under, then up and away from Alteria as it headed out of the Alteran system.

Their voyage had truly begun.

Day 5: Bored, toy-less and a safety drill

Cherice sat down heavily on the seat and, as she set up the recorder, tried to put on a smile despite how she felt. She composed herself then did a quick gesture in front of the recorder which began working after a short delay.

"Hi Danny, sorry I haven't sent anything up until now but it is soooo boring that there wasn't anything to say. They lost my toy case, apparently it has been traced heading back to Earth for some reason and Daddy is trying to get someone important to have it rerouted to our next stop.

Mummy says that I shouldn't get my hopes up. Mummy is doing her best to help me with my off-world studies and she has managed to find a few things to play with, but as you know they don't normally have children on these sort of long duration cruises so there is little on board physically to help.

It won't be long before we get to our first destination of interest, the Rainbow Star of Anchi so, if you like, I will get some holo pics and send them to you. I wish I had someone to play with though, I do feel lonely at times and I know Mummy and Daddy are doing their best. Apparently, everyone thinks I am a very good girl. How boring is that?

I'll be in touch after we've visited Anchi.
Byeee."

Cherice sat and looked around her room as the recorder sent the message. She knew that she was lucky really to be on the ship but it still didn't help that her toys and games were lost somewhere on the inter spatial highways.

She wandered over to her comfy chair next to her bed, plopped down in it contemplating what to do next. The door slid open and her father stepped in.

"Now then, here you are. I thought you were going to come and join me?"

"But Daddy I'm bored. I want my toys! I want to explore but I'm stuck here and I don't like it." She sat looking quite miserable and Carl had to feel sorry for his daughter. It had been quite a discussion Natalie and he had had when the promotion was offered.

There had been no disagreement about taking it, after all it was one of the most prestigious offers any ambassador could hope for. But they knew it would have an impact on Cherice.

She would be spending the best part of the next ten years on the Ziancan home world and would have to form new friendships with the young Ziancans. She had, he was pleased to note, started trying to learn the language so that she could fit in, even though she'd had her personal translator inserted close to the cochlea in both ears for several months now to acclimatise to them.

Pretty much everyone of the GAA had the implants so in most cases translation was instantaneous, but it was possible to turn them off if needed, if you wanted to 'go native'.

He sighed and took her hand as she stood up and reluctantly headed out into the reception room of their lavish suite.

"Come on, someone wants to meet you." he said and she frowned, wondering who would want to do that. Then she remembered that so far in just five days, she'd been approached by over a dozen different groups, all wanting their picture taken with her and she sighed, hoping for once it wasn't going to be like that again.

#

"DANNY!!!" She shouted in glee.

Of course, he wasn't actually *in* the room, but by special arrangement with Captain Xaoping Shoo, Natalie and Carl had managed to arrange a very expensive two way holographic link up with their son.

Cherice had been very down since they had discovered it was her case full of toys and games that had gone missing. So, with the captain's permission, the holographic link had been established with the university where Danny was studying. Now he and his girlfriend stood looking at the assembled small group in almost real time with just a tiny delay between conversations. The advantage of the position of being the newly appointed ambassadors to Zianca.

"Hi Sis, how's it going then?" Danny beamed at her, whilst his girlfriend, Carrie, stood to one side looking as if she'd rather be somewhere else.

"It's a big ship! There are lots of other species aboard and sometimes I get a bit frightened when they come up and want their picture taken with me, but I'm getting used to it. I'm just *sooo* bored at times as my toy case is still lost."

The Last Voyage of the StarVista 4

Cherice's expression changed to one of sadness as she recalled that all her favourite things were in that one, lonely piece of lost baggage.

A brief flicker of a smile passed over her face as she wondered if her case was having more of an adventure than she was.

"Yes, I heard from mom and dad. I'm sure someone will find it and send it on to your next stop. I gather that it takes quite a while to reach the first of your official destinations, Anchi isn't it?" Danny tried to change the subject so his little sister wouldn't get too maudlin.

Carrie absentmindedly scratched her neck and tried to smile, but it was clear she would rather be somewhere else. Not very supportive, Cherice thought to herself and ignored her.

"Sounds an interesting place but we have the final safety drills and test emergency evacuations in the lifepods before then. If the captain isn't satisfied that all is well and everyone knows what to do then she could cancel the trip. Perhaps if I misbeha…"

"*Don't you even think about it young lady*, your mother and I would be horrified if the trip of a lifetime was cancelled due to you missing your toys and games." Carl interrupted her and Danny chuckled as Cherice dropped her head a little.

"As if I would do *that*… Anyway Mummy and Daddy want to have a chat to you both so I'll say bye to you. Hope you are OK Carrie?"

Carrie was caught a little off guard at the sound of her name being mentioned.

"Ah, yes, yes, and I hope your trip is going well and you are enjoying it." She'd clearly not been paying attention and even Danny turned to her with a slight scowl on his face. He turned back to Cherice.

"Bye Sis, don't torment mom and dad too much now will you?" he said as he began to wave goodbye to her.

"Me? Not much, I promise. Byeee." Cherice waved at him then stepped away from the holographic monitoring zone. From Danny's perspective she just stepped out of view and now his parents came on just as Carrie also stepped away.

He rolled his eyes in exasperation but kept his cool as he put a smile back on for them. He knew his parents were not really happy with his choice of girlfriend but it was up to him he thought as he composed himself ready for them.
Meanwhile Cherice saw her mother nod to her that she could go back to her own room and she happily skipped away but with just thing on her mind.

It was going to be a very long trip indeed.

#

"I thought we would have been first to do this."

Cherice pouted her lips in annoyance as she stood impatiently with her parents, along with another couple, two Ziancans, siblings apparently. Lariq was also with them as they now stood next to their allocated emergency escape pod having completed the safety drill and flight.

"Each pod is self-contained and can carry up to eight passengers of any species in comfort, able to support them for twelve weeks, far longer than is required as there is a star port always within a maximum time of just two weeks away to effect rescue.

Do you all know why all ships have to have very stringent safety measures?" Lariq looked around the small group and one of the Ziancans spoke up.

"The Qincieta incident?"

"Exactly!" replied Lariq. Carl and Natalie smiled knowingly but they could see Lariq was eager to tell the story and without hesitation, he did just that...

"It happened almost eight hundred of your human years ago, in Ziancan terms, era seventy-one. The Qincieta was a large cargo and passenger transporter ferrying materials, cargo of all sorts and around six hundred fee paying passengers en route from Scorios five to the Krelti outer colony planet whose name I can't begin to translate!

It was a three terran week journey, ordinary, nothing exceptional about it - the, how you say, run of the millr journey done several times per terran year." Lariq saw Natalie stifle a chuckle.

"Run of the mill, that's what you meant." she quietly said and Lariq waved and nodded gratefully.

"Ahh, yes, our translators don't always pick up on all the nuances of all our languages, my mistake. Where was I? Oh yes, except this one would change everything.

The Last Voyage of the StarVista 4

Regulations had become slack and emergency procedures were often overlooked in order to cut down on bureaucracy and time between flights.

It was also before interstellar ships could provide almost real time engineering data to the nearest star port, before Hyperwave manipulation technology had been developed. The Qincieta was almost a week into their flight when it developed a serious fault.

One that rendered its main propulsion drives inoperable and knocked out its navigation stabilisation micro drives, so it just coasted along its original path. With no means of stopping or avoiding potential hazards they were helpless but considering their flight path was pretty well known then there appeared to be little to cause alarm and the captain and crew worked at solving the problem.

What they didn't know, was that one set of starboard trajectory thrusters used for fine adjustments when on slow approach to a docking port, were stuck in firing mode but at a low almost undetectable level. However, it was enough over time to subtly change their course and over the next few weeks the Qincieta deviated from their initial flight path. Now as anyone who's studied Hyperdynamic space flight will tell you, interstellar ships used to rely on picking up the homing beacons from the next port on their journey in closest proximity and if there was a slight discrepancy, they could easily adjust for it.

What they didn't know was, they were by now well-off course and unable to pick up the location beacon, so they coasted along helpless.

The Last Voyage of the StarVista 4

Now you would think that they would send out a Mayday distress call. But they couldn't because in those far off times the power for the long-range comms was routed through, and depended on, the main drives, which of course were malfunctioning and unable to operate."

"But..."asked Carl, "how did this result in such stringent safety routines and measures?"

"They were so far off course that they entered a dangerous and normally off-limits zone close to a neutron star. They began to feel the gravitational effects of the neutron star, and one of the bulkheads popped, so the captain, fearing the worst, ordered abandon ship. But at that time, they had quite simple escape pods that had no flight capability of their own.

A third of the pods launched got caught in the neutron stars strong gravity, and were sucked in and perished, whilst the rest were subjected to intense radiation and the occupants too eventually died.

Once rescue ships had managed to locate the Qincieta, they found it had passed the Neutron star system safely after all and if the passengers and crew had stayed aboard, they would have all survived. A large ship is better shielded than the escape pods and they could have gone to the Qincieta's cargo bays for extra protection. But even if the captain had realised her error, the pods couldn't fly back and re-join the ship, so once launched the passengers and crew were doomed from that moment on.

It caused a huge outcry at the time and led to all ships having powered and flight worthy escape pods with mandatory safety drills from then on. The StarVista corporation are very stringent on ensuring all their ships are safe, hence the drills and emergency test evacuations are rigorously done with no exceptions."

Lariq looked pleased with himself with his knowledge of the incident and one of the Ziancans patted him on the arm as they bade him farewell.

Surprisingly, Cherice had hung on to every word that Lariq had uttered.

"Do you know any more stories like that?" she asked inquisitively, forgetting about how bored she had been on the actual safety drill. Natalie and Carl looked at Lariq with the hope in their eyes that he had many more like that which could take Cherice's mind off her lost baggage.

Lariq carefully lowered himself to Cherice's eye level and smiled.

"Yes, indeed, lots more…" as he opened his eyes wide and smiled.

#

The StarVista 4 reached the apex of its flight curve above the galactic arm and slowly began the descent towards its first destination, the Anchi system. As it would still take them another ten days to reach it, at the apex of the flight, Captain Xaoping Shoo announced that the StarVista corporation had given her permission for everyone to enjoy a one-hour shuttle flight for free.

The Last Voyage of the StarVista 4

It would allow everyone to enjoy the emptiness of space, whilst taking in the view of the disk of the Milky Way from such a high vantage point, without the bulk of the ship around to detract from the view.

A real chance to experience the solitude of space.

A small number of the passengers decided that was not for them, despite taking a cruise on a star cruiser that spends a large amount of its flight time in the empty depths of space. The irony was not lost on some of the other passengers. Cherice herself also had her misgivings.

She sat in the lounge of their luxurious cabin and tried to look as miserable as she could.

"But Mummy. I don't want to go into space and have the ship leave us floating there on our own."

"Now darling, the captain wouldn't let us if she didn't think it was safe." Natalie had wondered if her little girl would react like this and hoped she could bring her around.

"But you heard Mister Lariq, look what happened to that other ship all those years ago. It might happen to us!"

"Oh no, of course it can't. As Lariq said, modern shuttles and escape pods are flight worthy in their own way and can keep supporting passengers for several weeks. They can fly back to the StarVista 4 any time if needed and the ship won't be that far away.

So you'll be all right, I promise. Just think of what you can tell Danny next time you message him.

Remember, you are the one out here doing all these amazing things and he isn't, so you could say you're one up on him!"

Cherice perked up at that thought and, yes indeed, it would be something good to remind him. As far as she knew, he'd never been out above the plane of the galaxy this far and then left for an hour, so, yes, perhaps it could be a good thing. She was still nervous but now decided it was time to be brave.

They all headed down to the allocated shuttle bay with Lariq and the Ziancan couple Trilac and Zilphan who were technically their neighbours. Lariq had a crew cabin relatively close to their section of the ship too.

Lariq stopped at the entrance to launch bay *B5* and activated his comms.

"I have my group here ready for embarkation."

They all heard a faint reply, then the doors opened and a very smartly dressed, uniformed Alteran greeted them.

"Ahh, Lariq, thank you. I will take over from here and when we get back, I'll alert you to collect them, that's if we get back..." the Alteran said slightly mischievously and Cherice's eyes went wide with fear. Natalie and Carl were about to say something when the Alteran bent over and smiled at Cherice.

"My humour, miss Cherice Richmond. I am Chief Helms-Pilot Delieezas and the captain has asked me to personally look after you on this very special shuttle flight.

The Last Voyage of the StarVista 4

I will not let anything happen to such a special person, indeed such a special group of passengers."

Cherice eyed him up and down.

"You're male then?"

Natalie and Carl did a quick double take, lost for words but Delieezas chuckled and again bent down and whispered in Cherice's ear.

"Yes, but don't tell everyone will you? It's our secret!" He stood up and managed to do a sort of wink of the eye and she knew from that moment on that she could trust Delieezas. She looked up at her parents with a cheeky grin before turning back to Delieezas.

"Can we start then sir?" she asked in an official sounding voice.

"Certainly, follow me." He led them inside the hanger deck as Lariq smiled and left them so he could continue with his other duties.

#

"Danny, Danny, Danny, that was brilliant!!" Cherice excitedly exclaimed as she recorded her latest message. *"We ever so carefully lifted off and left the hanger bay and along with loads of the other shuttles we hung in space with our galaxy below us, then the ship slowly departed and disappeared quickly into the blackness.*

I thought I'd be scared but our pilot is the one who normally flies the StarVista 4 and he was funny and really kind to me. He wouldn't let me sit in his seat though, but I guess that he couldn't really let me do that, so I'll let him off.

The Last Voyage of the StarVista 4

The galaxy below us, well, I've never seen anything like it for real. Lots and lots of tiny pinpricks for stars and in many places great dark clouds.

Delieezas, that's the pilot's name, tells me they are of clouds of interstellar dust that, with some gas he mentioned, might one day form new stars. As we looked, something even more special happened; a sudden star appeared way off in the distance, Delieezas says thousands of light years away and not in the GAA. It was a supernova, I think he said.

"Wow, I really wish you could have been with us to see it! Anyway, almost to the second, the StarVista 4 came back and we quickly docked and that hour seemed to be the fastest hour I've ever known. I hope we get another chance to fly outside the ship again. Hope you are okay and that Carrie isn't being silly like she was when we were able to chat properly the other day. Got to go so will message you after Anchi.

Byeee!"

The Last Voyage of the StarVista 4

Day 17: Rainbow Star of Anchi

The StarVista 4 continued on its way back down into the galactic plane and just a couple of days before the approach to the Anchi system the Hyperdrive was brought back into action. The giant ship slowed enough to resume normal flight along the hyperways and being back on the normal route the ship encountered several large freighters travelling in both directions.

One of those flying in their direction was just out of range to see detail but was a bright speck of light travelling off to the right of the StarVista 4 and Lariq had a surprise for Cherice.

They were on the starboard midlevel observation deck, deck 'C' and Lariq was keying in a special code to the info booth next to the translucent wall that separated them from the cold depths of space.

Cherice knew they were safe but even so she still felt a little unease at how flimsy the wall seemed, despite Lariq's assurances that it was a metre deep and quite safe.

"Here we go. Look at the wall next to us." He began to adjust the wall and that section, only about a metre across, began to show a zoomed in view of the outside.

It was centred on the nearest freighter that was travelling the same direction as the StarVista 4. Cherice gasped as Lariq zoomed even closer and they could easily see lots of detail on the ship.

The forward bulbous section contained the crew and control centres with massive metal girders extending out towards the back of it. Attached was the huge cargo container which had various alien looking symbols and, Cherice presumed, the company name and logo on the side.

"What do you think they have on board?" she asked.

Lariq tapped on the side of the info booth.

"It's the *Aeclinoor* a ship from the *Transiliat Gathering* system of worlds. It carries engineering parts, consumables and colonists to the Anchi system.

I expect the colonists are miners adding to the current workforce at Anchi. They are travelling faster than we can, so will arrive a couple of days ahead of us. We won't be going straight to the mining colony as the prime reason for our visit is to show everyone the unusual rainbow effect caused by the waste material which is directed to spiral in towards the central star, Anchi, where it will be absorbed and destroyed."

"You think there may be people like me on board?"

"No, very doubtful as we are already a long way from the Terran system."

"We call the main planet, Earth."

"That is true but the overall GAA official name is Terra so as a rule that name or variation of it is used for official business."

"Oh. I didn't know that. I was born on the Charon-Pluto orbital outpost and so I've only ever called our main world Earth."

"Ahh, you see, we call the main world of each interstellar species, the Primary World. So, for the GAA, your system is the Terran system and the Primary World is Terra. Have you been to your Earth?"

"Yes, a few times for holidays and a couple of times when I was very young as Mummy and Daddy were doing their jobs. Have you been?"

"No, it is a long way from Alteran and I have such a busy life that I don't go to other systems except when I am working on ships such as this one. Then I get to see lots of places and planets, but Terra, sorry I mean Earth, is not one I've been to. Perhaps one day I will visit but not yet. Have you noticed that the *Aeclinoor* is now a lot further ahead of us?"

"Oh, wow, yes it is. They are in a hurry!" Lariq consulted the display and rocked his head slightly which made Cherice giggle a little before she stopped herself.

"Sorry. That was not nice of me."

"That is no problem. I have to get you back to your parents but you can tell them what you've seen."

Cherice smiled up at this warm and friendly Alteran, took his outstretched hand and together they headed towards the nearest travelator.

#

Meanwhile in the Richmond quarters…

Carl looked at the communiqué and passed it to Natalie who stared at it incredulously.

"So why involve us?" she asked as she frowned at it.

The Last Voyage of the StarVista 4

"I'm not too sure but I do know that we are considered trustworthy. I thought it was too easy to get them to agree to Cherice coming with us. The price they are willing to pay for us being on this particular cruise.

I had asked for the voyage with the StarVista Two as it was a much shorter trip, but they were a little cryptic in declining that one and insisting we take this cruise." Carl replied, his mind wandering over what their superiors had planned for them. Natalie passed the communiqué back to him and he looked at it again:

StarVista 4 itinerary confirmed changed with additional stop added at the end of the cruise.

Final destination classified.

Discover what you can as to the reasons why another distant system has been added but wait until the captain has officially announced the new addition to avoid suspicion.

An agent is being dispatched to join the voyage at Falaise-c-puc Starport and will make themself known to you, if and when required.

Top priority and no further communications on this topic to be undertaken unless new information comes to light.

End.

"Well, all we can do is see what happens and enjoy the voyage as best we can. I do hope it's nothing dangerous, otherwise the Terran authorities will have us to answer to if anything happens to our little girl." said Natalie with her hands on her hips and a serious look about her.

Carl nodded in agreement, then destroyed the instructions.

The Last Voyage of the StarVista 4

#

"Attention all passengers, this is First Officer Graylor xZanders. We are on our final approach to the fabled Rainbow Star of Anchi and will use a spiral orbit to steadily bring us closer to the asteroid belt that causes the phenomena. As we do so Captain Xaoping Shoo has instructed our chief helms pilot to undertake a series of undulating manoeuvres to enhance the rainbow effect which will primarily be on our port side. Please make your way to port observation decks, 'A' through 'E'.

Refreshments will be available from our highly trained staff from the moment the captain signals we have reached our optimal flight path to give you the very best view. Please note that the interior lighting will be dimmed to twenty percent of normal in order to view the unusual effect without compromising your safety.

The StarVista corporation hopes you enjoy our first official stop of the voyage despite there being no star port in this system. However, we have arranged for anyone interested to have a tour of the mining facility on Anchi Seven's moon. Please ensure you have indicated if you wish to partake of this addition to our itinerary so that we can arrange the appropriate number of tours with the GAA Mining Guild. Note there is no additional cost."

On the StarVista 4 command centre bridge, Graylor xZanders appeared to relax once the communication was ended standing to one side of the captain's empty chair. Helms Pilot Delieezas looked at her and smiled.

"Good job. Something I wouldn't want to do, announcements where everyone hangs on your every word."

"Don't you believe for one moment that every single passenger is listening in, Delie.

There's always someone who sleeps through the announcement then is the one asking what are we doing, when will we get there, and usually the most important, when do the bar facilities open!"

"True. I'm still glad it's you who does the announcements!"

"So, idle chatter whilst I'm off the bridge, eh First Officer xZanders!"

Captain Xaoping Shoo had entered the bridge quietly and had been standing for a few moments smiling as she listened to her colleagues. This despite Comms Officer Carson spotting her arrival whereupon she indicated to him not to say anything as she listened in. Carson was one of the few human crew on board as most were either Ziancan, Scorran or Alteran.

Graylor, however, was a Krelti, similar to her own species of Gu-alt, the two species indeed being distantly related. There were just a handful of them on the ship.

Both xZanders and Delieezas stiffened to attention as Xaoping took her command seat.

"Relax you two. Anyone would think I am a terrible nasty captain. By the way Graylor, nice job on the announcements, I know you really enjoy that aspect of your work."

Graylor didn't speak but just shook her head, a human gesture many of them had picked up since Carson had joined the crew, although when Delieezas did it he did look as if he was in excruciating pain.

"Delieezas, report our status?"

The Last Voyage of the StarVista 4

"Yes Captain, on approach and I have configured the flight path to provide what I hope is the best view for the passengers."

"Don't hope, *make sure of it!* We have two thousand passengers and I don't want any complaints that we're too far away or that it wasn't what was in the brochures."

"Yes Captain." Delieezas went back to looking at his console and began to simulate various flight paths on approach to, and in the plane of, the Anchi system.

#

It was indeed spectacular. The StarVista 4 settled into what in effect was an orbit around the star Anchi at a distance of three hundred and eighty million km. At that distance most of the planets in the system lay inside their orbit and they were only five million km from Anchi 7 and the mining colony. The gas giant planet, three times larger than Jupiter in the Terran home system lay off to the right almost ahead of the ship and looked almost like a half planet due to the phase angle between it, the ship and Anchi.

As Delieezas piloted the StarVista 4 into the plane of the planetary system the fine diamond dust created a faint but hazy patch of light, reminiscent of the zodiacal light seen from Earth. However, once level with the disk of material it darkened until as they became lined up with the central plane of the dust, it hid the Anchi star, creating a series of optical effects in a halo centred on where the star should be.

Then as Delieezas slowly adjusted their orbital inclination the light scattering off the fine particles began to glisten and suddenly erupted into the most fabulous colours imaginable.
`Fleeting patterns rippled out from the display to gasps and indeed shouts of delight from the assembled passengers. As the command crew listened in to the observation decks, Captain Xaoping Shoo nodded and smiled at Delieezas.

"Good job Delie, great start to our official engagements, so we have a lot to live up to now. Keep us like this for the next fourteen hours then Graylor can make the announcement that we're heading for Anchi 7."

"Yes Captain." replied Graylor who smiled as Captain Xaoping Shoo got up and headed out to her quarters leaving them to get on with the important business of operating the ship.

#

Cherice set up the recorder and almost dropped it in her excitement.

"Hi Danny, Oh wow, take a look at the pics I'm sending you. Anchi really is a Rainbow Star! They say it has lots and lots of tiny asteroids made of that highly compressed stuff, carbon. Daddy calls them diamonds and says that centuries ago they were very special and important on Earth but there are LOADS of them in a sort of belt around the star.

As we flew slowly up and down next to them the whole thing shimmered through the colours of the rainbow and sparkled. I've never seen anything like it and I cried.

The Last Voyage of the StarVista 4

I know, I'm soppy is what Daddy called it but he and Mummy were also crying and Mummy said it was so beautiful she wanted to stay there forever.

Even the other races on board seemed to enjoy it. The Alterans and Ziancans in particular seemed happy but some Scorions just said it was pretty but nothing special to them. Boring lot aren't they! There is no star port here but we did go into orbit around the moon of a giant planet that has people on it and the captain allowed us a day exploring on that moon."

Cherice had a sudden thought and keyed in the code to link up with the ships database on the star system and began to quote from it.

"It says here that the Anchi system has no natural sentient species as the star is too hot and although there are fourteen planets, most are small airless worlds orbiting too close to their star. There are three what we call gas giant planets and the third one of those out has a large rocky moon that has a colony of mining engineers.

They maintain the vast GAA operation that supplies a large proportion of the nearby systems with raw materials rather than ruining their own systems natural state. The mining of several highly compressed states of carbon from the innermost five rocky planets has led to an unusual formation of carbon dust waste that is shunted into a spiraling orbit which feeds directly into the star.

This carbon 'asteroid belt' provides for some spectacular optical effects that have given rise to the unofficial name the 'Rainbow star of Anchi'. This in turn has led to an increase in tourists visiting the system and there are now proposals to build a huge orbital hostelry to cater for the increasing needs of this new industry." She finished quoting from the database and resumed normal conversation with her diary entry.

The Last Voyage of the StarVista 4

"It was amazing and I hope that one day you too get to come and see it.

Now we have just set off for our next special sight so when we get there I will message again.

Byeee"

She set the recorder to 'send' mode and left it to do its work as she flung herself onto her bed and smiling at the memories she had of that first stellar encounter.

The Last Voyage of the StarVista 4

Day 31: Famous and Human Lasagne

Cherice rushed into her room which lay off to the side of her parents bedroom and quickly found the holo recorder. As she fumbled with the controls it leapt into life and she calmed herself down by taking deep breaths just as she had been taught.

"Oh Danny, I am famous! The Captain, she's a Gu-alt, you know like an upright octopus on Earth, and she's called Xaoping Shoo. Yes, I giggled at that as it did sound like she was called a shopping shoe, ha ha.

Anyhow she held a special evening for Mummy and Daddy in celebration of them becoming the ambassadors and I had to sit at the top table with them. The Captain said lots of lovely things about them, then said I am very special and that everyone should treat me well and help me enjoy the voyage, something like a queen!

I'll have to look up what a queen is but it sounds important! I always told you I was the special one, now it's official!

Well, everywhere I go with Mummy or Daddy people of all planets wave and have their photo taken with me even more than before, so I must be famous now! I'm getting used to it. See! You should have come with us, I do miss you and I'm glad your studies are going well but we would have had so much fun if you'd been here. Mummy and Daddy are really pleased that you have managed to arrange some time away to be at our final port to welcome us back so that will be really good as I know they miss you too.

Anyway, I'd best go, the ship's top cook has promised to make my favourite meal, lasagne, although she did say human lasagne so I do hope she didn't mean she's going to use me for it!

Just so you know there are at least a few hundred humans on board so I wonder if anyone would notice if one of us went missing!

Byeee!"

She almost dropped the recorder onto the bed in her excitement and then quickly tidied herself up before going into the reception lounge to wait for her mother.

Almost getting bored again, Cherice suddenly saw her mother open the door from her bedroom as she stepped out into the reception lounge. Cherice smiled at how lovely her mother looked.

"Do I meet with your approval young lady?" Natalie asked and Cherice smiled, nodding enthusiastically. "Good, well, let's go and see this chef. She's called Clarac Ziqual and she's a younger Alteran than Lariq which is why she is still female, so make sure you are on your best behaviour. It's not every young lady that is invited to the premier kitchen of a top interstellar cruise ship and she specifically asked me what your favourite dish was."

"But Mummy, she says human lasagne, I'm worried she might want me for an ingredient!"

"Ha, very funny dear, but I think the lack of noise you normally make would make the silence deafening! Your absence would be quickly noticed, especially by your father and I!

No, it seems that lasagne has become quite an interstellar favourite throughout the GAA and many species now use their own version of the meat substitute that we are familiar with, so each now has their own particular recipe.

I made sure Clarac knows what to put in ours to make it just right. I'm sure you will enjoy it but for now we'd best get moving."

Cherice checked in the long mirror to make sure she was smartly dressed then took her mother's hand as they exited the room out into the corridor. Natalie smiled down at her.

"You know that before joining the StarVista fleet she was an award-winning chef who worked at the GAA headquarters? She planned and arranged the most elaborate of luncheons for when there were special occasions."

Cherice's eyes went wide and she skipped ahead as she wondered about all the meals the chef must have cooked for all those dignitaries.

Ten minutes later they approached the entrance to the main dinning centre. Natalie had a quick word with one of the waiters who then smiled and disappeared through the double door. It felt like an eternity to Cherice but was merely a couple of minutes, when a tall Alteran in a somewhat stained overall came through the doors and looked down at her.

"Ahhh the young humarling." The Alteran slowly walked around Cherice as if sizing her up then looked at Natalie. "Very little meat there, I believe she will need a few more months on board to fatten up before I can use her in the 'Human Lasagne'…"

Natalie stifled a chuckle as this exchange had been planned but she quickly bent down to a, by now quivering, Cherice.

"She's funny, isn't she? As if I'd let her use you for food!"

Cherice put her hands on her hips and was about to storm out in a huff when Chef Ziqual stood in her way and opened up a box she had been hiding behind her back. Cherice's eyes went wide with excitement and she looked eagerly at the contents.

"Orange chocolates!"

That was it, she was now happy. Chef Ziqual smiled and took her by the hand, leading her and Natalie into the kitchen.

#

She felt fat!

Stuffed full with eating all that lasagne, Cherice, and indeed her mother, sat or rather sprawled on the long sofa in their living room and relaxed letting the enjoyment of the meal settle down. Carl came into the room, shook his head and smiled at the state they were in.

"Guess you won't be needing the evening meal then you two?"

The look on both of their faces was enough of an answer.

"OK well, I have a meeting with an important person so I'll be back soon." He turned, expecting there to have been an answer, but both were now half asleep and not taking any notice.

With that Carl just shrugged and headed out, making sure their quarters were secured, he didn't want anyone just barging in on them whilst they were seemingly so vulnerable.

His private comms chimed and he clicked his right molar to open it.

"Yes, I'm on my way. Yes, all is in order as long as you can confirm we can go ahead with the plan."

He ended the communication and turned to look back at the entrance to his family's quite luxurious accommodation and smiled, knowing he had to set things up quickly and without his family knowing what he was up to…

Day 36 to 42: Freedom and the shopping stops

Cherice was nervous. She had received a summons from no less a person than the captain and there was no explanation as to what she had done. Her father looked at her and she couldn't tell his mood, he was clearly not angry at her but then again, he didn't look pleased either.

Even her mother didn't know what was going on so she took both their hands and together they headed towards the nearest travelator.

Pretty soon they changed to a vertical travelator and it wasn't long before they stood in front of an odd looking door. Carl passed his hand over a barely visible panel.

It opened and there stood Captain Xaoping Shoo and the first officer, Graylor xZanders, looking quite stern. Cherice racked her brain but could not think of anything she had done wrong and took a deep breath as they were welcomed into the captain's quarters.

The door closed behind her and she felt a rising sense of fear. She thought she had been a good girl and knew that any moment now her feelings would erupt into tears as she felt trapped, but for no reason.

"Ahh, my dear Cherice Richmond. Don't look so frightened, it is for good news that I ask you here."

Cherice looked at the captain with a blank stare, not quite knowing what was going on, but this

The Last Voyage of the StarVista 4

time Graylor did her best imitation of a smile and gently took her by the hand.

"We have some news for you. We don't want you to get upset but we have come up with something to compensate for your loss."

Now Cherice was stumped for words but then a thought came to her... her toys?

They were led into a side chamber of the captain's quarters and all of them sat down. Captain Xaoping Shoo cleared her voice and looked at Cherice.

"As you know, your final item of baggage, the one that contains many precious items for your own enjoyment, didn't make it to the ship before we left. Indeed, there was much confusion as to its whereabouts and on behalf of the StarVista corporation we give you and your parents our most humble apologies.

I'm afraid it has now been located but it is, let us say, a very long way from us and it will be impossible to get it to us until our voyage is almost over.

You see instead of Star Port Atricia, it first went to your Terran system, Earth, then was directed to return to Star Port Atricia, but there was an unfortunate mix up in the name. It is on a long-haul medical freighter heading in the opposite direction to us, out to a distant colony called Alritzia. They are taking important medical supplies and cannot turn back or divert to a nearby star port. I am very sorry we have let you down Miss Cherice."

Cherice's face was the epic picture of a young lady about to burst into tears. Her mother quickly held her hand.

The Last Voyage of the StarVista 4

"Cherice, you are quite a big girl now and you've already had some amazing adventures, far more than most children of your age ever get to do. The toys will be back at home for when we get back…"

She looked at the Captain for support.

"Oh yes, indeed your parents have given us the details of your new home on Zianca so we are arranging for it and several surprises to be sent there for when you move there after this cruise. But I have another surprise and one which I hope will help you enjoy your stay with us even more and perhaps compensate for your disappointment. Please stand up to attention for me."

Cherice looked puzzled and quickly glanced at her parents. They both had smiles on their faces and nodded for her to stand to attention for the captain.

She did as she was instructed and waited. Captain Xaoping Shoo and Graylor xZanders stood towering over her but each had a smile so her natural fear began to ebb. With her parents both there and appearing unconcerned she calmed herself down as the captain held up her multi tentacled appendages.

"Cherice Anastasia Maria Rosalind Anne Richmond. On behalf of the StarVista Corporation and in consultation with myself, Prime Officer Graylor xZanders and your parents, you are hereby accorded the status of Very Important Passenger and granted the Freedom of the Ship for the duration of this cruise.

Subject of course to a few necessary limitations such as passenger and crew private quarters, sensitive areas of the ship and the like. You will be issued with a special biopass that will guide you as to where you can and can't go.

As our passengers are highly vetted, we and your parents consent to you exploring the ship on your own as long as your parents know when you will be out exploring and we also expect that if a crew member specifically tells you not to go into an area of the ship, then you will dutifully obey them. If you contravene any of the above then this unique privilege will be rescinded..."

Xaoping Shoo noted her slight puzzlement at the last word and Natalie bent down and whispered in her ear. She looked back up at the captain and smiled, nodding at the same time.

"...and your status will be returned to that of a normal passenger, the biopass returned to us and your parents will be required to be with you at all times.

Do you accept this offer?"

Cherice was open mouthed as she thought of the balance between having her toys and games compared with roaming the huge StarVista 4 ship. No contest, she decided.

"Yes Captain Shopping Shoe, oh sorry, Captain Xaoping Shoo." That was it, she knew she'd already blown it and waited as the slip of the tongue wrecked the amazing thing that had just happened. Captain Xaoping Shoo looked down on her then began to laugh as Graylor xZanders bent down and whispered in her ear.

"I said that's what it sounds like but the Captain didn't believe me." Graylor stood back up and looked at her captain who just did the Gu-alt version of a nod and they both did a little bow and gestured to the door. It was opposite the one they'd come in through and Cherice was puzzled.

"You are all invited to a tour of the command centre bridge of the StarVista 4" said the captain and she ushered them in through the now open door to begin their VIP tour of the control nerve centre of the vast ship.

Carl and Natalie had not expected this and it was hard to decide who of the three humans was the most excited. Graylor took up the rear of the little group and indicated for them to follow the captain and in a state of wonderment and surprise, they stepped onto the StarVista 4 command centre.

#

Diary entry
"Hi Danny. Wow, you won't believe this! Don't get too jealous, OK just a little then but... I've been given the freedom of the ship as the StarVista corporation has sort of lost my toys and games baggage. The good news is that as everyone had to pass very hard tests to be allowed on this huge ship, Mummy and Daddy have agreed with the captain that I can explore the ship on my own but if a member of the crew tells me not to go somewhere then I have to be good and obey them. So now I have a special Biopass and a map of the ship on my holo player so I know the places I can go.

It is just in time as the last two destinations have been very boring as they were special shopping stops. Shopping Stops! Trelieese and Coriqz are supposed to be the places to visit for strange and exotic markets but for some reason I wasn't allowed to go to them, apparently it is for grown-ups only. I had Lariq stay with me for the two

The Last Voyage of the StarVista 4

days and he was fun because he loves our culture and so knew lots of games we could play.

So although I couldn't go down with Mummy and Daddy, I had lots of fun playing games with Lariq and hope we have another stopover like that again.

Mummy and Daddy came back and for a few nights I could hear strange sounds coming from their room and they looked very tired when we had our meals but they said it was an adult thing and not to worry.

I know what they were doing.

I know what they were doing.

Bleurgh! I hope there isn't a surprise in nine months' time! You know what I mean!

Byee for now!"

Day 49: Slip up at Plckendar

"Hi Danny. I KNOW! You don't have to spell it out for me! They taught sex at school last year, so I know all about it, but yee-uck! Mummy and Daddy doing it - I can't bear to think about it. I don't want another you or me running about our new home when we get to Zianca. With you away at university I have them all to myself and I want it to stay like that!

On to better things. Goody!

We're on our approach to our next holiday destination and it is the planet Plckendar, I think I have said that right. We're manoeuvring into the right position as we orbit the planet so that we get a high up view of the towering waterfalls of Marlt. After a few hours we have permission to go down in the shuttles and hover nearby to view them close up and, guess what? We are on the first shuttle! It's really exciting as the falls come off what we call a continental plate that has been thrust up almost fifty kilometres whilst the other plate has been pushed down almost the same amount creating a huge trench almost as deep.

So the waterfalls are almost a hundred kilometres high. I gather most of the water doesn't make it to the bottom but becomes heated as steam and rises back up but when the sunlight is right, there are lovely rainbows and you know I really like them! Mummy says that there are plans to put a huge sort of lift to take passengers up and down close to the waterfall to get an even better view but she also thought it could be dangerous and expensive so who knows if it will ever get built. I'll send pics when we get back as I've just heard Daddy calling me to join them so I'll have to rush off for now.

Byee Bro!"

The Last Voyage of the StarVista 4

Day 50
Cherice diary addition.

Cherice fiddled with the controls. *"Not sure if this is on or working, oh, it is, sorry about that Danny. Now don't go making fun of me, I'm not as old as you so am only just really getting used to this holo recorder.*

Well, what a disappointment! Mummy says that someone didn't tell the planners that we would arrive at the worst time of season for Plckendar and that we could barely see the waterfalls of Marlt from orbit! The cloud deck was so low they even cancelled the shuttle trips! Daddy says the planner ought to be sacked and with Mummy, has suggested to the captain that there should be compensation as many passengers were very unhappy.

I felt sorry for Captain Xaoping Shoo as she too was unaware until we arrived in orbit and has apparently sent a 'strongly worded' message via hyperbeam to her bosses about it, according to Daddy.

We did get a bonus however as the captain discovered, or was it someone in her crew..., I don't know, anyway someone discovered that if they manoeuvred the ship into the right position behind the fourth planet's largest moon they could create a total eclipse of Plckendar's central star and it was amazing!

There is some sort of highly inclined fine asteroid belt close in to Plckendar that we could see shimmering either side of the star's corona, I think that's what the captain said when she gave a running commentary. It was similar to the Rainbow Star earlier in our voyage but the small stuff is apparently lumpy and shiny asteroids this time.

The Last Voyage of the StarVista 4

As a bonus the second and third planets were far enough to one side of the star that we could see them as really bright 'stars' compared with the usual stars we see as we fly through normal space. I've started to upload the pictures so hope you like them, of course there is nothing about the waterfalls of Marlt so can't help that, but the rest are really pretty.

Anyway, Mummy is calling so I'll be in touch soon.

Byeee!"

The Last Voyage of the StarVista 4

Day 53 to 68: Flying lesson and a long gap

"Attention passengers of the StarVista 4, this is First Officer Graylor speaking. Shortly the ship will pass back into normal space and over the next few days we will be arranging special fly around shuttle trips for you to enjoy the experience and get to see our stunning star cruiser from the outside once again, rather from your normal viewing on the inside.

Please check the in-cabin consoles for your allocated time and which shuttle bay to report to. Each flight will last around thirty Terran minutes per passenger along with ten minutes preparation and debrief time. Please consult with your section steward as to the allocated time slots. Thank you for your attention. This message will also be available on your room consoles with links to further information if required."

The door opened and once again there stood Helmspilot Delieezas who performed a slight but comical bow to Cherice and her parents.

"Why it's the humarling, Cherice and her family. How we are nice to see you again." Cherice chuckled at how well he spoke in Terran despite the slight grammar slip up.

Carl stepped forward as Natalie took Cherice by the hand and together they all headed over to the suiting up area. Delieezas stopped and motioned for them to don the flight suits, that had been prepared for them for the first flight just a few weeks earlier.

Cherice didn't wait to be told and was quickly climbing into the suit in her eagerness to be in space outside the ship again.

She was a little puzzled about the flight suits and it had been bothering her since their first flight. "Why do we need special suits if it is safe to fly in the shuttle?"

"Ahh, a very good observation indeed. As we are a passenger ship, we have to follow even more stringent rules about safety than, say, a commercial cargo or military ship. So, this helps ensure that passengers on StarVista ships are safe no matter where they are. The main ship has a lot of protection compared to these shuttles which are very well built but even so, much smaller, so there is less protection between you and outer space."

"Oh, I'm glad then to have the suit. Can I fly the shuttle this time?" she asked cheekily and Delieezas smiled at her.

"First things first, little one. I will take us out to a safe distance and we'll do a steady fly around of the StarVista 4 so you can really appreciate the ship in all its glory. Did you know that actually the StarVista 4 was not the fourth to be built in the fleet, but the fifth?"

"Well that's a bit odd Mr Delieezas, is there more to this tale I wonder?" asked Carl and he could see Cherice was eagerly awaiting a new story. Delieezas again smiled, knowing he'd got them hooked.

"First things first, now you are suited up let us board the shuttle, this one is my favourite and it's called 'Trallaac' which means 'trusty or trustworthy' in Terran. It always flies well and smoothly which is why I enjoy flying it."

Delieezas indicated for them to head over to Trallaac and as they did so the shuttle door opened automatically for them; they climbed in and took their seats. Cherice looked longingly at the pilot's seat as Delieezas entered and closed the door behind him. He saw her look pleadingly his way but subtly shook his head whilst smiling at her enthusiasm.

Flight checks done, he talked to the shuttle control centre and the hanger bay doors opened; the craft ever so lightly took flight and headed out into the blackness of space beyond. Despite seeing the star filled sky so many times Cherice still looked on in amazement as the wide curved view screen wrapping halfway around them gave them a grandstand view.

At first the StarVista 4 was hidden behind them and once they were far enough out, Delieezas brought the Trallaac around so they could look straight at the ship. The shuttle bays were arranged two thirds of the depth of the ship all around it so multiple shuttles could launch without impediment and they watched as the doors closed on their bay.

Three more bays opened up and silently and majestically three more shuttles launched, joined them, spaced well apart from each other.

"At this time, four more shuttles are being deployed on the other side of the ship and once they are in position we will all begin a slow fly around of the StarVista 4 whilst she is coasting along with the main engines offline. They should be in position in around two of your minutes." stated Delieezas as he then began to talk to shuttle control.

The Last Voyage of the StarVista 4

Cherice just sat and gazed in awe at the sheer size of the space cruiser. For their first flight the SV4 had moved away quickly so they could experience the emptiness of space.

Now it was suspended in space and Cherice realised that she could see the band of the Milky Way galaxy diagonally passing behind the star cruiser.

"Mister Delieezas, sir, where exactly are we now in our galaxy?" she asked inquisitively. Natalie looked at Carl and they both smiled at how she was so inquisitive and always wanting answers. They hoped Helmspilot Delieezas didn't mind.

Of course he didn't. Too often he had passengers who in reality couldn't care less where they were, they just wanted to get to each special destination and in some cases never even bothered to venture away from the ship. So to Delieezas it was a delight that he had passengers who had an insatiable thirst for knowledge and exploration.

"Well Miss Cherice, we are coasting between destinations and as such are not very far above the plane of our part of the galactic arm. As there is no 'up or down' in space we happened to be flying at a slight angle to the galactic plane but this is so that we can get a good view of our part of the galaxy. Did you notice that compared to when we were high above the galactic plane last time there were fewer stars close by?

Now we have a more stars around us, most at about eight to fifteen light years away, so this is a low stellar population region, whilst we are just out of the main galactic plane. Does that make sense?"

The Last Voyage of the StarVista 4

"Oh yes, thank you." Cherice settled back as Delieezas coordinated with shuttle control and began to move the Trallaac in sync with the other seven shuttles as they slowly flew around the vast StarVista 4 interstellar cruise ship. A wide-eyed Cherice, and to be fair, also her parents, took in the view of the ship.

The view screen began to display the basic details of the parts of the ship for them to identify as they passed them in a slow spiral that gradually took them around and over the ship.

Cherice motioned to Delieezas to ask if she could take images with her recorder and he nodded, tilting the Trallaac so she could get good views. Danny would have a lot of pictures of the StarVista 4 to look at soon!

Ten minutes later they had completed the fly around and each of the shuttles was given permission to move away further from the StarVista 4, much to Cherice's puzzlement.

Delieezas turned to them.

"Mrs ambassador, Natalie, I understand you wanted everyone to have a chance to try flying the shuttle. Do you wish to be first?" Natalie looked over to Cherice.

"Well my, how about you first then Cherice?"

The look on her face however was a little different to what Natalie had expected. Cherice went coy and looked down at her feet.

"Can I watch you and Daddy fly first?"

Carl saw the nervous look about his daughter. "Yes of course you can, no need to worry and if you don't want to do it later, then that's fine my little poppet.

You go first then Natalie and we can see how it's done."

Natalie proved a natural whilst Carl clearly was not meant to fly anything, let alone a shuttle, so Cherice knew, as she now took the controls, that she had to make an impression.

Delieezas just smiled at her and carefully went over the basic controls several times. Cherice however was eager to get started.

"Mr Delieezas, I think I'm ready as I have been watching Mummy and Daddy, especially Mummy." She quickly looked back at Natalie and winked as Carl cringed at the thought that the two ladies in his life might prove to much better and natural flyers.

Indeed it proved to be the case.

Cherice had a natural instinct and after a couple of quick tests she began to fly the shuttle with ease. Even Delieezas nodded in approval and relaxed for once, but still kept an eye on things.

All good things come to an end however and Delieezas spoke up.

"Well now Miss Cherice. Looks like I have to watch out for you as you might be taking over my job! Time for us to be heading back so level up and stabilise the flight, bring down the speed to zero please."

She did so and Natalie felt so proud of her little space pilot. Delieezas took control but just before he had chance to do anything Cherice remembered something he'd said at the start of the flight.

"Mr Delieezas, why is the StarVista 4 not the fourth ship?"

The Last Voyage of the StarVista 4

He smiled, knowing he would now have to tell the story.

"Well, I'll just confirm we are cleared to head back and as we head in, I'll tell you."

A few moments later he set the shuttle on standby whilst the other shuttles duly headed in.

"It's nothing really. The first three StarVista cruise liners were already operating and the order had gone out for three more. StarVista 3 was the last to use a particular engine design and StarVista 4, 5 and 6 would have a newer more efficient design of engine.

This cruiser should have been number 5 but when the original StarVista 4 was launched and was undergoing its star trials, a serious malfunction in its new engines left it stranded for over three of your Terran weeks. As the engineers raced to work out and fix the problem, what should have been StarVista 5 was kept at its space dock and once they knew what the problem was, they modified its engines.

So as the last three ships had not yet been given their official designations, the fifth ship to be built, this one, became the fourth ship of the fleet to become officially operational and so it was named StarVista 4.

Meanwhile the fourth ship was brought back to space dock and its repairs took longer, so it ended up becoming the last of the fleet to become operational. In a twist of fate, what should have been StarVista 4 became StarVista 6 and the sixth ship was launched as the StarVista 5.

So there you have it."

Cherice was still thinking about it as her head spun at keeping track of which ship was really which as they headed back in. She couldn't help but feel a little sad for the original StarVista 4 as it felt to her that it had been relegated to the back of the line.

#

Diary entry

"Hello again brother!

The captain decided to bring us out into normal space for a week so that those who wanted to and could afford it, could have flights aboard the shuttles around the ship and Daddy, Mummy and I had our go yesterday. Wow! I knew the ship was huge but it really is HUGE!!

They let Daddy and Mummy fly the shuttle after they had been shown how to then, get this, get this, they let ME fly it as well! Daddy wasn't very good but you know how he is with technical things like that.

The captain let her top helmsperson Delieezas take us out and he said afterwards that I was a natural and I should think about it in the future. Daddy was not so happy at that, but Mummy thought it was really, really good. I so love Mummy and Daddy and of course you too. Miss you Bro and I wish I could fly a shuttle to come and fetch you.

Mr Delieezas said though that I would need a bigger and faster ship. But perhaps one day?

Byeee!"

The Last Voyage of the StarVista 4

Day 70: Upset at Qrianlairing

"Hi Danny, Sorry it has been a while but you knew we would have several long stretches between some of our destinations. We are approaching the Qrianlairing Nebula and I'm a bit nervous. The captain says we are perfectly safe as we pass through it and that the diffuse gas and dust will glow and fade as we travel through it on slow speed, so that it will apparently look beautiful. I hope she is right.

Daddy says not to worry but Mummy and I are not too sure. The captain informs us that the main observation decks on both sides of the ship will have free food and drinks available all the time as we pass through. So, it doesn't matter what time anyone wants to go up and have a look or sit out in the special loungers and either watch or just rest and enjoy the view. I might stay in my room.

I'll call soon.
Byeee for now."

#

The StarVista 4 approached the outskirts of the Qrianlairing Nebula. From several lights years away, it had seemed quite dense with towering columns of gas and dust looking like an outstretched hand which didn't look too inviting. The name Qrianlairing, as Cherice discovered from the information consoles in their living quarters, was an old name from the Scorion star charts that meant *Hand of the Old Ones* as to some it looked like the crinkled old hands of a being with six fingers.

The Last Voyage of the StarVista 4

It was a star forming cloud with at least a dozen new stars and several hundred proto stars forming deep within its cocoon and yet, as they approached, the outer layers were quite thin and in places see through.

Their path would pass a third of the way through the lower part of the great cloud which was at least fifty light years wide, but would afford glimpses of the newly forming star cluster towards the centre through the thinner patches of the nebula.

They approached the outer edges…

"Command crew to control centre, Command crew to control centre."

The StarVista 4 could really fly itself and Captain Xaoping Shoo and the main flight officers could do their jobs from any part of the vast ship. But sometimes protocol demanded that the full command crew be in the control centre bridge of the ship when passing near to and through nebulae as they were known areas of instability. Strong magnetic fields and violent 'winds' from the emerging protostars were the main contenders to look out for.

Graylor entered along with Science /Engineering Officer Calsohn, a Ziancan and Helmspilot Delieezas. The Captain, Chief Engineer Ahanascal Coaraskk a Krelti along with the only human command officer, Comms Officer Carson, were already at their stations. Captain Xaoping Shoo looked at them and smiled.

"Good of you all to join us. Standard procedures everyone. Looks like a nice trip and we have about five thinner sections that will allow our passengers to view the cluster towards the centre."

The Last Voyage of the StarVista 4

The team took up their places as various crew members reported in that passengers were already making their way to the observation decks.

The views were fairly monotonous to the command crew as most of them had done upwards of eight or so flights over the last twelve terran years. Crew rotations meant that most of the normal crew positions were alternated on consecutive flights as they were such long trips. However, the command crew was on each flight. Every cruise had a similar length of break between cruises so that the vast ships could be looked at in fine detail and any modifications or upgrades performed ready for the next cruise.

"Entering a denser patch of gas, mainly hydrogen, oxygen, carbon and silicon grains plus many of the normal inert gasses in trace amounts. No danger to the ship, Captain, our shields can easily deflect them."

"Very good Calsohn, time to closest approach to the central cluster?"

"Five hours, twelve minutes."

"Good, plenty of time for our passengers to enjoy the swirling clouds as we pass through them. Let's keep them informed of the best views as we happen upon them.

Delieezas, distance at closest approach?"

"One light day, Captain."

Graylor leaned forward over Delieezas's console and looked a little puzzled.

"Unusual that we've been given this course, Captain. It's a lot closer than we've ever gone past the central cluster and they are quite young, temperamental stars.

Lots of radiation spikes from them, so normally we're around a light week out."

Xaoping Shoo turned and looked at Calsohn in turn for an answer.

"As far as I can see from our scanners and monitoring ships systems there appears to be no danger. I'm sure Mister Delieezas could get us away if a flare up occurred and at a light day we still have plenty of leeway for a quick exit."

"Very well," Xaoping Shoo looked towards, and did a polite nod, to Graylor. "Close monitoring team, let's have no errors on our part, we have plenty of people on board to look after and as far as I am aware there has never been a…"

"Err Captain, don't say it…" Comms Officer Carson butted in and regretted it instantly, but Captain Xaoping Shoo just did the equivalent of a chuckle.

"Ahh, you terrans, some of you still have little superstitions. Very well. I won't say it just for you Carson. Graylor, keep an eye on things and I will have a little wander amongst our passengers. I know a certain little passenger is worried about this excursion and I think I will pay her a visit."

Xaoping Shoo stood up and headed out as the view screen switched to wide view and the command crew settled in to monitor and enjoy the relatively familiar, yet closer than normal view.

#

Cherice was close to the observation deck wall screen as Lariq joined her and her parents.

The Last Voyage of the StarVista 4

They watched the slow motion of the nebulous swirling clouds as the StarVista 4 cruised through the Qrianlairing Nebula. She looked out watching for thinner gaps in the hope of being the first to spot the inner star forming region, but she was a little puzzled.

"I'm confused." she said out loud to no one in particular. "Isn't this one that can be seen from home? In the photographs it's pink, blue and green but I can hardly see any colour, it's quite dull!"

Lariq looked at Carl and Natalie and they nodded to him to explain. They knew he loved to help educate Cherice and she seemed to hang on his every word.

"You are right Miss Cherice. This is the one that your species calls the egl nebular, oh, sorry, Eagle Nebula. It is a star forming region full of dense gas and dust where stars are forming inside the dense clouds that you can see outside. But we are on the other side and so it looks quite different to you.

The colours are better seen from a greater distance, we are inside the nebula so the gas appears thinner and so less bright. It is the brightness that helps your eyes see the colours, but they are quite subtle really when seen so close up.

However, I can enhance this section of the view screen. He quickly did the required hand movements above, but not touching the screen and lo and behold the colours became evident. Several Scorion and Tiancan passengers saw what he did and they too quickly changed the view screen settings much to gasps of delight from many around them.

Pretty soon the whole of the observation deck's screens were showing more colour and several of the passengers put up whatever appendages they had in a show of appreciation to Cherice and Lariq. Lariq bent down a little and whispered in her ear.

"That's their way of doing what you terrans call a 'thumbs up' gesture." Cherice smiled and, turning to the other passengers, put her right thumb up in return, much to their appreciation.

She turned back to the screens just in time.

"Oh look, there, I can see deeper!" They watched as a thinner area of the nebula allowed a view, but not quite, of the young star cluster at the core of the nebula. Even so, she was excited and Carl looked at Natalie, then turned to Lariq.

"Lariq, are you able to stay and be with Cherice for the time being, and if so, how long for?"

"Oh, no problem, the passenger assignments for myself are for you and the passengers you met when we did the emergency drills and they are just over there. I'm sure they won't mind if I stay with Miss Cherice and indeed the Captain gave me special dispensation to help you in any way I can." Natalie nodded approval and gave Cherice a little kiss on the cheek.

"Now you be good for Mr Lariq and we will see you later." They left as Cherice busied herself with looking out at the vast nebula watching for any more gaps. Off to one side a subtle flash took place and she blinked but didn't think anything off it.

The Last Voyage of the StarVista 4

Ten minutes or so later Captain Xaoping Shoo finally found Cherice and Lariq after answering questions from passengers along the way. The price a captain of a cruise liner had to pay, dealing with passengers. Most were usually pretty good but there was always a small contingent of annoying ones on every trip. So far she felt she had been lucky and there had been no one like that.

So far.

"So little humarling, how is it so far for you?" she asked Cherice who beamed at her with a broad smile.

"I've seen several gaps and Mr Lariq and I think we spotted the central group too for a moment."

"Well done. See there is nothing to worry about." Xaoping Shoo's attention was briefly caught by another faint but discernable flash off to one side a considerable distance away. She didn't say anything but mentally made a note of it.

"I hope Mr Lariq is informative and helping you enjoy what we are passing through. Most of our flight paths take us much further out, but if I am not mistaken we seem to have been given special dispensation to travel a little deeper than normal. Hopefully you will get to see many more unusual things that are normally hidden from a more distant view."

Xaoping Shoo was about to leave when there was another flash of light deeper into the nebula and she stopped and stared in the direction of the flash.

Cherice had seen it too and frowned.

"That was a bit bright. Are we safe, Captain?" She asked a little hesitantly.

"Yes, of course my little one, there are very young stars forming and sometimes they can throw a baby tantrum as they try to settle down. You must arrange to talk to our in-flight astrophysicist, Crayt, a mine of information. He's currently with a group that specifically paid extra to have him as their guide for this venture into the Qrianlairing Nebula, otherwise I would have requested Crayt come and speak with you instead."

Another flash, somewhat more intense now caught all their attention and this time Cherice flinched.

"Indeed Miss Cherice, if you excuse me I will head back to the command centre. Please do enjoy the views of the nebula and proto star systems forming." With that the captain smiled, turned away and left. Rather too briskly, thought Lariq. His side lit up with another bright flash and this time Cherice closed her eyes tightly as she was beginning to dislike the turn of events. She slowly reached out and instinctively held Lariq's hand as the flashes became more intense and she began to tremble.

"Why is it doing that? I thought we were looking through gaps in the dust clouds but no one mentioned these flashes before. I don't like them!" she muttered. Lariq could only watch, a bit bewildered, as he had been on several flights through the same nebula with the ship and had not seen anything so intense. He watched as several flashes occurred in quick succession and Cherice , along with a number of other passengers, were now becoming genuinely frightened.

Suddenly Graylor xZanders voice came over the intercom.

The Last Voyage of the StarVista 4

"May I have your attention please. Please note there is no cause for alarm at the increase in the interstellar lightning. This is an effect often seen with the strong magnetic fields associated with the denser clouds of gas and dust. We will shortly be clear of this region and so hope you will instead enjoy this particular extra light show, as it is an unusual occurrence for us to get such a unique close-up glimpse into the early stages of star formation."

A brighter flash ripped through the nearest dense part of the nebula and that did it for Cherice. She burst into tears despite what Graylor had just announced and Lariq quickly scooped her up and took her back in the direction of her quarters.

#

"Good idea, Graylor, let us hope that has settled the passengers." Captain Xaoping Shoo had reached the command centre and shortly after, astrophysicist Crayt had joined them as requested by the captain.

"What do you make of it then Crayt?"

"Quite odd, I've never experienced such unusual effects in a star forming region like this. I'd expect something similar to this but a lot closer in where the magnetic fields are very strong and in polar opposites. Worth investigating if we can?"

"No, we have passengers, we're not a science vessel, but I certainly think we ought to put in a report once we're clear of the nebula and request a science support vessel to be sent to check out the activity in it.

The Last Voyage of the StarVista 4

I've not experienced anything like that in all the years I've been captain of a cruise ship, and that's a long time indeed!"

"I'll go to the astrophysics centre and monitor it from there in as much detail as I can. I may not have all the facilities of a proper science ship, but I can at least gather some info to help if needed." Xaoping Shoo looked and nodded approval.

Crayt left as Graylor looked up from near Comms Officer Carson's station.

"Captain, we're getting reports of some of the passengers not too happy with the unusual flashing, indeed it seems Section Officer Lariq has taken the little humarling back to her quarters as she is frightened by the unusual display."

"Oh dear, I'll probably get a report from her parents about it. Mr Delieezas, please change course and take us out of the nebula, then resume normal course for our next destination."

"Yes Captain."

With that the visit to the Qrianlairing Nebula was officially over.

Meanwhile back in her quarters as Cherice tried to settle down, she hurriedly set up the holo recorder.

"Danny! She lied! The Captain lied to me. There was lightening and flashing and I was really scared and I have been in my room crying ever since. Mummy and Daddy have tried to help me but I don't like it and can't wait to get out the other side of this horrible nebula thingy.

I hate this ship and they still haven't found my toys!!

Bye!"

The Last Voyage of the StarVista 4

\#

Meanwhile, deep in the Qrianlairing Nebula...

> *"Have they detected us?"*
> *"No your excellency.*
> *"That is good for your sake. Wait until they have completely left then restart operations. Nothing must stand in the way of our mission.*
>
> *What I want to know is, why was their flight plan a lot closer in than normal. We worked on the basis that any of their pitiful holiday ships would not come into the nebula this close. Once they are gone, send a coded message to our contacts in the GAA council and order them to discover why that ship was sent on that path. Let us hope we have not been compromised.*
> **For your sake."**
> *"Yes, your excellency."*

\#

Meanwhile in cabin C2001, Sicanrinka was puzzled after returning from observation deck A. The itinerary had mentioned they would skirt the Qrianlairing Nebula and knowing its importance to the overall mission she had been shocked to discover they had gone deeper inside the nebula instead.

Fortunately, her comrades had not been discovered. She knew she had to report back and that would be risky, but not impossible. She had a deep suspicion that someone in the GAA suspected something was going on.

The Last Voyage of the StarVista 4

Somehow they had influenced the StarVista corporation to make a slight change to their flight plan of the StarVista 4. It was a worrying development.

Quickly she set up the equipment that could hijack the comms system and began to compose and transmit her message…

#

Day 74
Diary entry.

"Danny, I'm sorry. I was really scared and upset so I'm sorry I sent the message and that you are upset about what happened to me. It is all right now, we left the nebula yesterday and there wont be another sight like that so close that we have to go through it. The Captain has promised me when she came and visited and she was upset that I was upset. So, to say sorry, she has asked Delieezas to take me on a special extra trip around a comet in the next system whilst they get ready for the sights at the eighth planet of the Brinlack system.

Brinlack eight is still quite primitive and has animals that on earth we called dinosaurs, so the two hundred humans on board are especially excited, although the Scorions again don't seem too bothered about this stopover. I sometimes wonder why they are on the voyage, but Daddy says that they often say the opposite of what they really think. Silly people! Must go now but will tell you soon what the comet was like.

Byeee!"

The Last Voyage of the StarVista 4

Day 77 to 78: Bonnie and Clyde

On hearing the captain had requested a special flight for her, Cherice's spirits were raised as she headed along with her parents. Cherice really, *really* wanted to run along the corridor, her excitement was unbounded, but Natalie and Carl insisted on taking the travelator instead, much to her annoyance. They reached the shuttle bay and her father pressed the intercom.

"Cherice Richmond reporting as instructed by the captain." There was a slight delay and then the doors parted to reveal Delieezas with his flight suit on and one, much smaller, in his left hand. Cherice's eyes went wide as she carefully reached out and took it from him. Delieezas smiled, nodded to her and they all headed into the shuttle bay prep room.

"Yes, we've had a special official crew person suit made for you to wear when we go out on a shuttle ride. I hope it fits you?"

Cherice was too stunned at first to reply until her mother prodded her.

"Oh yes Mr Delieezas, wow, this is amazing!"

Natalie tapped Cherice on her shoulder. "Now, you behave yourself and do everything Mr Delieezas tells you to do as he is in charge."

"Aww, Mum! I've done this before with you two!"

"Yes, poppet but this time you are alone on the flight and it won't be just flying around the ship, it's going to a comet. Mister Delieezas, any trouble from this little one and you come straight back, is that understood?"

The Last Voyage of the StarVista 4

Natalie said in a stern voice as Carl also looked at him with a 'don't argue with the wife' look, and Helmsman Delieezas stood to attention.

"Yes ambassadors, I'll take great care out there and I'm sure Cherice will enjoy our trip."

The two passed through into the primary sealed area; through the small glass window they could watch as Delieezas helped Cherice into her own flight suit, one Captain Xaoping specifically had made for her as such a valued passenger, much better than the more ungainly and large flight suit she had previously had to wear. Once done they turned to face her parents and Cherice gleefully waved before they headed out of sight to embark into the shuttle.

Carl looked at Natalie.

"She'll be OK, Mr Delieezas is an exceptional pilot and the captain wouldn't let them do this if she had any concerns."

"I know, she's growing up so fast and on this voyage she's really matured for one so young. I'm pretty glad there was no one else her age as I suspect she'd have not done a fraction of the things she's achieved since boarding."

"We can be proud of her, that's for sure my love. Let's get up to the captains quarters and take up her offer of watching their flight from there." Natalie nodded and together they left the prep room and headed out.

Meanwhile in the shuttle Cherice was settling into her seat to the right of Delieezas as he took her through the preflight sequence.

"Outer hatch - sealed?" he asked.

The Last Voyage of the StarVista 4

"Confirmed sir, outer hatch is showing sealed."

"Manoeuvring thrusters and systems check?"

"Check."

"Power banks showing fully charged?"

"Check."

"Safety systems online?"

"Check."

"Very good miss Cherice. Here you are, press your chinguard microphone and ask shuttle bay control for clearance to launch and to open bay one doors."

Cherice's face lit up with glee as she'd not been asked to do that before in the practise runs she'd had to undertake with Mr Delieezas. She touched the control under her chin but momentarily froze with doubt. She looked up at Delieezas; he smiled and tried to wink, although for an Alteran it was never an easy thing to achieve convincingly. Cherice understood, however, bolstered by the clear show of confidence her mentor had in her, she took a deep breath and spoke into the microphone.

"Shuttle Bay control, we request permission to leave, acknowledge?" She quickly looked over at Delieezas and he nodded encouragingly as a voice came over the comms.

"Shuttle 'Trallaac', bay doors opening and you are cleared for launch, have fun you two but bring it back in one piece."

Delieezas tapped his comms.

"For that cheeky statement, Cherice will now fly the shuttle out." He cut the comms but indicated that he would do the flying and they lifted off the bay floor.

He deliberately wavered the shuttle before shooting out the open doors as the shuttle bay controller almost had a fit. Cherice burst into giggles but a new voice came over the comms.

"Very amusing helmspilot but as your captain I'd advise against another trick like that, you understand me?"

Delieezas swallowed hard.

"Sorry captain, I was the one actually piloting but I assure you it won't happen again. Setting course for the comet in the Brinlack system, we'll transmit holo screen images as we fly round and through the comet's tail. Permission for *extra activity*?"

"Granted. Looking forward to it."

Delieezas appeared to grin then set up the coordinates before asking Cherice to confirm and finish the final number input. As she confirmed it the shuttle moved to high speed and changed course, much to her excitement.

Just fifteen minutes later the view screen directly ahead showed the comet with the Brinlack sun off to the left and the comet's tail streaming out to the right, curved and split into two. Cherice pointed to them.

"Why two tails?"

"Ahh, it is because one is made of gasses and the other is denser material called dust. See the gas one is straighter than the other?"

Cherice nodded, fascinated. Delieezas continued his little astronomy lesson.

"The straighter one is the gasses as they are so light they are easily swept behind the comet by the solar wind of the Brinlack sun.

The dust is heavier so isn't affected as much and so from some angles is curved as it still has the motion of the comet along its orbit. Have you met our on-board astrophysicist, Crayt?"

"No. I've met lots of amazing people so far but not him/her?"

"Crayt and his species doesn't have er, well, I'm not sure how to say this or if I should I.."

"If it is about sex, no worries as we did that at school last year. Not all species have two genders, or even one, so what is Crayt?"

Delieezas carefully shook his head and could only smile at how mature for a human Cherice was.

"They don't have any gender. Crayt is a Bilastronon and something inside them tells them when to produce another Bilastronon, there is no mating or male/female. To them, most of the species of the GAA are, in their opinion, a little backward by having two or more genders so even for us open minded Alterans, it is still an odd concept. Our chief engineer, Ahanascal Coaraskk, is also a Bilastronon, as are some of our service crew.

Ahh, here we go. For now, I will fly the shuttle but when I say so, take your controls and remember how well you flew the first time we went out around the ship."

"Yes Mr Delieezas. The shuttle's name is difficult for me to say. Can I call it…Bonnie?" Cherice looked sweetly at Delieezas and he looked puzzled.

"Bonnie? Why that name?"

"I don't know, I've heard it somewhere and I like it."

"OK then, between us and only us, Bonnie it is."

Delieezas then flew shuttle 'Bonnie' close in and around the small ice and rock nucleus, avoiding the occasional sudden jets thrusting fresh ice and dust into space at high speed. Cherice just looked on in wonderment, then had a thought.

"What's it called?"

"Sorry?"

"The comet's name, what's it called?"

"Oh, I see. It is a newly discovered comet in this system making its first approach to the Brinlack star, so as far as I am aware they haven't given it a common name yet, just a complicated designation of which even I can't work out the meaning." Delieezas thought for a moment then an idea popped into his head. "Clyde, we'll call it 'Comet Clyde'."

Cherice looked puzzled.

"When we get back, look into your history library for Bonnie and Clyde." replied Delieezas as Cherice shook her head and concentrated on the view screen in front of her. Delieezas flew them round and partly through the gaseous component of the tail; as he did so the localised magnetic field of the shuttle disturbed the particles.

He deftly manipulated the flight path, then moved them away turning the shuttle to face the tail section they'd just been through. Cherice gasped in wonderment at the slowly spiraling patch of the tail and Delieezas smiled, knowing he'd achieved the right reaction. He headed them back into the tail and started a series of complicated turns and dives through it as Cherice clapped her hands with glee.

The Last Voyage of the StarVista 4

From the StarVista 4, Captain Xaoping informed the passengers to enjoy the artistry of Helmspilot Delieezas as Natalie and Carl too enjoyed the view from the captains quarters..

Back on the 'Bonnie', Delieezas set up a complicated series of manoeuvres and showed Cherice how to follow the flight path on the flight screen. She took control a little nervously but quickly found it easy to follow the path laid out. Very soon Delieezas indicated for her to take the shuttle out of the remains of the tail and off to one side to enjoy their handiwork.

Cherice was almost in tears at the wonder of the expanding form of a flower drawn in space from comet dust.

"How long will it last?" she asked quietly.

"Only another few minutes, the comet is racing towards a close encounter with the Brinlack sun so there will be lots of gas and dust to replace what we've disturbed. Well, I hope you've enjoyed it and now we have to head back so why don't you turn us towards the ship and fly us close until I take over?"

She did as she was told, gleefully taking the controls and they headed back.

Cherice was ecstatic…

Diary message supplemental:

"Hi Danny. Wow, Wow Wow! Delieezas took me to that comet, it hasn't got a name, the StarVista 4 science person had found it as she scanned the system on our approach. Mr Delieezas let me fly the shuttle again.

The Last Voyage of the StarVista 4

I've called the shuttle Bonnie and for some reason Delieezas decided to call the comet Clyde. I don't get it, but he says I should check our old history files, so I guess I had better do that at some point. We flew around, along, then through the thinnest section of the tail and it was really pretty!

As we flew through the tail our wake caused particles to flow around us and swirl so from the ship it looked really pretty. Delieezas asked me to follow a special fight path and as we did some amazing manoeuvres it made the cloud look like a flower and everyone cheered us on. It was awesome! Mummy and Daddy were so proud and have been telling everyone that their daughter was flying the shuttle!

After we got back, the StarVista 4 arrived at Brinlack Eight and they used the high resolution scanners to show really large images projected onto the observation deck screens which made the dinosaurs look really big. Then they sent a team down and showed that they are really very tiny!

It was quite a scare really when they started showing what seemed like a large dinosaur, then they panned back and it was barely any higher than me! And that was the largest! So I really enjoyed this stop, especially with my special extra fly round the comet and I do hope you like the images I've added to this message. It has really made up for the awful nebula thingy so I'm quite happy now.

Love you Danny!
Miss you still!
Byeee."

Day 83: Engineering

"Cherice Richmond." she stated to the intercom quite matter of factually. "May I enter?"

Cherice was inquisitive to the core and so far, had managed to visit several of the main sections of the ship that she was allowed access to. She stood outside the entrance to the engineering department and patiently waited for a response.

It came to life, catching her off guard as she had begun to wonder if the intercom was working.

"Ahh, the small human. Enter." the voice said, and the door opened. Cherice carefully, and a little nervously, stepped through and the door whisked shut behind her making her jump a little.

"So, freedom of the ship then?" Chief Engineer Coaraskk was always straight to the point, eyeing her up suspiciously. Cherice hesitated as she wondered if she was already in trouble.

"Yes sir. Captain Xaoping Shoo herself has granted it. Am I in trouble?"

Coaraskk relaxed, tried to smile in a friendly way, but a Bilastronon could look quite fearsome at the best of times.

"Very well. I was not too happy about having a civilian child allowed to roam my ship freely, but as you are so small, I can't see you being a spy now...or are you a spy?" Coaraskk looked down at her and Cherice almost felt like turning tail and running away.

But then she thought, she was a Richmond, and according to her Mummy, no Richmond ever runs away from trouble. She stood firm.

"Well, the captain gave me permission to explore HER ship and so here I am. I hope you don't mind, but I've never, ever seen an engine room!"

Chief Engineer Coaraskk roared with laughter. Two colleagues, one a Scorion the other a Ziancan came running around the corner, presumably from the main engineering section, to see what the fuss was about. They smiled when they saw Cherice standing defiantly in front of their chief.

"Very well said little human. What do you say Ziik and Beskq, I think we shall have to let this tiny, mighty one in!" The chief bent over her and Cherice again didn't know whether to run away.

"Good, you are a strong one Miss Cherice Richamondal."

"Richmond, it's pronounced Richmond." she said defiantly; the chief stood back up straight again.

"Cherice Richmond, I welcome you to the most important part of the StarVista 4, otherwise in here known as *MY* ship, for I and my trusty colleagues here keep her running smooth as Chinarian smooth weave.

Ziik, you and Beskq look after things whilst I take our honoured guest on a tour of our little sanctuary."

They did a polite but unnecessary bow to their chief who gave them a scornful look, tinged with a hidden playfulness that you wouldn't expect from such a strong minded person.

Cherice was in for a treat.

The Last Voyage of the StarVista 4

They walked through an ancillary room which Coaraskk stated was a safeguard with added bulkheads in case of shielding failure in the main engineering deck.

To Cherice it was just a plain room with little of interest and politely said so, much to the amusement of the chief.

They then approached the main engineering section and Coaraskk carefully approached its door. It hummed a little, then opened. He stepped through but held up an appendage.

"The entrance opened for me as it is keyed to my biomedic data. However, let it close then you try to approach and see if it opens."

Cherice nodded, the door closed and she approached but stopped right at the door with it still firmly closed. It then opened and the chief smiled at her.

"Only certain crew may enter so it is impossible for anyone to get in who is not authorised. Step through now and join me." Cherice gladly did so and looked at the large room with its complicated consoles, lights and panels.

"Technically, the ship's own automation systems can monitor and manage the ship's engine status, but it is standard practice to always have personnel oversee operations as a precaution. Have you heard of the *Qincieta incident*?"

Cherice nodded enthusiastically.

"Yes, Mr Lariq probably told you. He can be a little flamboyant in his description of what happened. It was a serious engine failure, or so it seemed, as the engines were in those days solely controlled by the onboard ship's master computers.

The Last Voyage of the StarVista 4

Unfortunately the latter had suffered from a glitch making the captain and crew believe the ship was in danger of exploding. The engines went offline and without anyone's knowledge the navigation systems were also giving false information.

If they had kept a normal engineering crew on board, instead of running a bare minimum, then it is believed it could have been averted. So here, Ziik, Beskq and I, along with two others off duty at the moment, keep an eye on things. We run checks on all vital systems, ask the ship to also conduct tests on the engines and we compare results. Since these protocols were introduced, there has not been another Qincieta incident and there won't be on my watch."

"So you keep us safe then Chief Coaraskk?"

"Yes, indeed little one, yes indeed. Come over here to the yellow console. That's the navigation systems. Now press the illuminated path to highlight our course." Cherice did so and the holo display lit up to show the overall path the StarVista 4 was taking between stopovers. Coaraskk pressed a small patch on the console.

"Captain, we're just about to perform a small series of very minor course corrections, nothing to worry about, so Mr Delieezas shouldn't panic. It is for our young guest." The chief turned back to Cherice.

"Now just highlight this position ahead of the course and tap just slightly to the left side. Good. Now I'll tap here… There we go, you have just made a small course correction and for a short time been in control of the whole ship.

Mr Delieezas spoke very highly of your skills at navigation in the shuttle so I was not worried about allowing you to do this.

Nice work little humarling, perhaps you might make a good engineer one day?"

"We didn't seem to change. I didn't feel anything! Also technically I think I acted more like a navigator than an engineer?"

Coaraskk roared with laughter and held his left side briefly.

"Very well observed, you are quite right. Have you noticed any of our course changes so far in the cruise?"

Cherice thought about it and realised she had never felt anything at all. She shook her head, smiled then looked over to a solid looking bulkhead. "What's behind there?"

"Ahh, well spotted. This is the main bulkhead that the hyperdrives lie behind. Very dense shielding as it can be very nasty if you are exposed to the raw energy they contain. Completely safe so no need to worry. Well, little humarling, the tour is over for now so I hope you have enjoyed it. Time to leave. But first, here you are."

The Chief brought out a small embossed metallic badge. "There you go, your own official engineering badge. Doesn't allow access, you are too young for that, but it is a symbol to wear with pride. It will alert me to your presence if you wish to visit again and I will let you in.

If however the badge is highlighted red then you will not be allowed in as we may well be performing important work on the engines and system. Understood?"

Her beaming face suggested that she did!

#

Diary entry

"Hi Danny, I'm now going to be an engineer! Chief Engineer Coaraskk heard that I was a good pilot and asked me if I wanted to see the engineering deck.

Daddy and Mummy asked the captain and she said yes, so today I spent some of the day with Chief Coaraskk who let me tap some controls that changed our course and I also kept the big hyper engines in best condition.

The chief is a Bilastronon so doesn't have a gender so we can't say he or she which is a bit odd to get used to. Chief Coaraskk had a present for me, my first engineering badge. So now I can go down there whenever I want unless the red light is on, then I have to come back to my room.

I don't think about my toy and games case anymore, well at least not until now and I feel like the ship is now my playground, that is what Mummy calls it.

Everyone is so friendly. I am being good so don't ask again!

Tomorrow we reach the storm planet of Zeial. It is a very big planet with five huge storms swirling that no one can explain, as they have always been there. No one knows when they started but they make the tales of that red spot our Jupiter used to have seem like it was a tiny thing.

Daddy has put me in charge of taking our official family photos now and has given me my own personal holo recorder instead of a borrowed one, so I'll make sure I get lots more images for you.

Byee for now!

The Last Voyage of the StarVista 4

Day 84: Storm planet Zeial and a breakup

The StarVista 4 approached the storm planet Zeial from below the orbital plane and slipped into a wide orbit around the massive gas giant planet. Cherice sat patiently as astrophysicist Crayt opened up the ship wide passengers com system for a brief lecture on what they were to look out for.

"Passengers of the StarVista 4, as you may have heard from our chief executive officer, Graylor zXanders, we have arrived at the storm planet of Zeial. We are orbiting in synchronous rate with the planet and you may have noticed we are currently looking at the night side. Look out for what appear to be small flashes along the belt systems, their size is deceiving as they produce more power than any of our major space ports combined.

The Zeilans have tapped into this, you may see a hint of their energy ports tapping into the storm areas on the close up monitors. Note that these are not the storms we will soon witness. In forty terran minutes, we will experience daytime as our orbital rotation with the planet brings us round to the daytime side. As we do so, look out for the five major storms that rage in the two main belts closest to the equatorial zone of the planet. Three lie in the northern hemisphere and two in the southern and current estimates suggest they are close to merging.

For scale, note the largest storm is the size of Alteran Six, itself classed a small gas giant planet!

Current estimates suggest the merger will take place over a period of a Zeialian year, in Terran terms that is nine hundred and fourteen days. Simulations of the merger always come up with different results, but overall, it is most likely to be a huge planet wide storm that could last centuries.

Zeial will be changed forever. The merger will not affect the orbit of the planet, but the Zeialians have become dependent on the energy from the current storm systems and so plans are being put in place to safeguard their civilisation.

Further information and graphical overlays may be found in our many information booths on the observation decks or in your own quarters if you so wish. Enjoy the view as the storms come into view soon."

Crayt settled back and looked at Cherice as together they began to watch the giant world before them as night gradually slipped into day. Slowly their first sightings of the storms brought gasps at the sheer size of them and the amazing colours.

"Why is that one deep red, the other two a light orange, yet the southern two are pale creamy white?" asked Cherice inquisitively.

"It is all down to chemical compositions and also to high level icy clouds drifting over the two southern storms. In the past they too were a reddish brown colour, but the last few years as they have moved closer the surrounding weather systems have been pushed up over them.

Trust me, they are still powerful storms indeed and you wouldn't want to take a shuttle down into them.

Can you see the smaller storms approaching the first of the northern ones? They'll be ripped apart and absorbed in the next few hours, adding energy to the first large storm. Nature is a powerful force wherever you are in the universe, little humarling, remember that."

Cherice stared at the unfolding drama, mesmerised by the seemingly slow dance of the smaller storms as they approached their end…

#

Diary Entry

Hi Danny. Sorry to hear you broke up with your girlfriend, I sort of liked Carrie but she did seem to boss you around a lot. That's what Mummy thinks too but I don't think I should have said that should I? Oops!

I'm glad my pictures of the storm planet of Zeial helped take your mind off her and guess you don't really want to talk about it, although you never know she might change her mind and come back to you?

As to the storms, they were amazing and seemed to rotate so gracefully, it is hard to believe that they have horribly fast winds and that the experts think they will merge shortly and change the whole planet's weather systems forever.

Let me tell you about our upcoming plans.
Daddy has been sent, via hyperbeam, something that now gives him and Mummy final confirmed official status as a full ambassadors for Earth on Zianca. We also have the details and images of our new home and it looks amazing!

The Last Voyage of the StarVista 4

I was a bit wary as I will have to make new friends, but I've been told the Ziancan young at the school where I will be going to, are eager to meet me and find out what I think about this voyage. I am making sure I keep all these recordings so I can look back and get things right.

We are on approach to the, let me get this right, Trianquarkalear system, wow that is a mouthful! One of its moons is made of ice but another moon crashed into it and there is only half the moon left. The brochure says it is one of the oddest sights to see, a half jagged moon that is a tenth the size of our Earth's moon so it looks really good. Yes, I'll take pics for you and send them in a few days. See ya!

Oh, extra bit before I forget. Daddy and Mummy were interviewed by someone called Sicanrinka about their new job. I didn't know we had an official reporter on board.

Why didn't she come and talk to me?
Oh well.
Byee!"

Day 96
Diary Entry

"Hello? Helloooo? Oh at last, sorry about that, the recorder had a bit of a fit and I didn't think it was on! Trianquarkalear was impressive! Apparently, we are seeing it quite soon after the massive impact that almost smashed it apart. There is still lots of it spreading along its orbit and Mummy says that gravity is beginning to pull some of the bits back as they hit the largest piece.

It is beginning to heat up and melt but we would have to come back in thousands, maybe even hundreds of thousands of years before it becomes a round world again.

The Last Voyage of the StarVista 4

We couldn't go too close either because of all the ice and rock close to it, but the captain sent several of the shuttles to fly in and out of the bits, something like an asteroid belt and we watched them on the observation deck screens. As they whizzed in and out of the ice chunks I got a bit dizzy and got a headache, so Mummy took me to the medical bay. I'd not been there as I didn't think I should, but Dr Sreisse was really nice and said if I want to go and see them then I could as long as I ask him or his team first.

My headache is gone now and he thinks it was just a minor blip so Mummy and Daddy are happy, so am I of course! I'll be in touch again soon, probably after our next stop at Etel Six.

Bye for now Danny, bye.
Byeee.

Interlude

The Last Voyage of the StarVista 4

2481 AC
The Hansone family home

Andrew James Hansone smiled as he watched the screen come to life with the documentary.

The programme titles flashed by, then the narrator, none other than the famous explorer 'Sir' Harley Ryker-Smyth began telling the tale. He chuckled at the old fashioned and almost hardly ever heard of 'Sir' moniker but loved the opening 3D holographic fly around of the vast StarVista 4 interstellar cruise liner.

Sir Harley also looked the part of an ancient explorer with his old-fashioned black waistcoat, cream frilled shirt, very large flowery bow tie and black neat fitting trousers. The moustache also made him look distinctive, especially as few men or women grew them anymore. Apparently long ago it was quite fashionable.

Sir Harley began...

"Hello fellow explorers, it is I, Sir Harley Ryker-Smyth, famous for charting the jagged scars of Eldered Five, exploring the savage jungles of Alteran Twelve and escaping from the ravenous hordes of Scorios. Tonight on *Mysteries of the Ever-Changing Universe* I'll be taking a look at one of the most mysterious and strange happenings of the last one hundred years that is still forcing us to ask the question: whatever befell the StarVista 4 with its two thousand passengers and seven hundred crew?"

As he spoke a holographic replica of the StarVista 4 swung around his body as if in orbit. Just

The Last Voyage of the StarVista 4

as he finished talking, he grabbed it out of the air and held it toward the viewer dramatically.

Andrew smiled and settled back, hooked already.

Sir Harley continued…

"The StarVista fleet was made up of the finest interstellar cruisers of their time, with six being built to take passengers far and wide amongst the primary civilisations of the Galactic Arm Association. They travelled all along the Orion arm of our galaxy including where the human race had explored and settled and met with many races who were also keen to explore the galaxy we all call home.

The first three ships were built in 2380 by the StarVista Interstellar Corporation, their strict safety guidelines were meant to guarantee the passengers could enjoy adventures amongst the stars and see strange worlds from the comfort of the vast observation decks.

Seven miles long, almost four miles wide they proudly boasted every conceivable luxury, sporting activity and leisure facilities to rival none and beings from many worlds flocked to book the limited places available for each cruise. For twenty five years the fleet enjoyed immense success until, that is, the tragedy of StarVista 4 on earth date July 3rd 2405 AC.

To this day there are conflicting accounts from officials as to what really happened on that fateful day. What we do know is that two thousand seven hundred *never returned to see their loved ones again.*

After this break we will take a deeper look at what befell the StarVista 4 and whether we have

The Last Voyage of the StarVista 4

been told the truth *or not* about what really took place on that fateful, awful date."

Andrew tried to skip ahead over the break but the broadcaster was canny and it would not fast forward, so as the boring old fashioned stuff of commercials played out before him he picked up his holo-tablet and searched for the official explanation for the StarVista 4 disaster.

He looked around the room suddenly nervous as if something was in there with him but he shook his head. "Hah, monsters or ghosts, not real so I don't care." he exclaimed a little bolder than he actually felt. He remembered stories of a distant ancestor being a so called ghost hunter but even now no one had ever been able to prove they existed. The feeling passed and he continued with his search.

'There you go' he thought, apparently the system they had been touring was a relatively new one, not fully charted and indeed they really shouldn't have been there in the first place. As the ship had entered into orbit it had encountered an uncharted small, icy moon and crashed headfirst into it, being destroyed instantly with no survivors.

Andrew cocked his head slightly to the left, puzzled. Surely, he thought, they would have been experienced enough to have done a basic reconnoitre first to ensure everyone's safety? He noticed the commercials had ended and the programme titles came back on, so his attention switched back to the programme.

Sir Harley stood, or rather, floated crudely in space as he again took up the story…

"Welcome back space mystery fans. To understand why StarVista 4 was where it came to be

The Last Voyage of the StarVista 4

as it met it's terrible end we have to know something about the star system that contains the gas giant planet, Tianca. Although many of our kindred space-faring civilisations knew of the system of planets of the star Cantrara, it was not until an exploration vessel from Alteran 11 in 2387 surveyed its largest planet, Tianca, that it became known that its sheer beauty surpassed even our own glorious planet Saturn. Yes, Tianca had a ring system. But a ring system like no other.

Five, yes, five bright icy rings lay around the planet with inclinations of up to twenty-three degrees from the equatorial plane with cascading ring falls spiraling down, connecting all five rings systems.

Speculation is rife but the best minds suggest we were living through a unique era whereby up to five comets strayed too close to the planet in quick succession and became shredded forming the rings.

With each of the five having different orbital inclinations to their capture and subsequent destruction it could explain why the system is unlike anything else seen in the eighteen thousand worlds of the Galactic Arm Association.

So beautiful is the sight that perhaps it should come as no surprise the StarVista corporation petitioned for decades to include it in its itinerary and fate meant that it was StarVista 4 that made that first, *and last*, commercial voyage to the planet.

After the break we will take a closer look at the StarVista 4 and ask: was there a design flaw? Did it fly into a dangerous area unprepared or was it simply a case of being in the wrong place at the wrong time. Come back soon as we unravel the mystery!"

Andrew shook his head, studied the official report on his holo-tablet and wondered for a brief moment whether to ignore the programme and find something else to while away his time.

But he was fascinated, hooked you could argue… and so he patiently waited for the commercials to end so he could take up the story once more…

StarVista 4: 2405 AC
Day 102: The Etel Six incident

"Hi Danny. Now today was really weird. Our latest stop was the strange planet known as the death world of Etel Six. If you like really ancient history then I guess you'd be happy as this world's people lasted thousands and thousands of years but they all died out!

According to our guides, they ignored all the warnings about not controlling their population and industry and their whole ecosystem collapsed. To top it all, Daddy says a small asteroid crashed into the planet's major ocean and that apparently finished them off. Scary or what?

They say that is why every major planet with people on it has a defence system in place to stop such asteroids or comets. Good idea after seeing Etel Six, I say!

I've taken images of the ruins that are left and some vegetation is beginning to grow again, but there are no large creatures left and I found it quite awful and sad really. I'm glad now our Earth realised the dangers in time as Etel Six really lives up to its name of a death planet.

Would you believe it but we've now visited half of the destination sites and I can't believe we've been on board over three months.

Did I tell you that my toys and games case is now back where we started at Alteran! I'll never see them again! Mummy says not to be too upset but they are my things! Having said that, I'm still exploring the ship so as Daddy says, it keeps me occupied between stopovers.

Must go but will be in touch soon. Byeee!"

Day 104/5

The Last Voyage of the StarVista 4

Watching the various species that populate the GAA worlds and take cruises such as this, always amused and allowed Senior Bar Officer Anatonyp to enjoy his work.

It was the variety of personalities that held a deep fascination for him along with his ability to remember most passengers on a cruise after just a few visits to his bar area on what he liked to think of as the main observation deck. As chief bartender, he spent time on all the decks at some point but knew the staff under him were fully capable of looking after the liquid needs of the passengers, be it alcoholic or not as the case may be.

But something was bothering him.

Pretty much every other day/night period, there were always two Ziancans who frequented the main observation deck bar for roughly an hour. He'd got to know them in a roundabout sort of way.

They belonged to a group of youngish Ziancans who were, by all accounts, very well off and had parents of high esteem. But these two didn't always see eye to eye with the rest of the group who it seemed were always picking on them for 'fun'. The age old, universal, well to do bully boys.

As Anatonyp prepared for the bar section to close for a few hours for the night period, his thoughts kept turning to the two Ziancans. He was also a Ziancan and knew that his species had to take in copious amounts of water to survive. That and to dilute the effects of any alcohol consumed.

Indeed his species could not partake of some types and so he always made a note of any Ziancans who frequented any of the ship-wide bars.

The Last Voyage of the StarVista 4

He made sure his staff were fully aware of how to ensure their Ziancan guests did not 'over do things' to put it mildly.

But he had not seen the two Ziancans since their last stop and something was pinging away in his mind that it was a break from their normal routine. He closed the bar and as the staff left, he tapped into the comms.

"Chief Zaclin. This may seem strange, but we are sure all of the passengers are accounted for?" A pause as he listened to Chief Security Officer Zaclin check his records. "Oh, so all bioscans show all accounted for. Perhaps it is just me, but I haven't seen two of the young Ziancan party since Etel Six and it seems to be stuck in my head now.

Oh, very well, I didn't know they were all in one of the largest suites. Yes, I'll meet you there in a few minutes."

He knew he was chasing the Scralaq up the wrong tree but something just didn't seem to add up. He set off to meet with Chief Zaclin.

#

At the plain door, the same style as every passenger suite on the StarVista 4 Chief Security Officer Zaclin signalled the occupants that he wished to enter as he and Anatonyp stood outside, both thinking they were on a fools errand.

No answer.

Zaclin signalled again then after a few moments, a third final time.

"Now, I don't like this, their bioscans indicate they are all inside. He overrode the door controls with his security clearance and the door slid open.

The group were all sprawled out on the floor, draped over seating, all in distress of sorts. The chief hit the comms button.

"Zaclin to medical bay, emergency situation on deck B, home in on my signals. Full team required, we have multiple casualties, Ziancans and I have Anatonyp here who suspects severe alcohol poisoning and likely dehydration."

As he was doing this Anatonyp had been moving through the room noticing there was another thing wrong. Three were missing despite all their bioscans indicting them to be there.

Zaclin spotted a contraption on one of the dressers and scowled.

"How did they get one of those inside the SV 4 and past my security team?"

"What is it?" asked Anatonyp whilst checking over another of the young Ziancans.

"A bio cloner. Clones the biochips and then creates a mirror that is independent and can fool the ship's systems into thinking the person is on board and healthy when they are not. This is serious. So where are the other three?"

Anatonyp looked around the room. "This looks self-inflicted, not malicious if you ask me. They partied but someone didn't check they had enough water to counteract the influence. Stupid youths! This is not good. What if... What if the other three are still on Etel Six?"

Zaclin's face changed and despite being a Krelti who always had difficulty showing their true emotions, it was obvious he was seriously worried. He was about to say something when Dr Sreisse and the medical team arrived.

"Doctor, it is imperative we get at least one of these rascals awake. We fear there are three of their number possibly left behind at our last stop.

"Well, I'll do what I can, but we need to get them back to the medical bay as they are unconscious." Dr Sreisse motioned to his team and they worked quickly to get the five Ziancans stabilised and off to the medical centre.

Zaclin looked at Anatonyp and shook his head.

"Now for the worst part. Informing Captain Shoo!"

#

Diary update.

"Hi Brother. Oh boy, Captain Xaoping Shoo is really angry! It seems that there is a mixed party of young very well off Ziancans. So, when we stopped and sent down people who wanted to visit Etel Six, you know the death world where everyone had died many years ago, it seems that some of the Ziancan party played a prank on three of their group and they've been stranded there for two days without food or water!

The returning party used holographics to make it look like all of them were on the shuttle and somehow did something to their bioscans, but I feel sorry for the pilot as she's had her pay docked for a week.

The Last Voyage of the StarVista 4

The party that returned apparently got really drunk and forgot about their friends whilst they were passed out in their rooms. Another good reason why I will never touch that stuff called alcohol! They have been put in a sort of jail for a few days to teach them a lesson.

The StarVista 4 can't turn round and go back as it has a fairly strict schedule but luckily several of the shuttles are long distance versions, so one has been dispatched back at high speed with a medical team on board and Mr Delieezas in charge.

It will still take a round trip of six days for the shuttle, as we are getting further away so it will take two days to get there and four days to catch back up with us. The stranded Ziancans are very lucky that Barperson Anatonyp became suspicious because he regularly served two of the stranded Ziancans every day.

When they didn't turn up, he began to ask questions. As you may know Ziancans need lots of water to survive and as there is no way of communicating with those stranded, then the shuttle is heading to where the Ziancan party were dropped off the first time. If they are sensible then they will have stayed in one of the ruins; there is very little wildlife that is dangerous so we are all hoping they are found OK.

Must go as Daddy and Mummy want me to meet someone. I think it is someone they have made friends with during the cruise. Not hard to do, I've made lots of friends now that I'm sort of famous. Hope you are not jealous!

Byeee.

The Last Voyage of the StarVista 4

Day 110
Diary supplemental.

Oh Danny, it is awful. One of the stranded Ziancans died due to exposure and dehydration and the other two are very ill. Dr Sreisse and his team are doing everything they can to save them, but we all are worried for them.

The young Ziancan party have now been charged and formally arrested and will stay in the jail, but that is too good for them according to Mummy. They will be handed over to the port authorities at our next stop at Igrocl.

It's so sad and it's the talk of the ship. I really feel for the shuttle pilot and Daddy has petitioned the captain to be lenient with her as everyone had been fooled by the holographics and false bioscans, even the security chief! Daddy is hoping to convince the captain to not charge the pilot as well.

Igrocl is almost three weeks away at standard cruise speed, but we've been given permission to go faster than usual to get to Igrocl so the awful Ziancans can be taken off the ship sooner. I'll keep you updated.

Byee.

The Last Voyage of the StarVista 4

Day 128: Igrocl diary report

"Hi Danny, so Carrie had been seeing someone else all this time I hate her now and it sounds like you do too. If only she could drop into one of those storms we saw on Zeial! Mummy says I mustn't talk like that but that's what I feel!

On other things, attached are images of our most recent stopover at Igrocl. I asked the captain about the names of these places and she says it is how they are translated into our language that makes many of them seem odd to us.

The Igroclians have built some of the most amazing structures we have ever seen, with buildings stretching miles into the sky with interlinking travelator systems between many of them. They also love to build deep underground. Apparently way back in their past they had two subspecies, one that lived on the surface, the other underground and they used to fight each other. Much like the Atricians and Alterans apparently. Then two of their leaders got fed up and they joined together to form an alliance which has lasted several thousand of our years.

If I understood Mummy and Daddy right, they were amongst the first to explore our galaxies spiral arm where we are and helped form the Galactic Arm Association. Isn't it amazing what can be done when we all help each other!

Oh, I almost forgot, the charged Ziancans have been handed over and I'm pleased to report the two that were seriously ill have been saved by Dr Sreisse and the medical team. They are awesome! I mean the medical team, silly!

The Last Voyage of the StarVista 4

The two survivors are still in a state of shock and have to stay under medical supervision for a few weeks so they can't leave the ship until Dr Sreisse gives them clearance.

We now have another long period between stopovers but if anything happens, I will send a message to you. Love you Danny. Keep strong and I'm sure someone will come along to keep you company.

Byee!"

#

Cabin C2001

The message was clear, their suspicions had been confirmed and the decision to allow her on board the ship had been the right one. If their intelligence was correct then as a bonus, the StarVista 4 was going to be allowed to go where no GAA ship had gone before, at least not a civilian one. Few ships had been to the Cantrara system on the very edge of GAA space and her instructions were now clear.

She was to try to prevent the StarVista 4 from getting to the system. It ran against her own personal needs as ideally the ship would be taking her straight to her final departure point from the retched GAA, but her needs were now of no consequence.

She'd successfully removed the medicom biochip and installed it in a special adapter that simulated her biorhythms and gave out false readings for her location at all times, giving her freedom to move about the ship without suspicion. So far it had worked like a charm.

Fortunately she was well equipped, the masking field had prevented detection of her smaller items of equipment and of her true form. She carefully made her way to engineering.

Adjusting the kit until she was invisible when there was no one around, she waited until a member of staff left and she quickly slipped in, unnoticed.

She went to work setting the tiny device in place. Once activated and its job done on the hyper engines, the device would be obliterated leaving no trace.

An apparent simple malfunction of the engines and the cruise would have to divert to the nearest star port and more than likely the ship would not continue any further. She had at least got this far and would have to make her own plans to get to the Cantrara system, but this ship would not now be the one to do it.

She bided her time.

Day 130: Dr Sreisse, and a party too!

Cherice stood outside the door and waited patiently. After a few minutes when she'd begun to think nobody knew she was there, the door slid open and a beaming Dr Sreisse indicated to her to enter the medical facility.

"Now Master Cherice, I want... oh dear, have I said something wrong?"

"No, well yes, Doctor Sreisse, I'm not a boy, I'm a girl so really it should be *Miss* Cherice."

"Oh dear, I am sorry and hope I have not caused you offence?"

"No silly, oops, sorry I shouldn't have said that should I?"

"Then that makes us even - now let's have a look around as we're quite slow today, I think you would say that is a good thing. With two thousand passengers and seven hundred crew it can get surprisingly busy at times but usually nothing serious, I'm glad to say. Not like the frightful events surrounding the Ziancan party, that was definitely a one off, at least I hope it was!"

Dr Sreisse gestured to her, turned and led the way through into the main theatre.

"Because of our long flights, we have almost every conceivable medical aid and equipment you might need whether you are Scorion, Gu-Alt, Human or Alteran as well as many of the other primary races of the GAA. As you know, most species have evolved on nitrogen and oxygen atmospheric worlds and over the long span of the GAA many of the

The Last Voyage of the StarVista 4

oldest species have adapted, until they all now require just one variation of the atmospheric mix.

I have looked at you and your family's records for this voyage and I'm glad to see you had been taking the extra supplements as advised."

"Why do we have to do that - they taste horrible!"

"Your worlds are a recent addition to the GAA and so you haven't had the same exposure to the standard atmosphere as the rest of us, so the supplements allow you to breathe the ship's atmosphere with no difficulty at all."

Dr Sreisse moved through into another room where a special adaptable bed lay off to one side and a bank of consoles and controls on the other.

"Kindly lie down on the bed and wear these special goggles to protect your eyes." Cherice did so a little warily as the Doctor indicated to a screen and a Ziancan nurse came into the room to check that Cherice was comfortable on the bed. She helped Cherice adjust the goggles to ensure they were in place, then retired out of the room, Dr Sreisse smiled.

"Now Cherice, this scanner will map your entire body in minute detail so we can check for anything that may be wrong. This is just a demonstration for you as I have your medical records and I have no worries at all. Close your eyes until I say you can open them. OK?"

"Yes Doctor." a slightly timid voice wafted over from the scanner bed as Dr Sreisse began the scan. Two minutes, but what felt like an eternity to Cherice, it was over and to her amazement a full-size holographic version of her appeared, standing in a nearby illuminated cubicle. It appeared fully clothed, much to her relief.

"Now, let me show you where and what your liver looks like." He adjusted a few parameters and a section of her body became semi-transparent, showing the liver in 3D. Dr Sreisse manipulated the controls and the liver appeared to float away out of her holographic body and then enlarged to ten times the size showing it in minute detail. He then peeled back the layers of data exploring the insides of the liver.

Cherice thought she would feel sick at this strange exploration of something inside of her, but she was instead fascinated, if a little squeamish, at the odd sight before her.

"Can I see my brain?" she tentatively asked and Dr Sreisse nodded, smiling at her inquisitiveness. The liver vanished and then the holographic person's brain appeared in front of Cherice. Gradually its layers were explored showing the intricate structure that was her own brain. She stood in awe as Dr Sreisse shut down the hologram of brain and person.

"With this, my team and I can explore in incredible detail what is happening to someone's body and we can see where something is going wro…" Suddenly a warning light came on and a voice sounded out of thin air.

"Dr Sreisse, medical emergency, three incoming from engineering with hyperspacetial burns. Medical teams assembling in bays one to three."

Dr Sreisse motioned to Cherice. "I'm sorry Cherice but you will need to leave as I don't know how serious this is for now, but once the emergency is over then I will inform you of the outcome if I am at liberty to discuss it."

With that Cherice was ushered out by the newly appeared Ziancan nurse who smiled at her as she left. She waved good bye as the door shut firmly behind her.

#

Chief Engineer Coaraskk stood quietly as Captain Xaoping Shoo sat in quiet contemplation in her command quarters after reading the chief's report. It seemed like an eternity to the chief. Being a Gu-alt, you could not easily interpret the expressions on the captain's face, all the chief could tell was that the captain was in deep thought and had to be concerned at events.

"So…" Captain Xaoping Shoo began, "We were fortunate in that whatever it was, the engines are unaffected, but somehow there was a small breach allowing some hyper radiation to seep through. Hence our casualties. Yet there is no explanation for the accident and no signs of any form of sabotage?"

"Correct Captain. I have been over the engine manifolds several times in the smallest detail and can find no sign of a possible device that may have caused the rupture. We have repaired the very small amount of damage where the worst effects occurred, affecting Ziik and Beskq along with ensign Dhall. They have all now recovered fully as we were quick to get them to the medical bay.

You mention sabotage, but why would anyone do that and to what end? We fully screen all passengers and crew before the voyage begins and Chief Zaclin is very thorough." The chief said with conviction.

"I agree. However we've had enough unusual events, what with the Ziancan pranks and now this. As I understand, none of the passengers are aware of the engineering accident?"

"Chief Zaclin has assured me none of the passengers know, well, err… all except one."

"Out with it Chief, I'm slowly losing patience."

"The young humarling, Cherice Richmond, was in the medical bay visiting when the three crew were brought in. As far as I am aware Dr Sreisse sent her away making her believe it was a drill and Chief Zaclin has made discreet enquiries with her parents and they appear to know nothing."

"Good. Let us keep it that way. The last thing we need is the passengers thinking they are on a dangerous voyage. The company would not forgive us if they had to deal with complaints or even passengers wanting to disembark early and asking for compensation.

Chief, I don't believe you or your team was at fault, but keep a close monitor of systems for any abnormal changes. I have a strange feeling about all this but cannot put my tichao on it. Dismiss."

"Yes Captain." Coaraskk left, also having a deep unwelcome feeling that something was amiss with the voyage but like the captain, could not understand what the underlying problem could be. Not enough to inform the company that the voyage should be halted as there was no evidence to present.

Coaraskk resolved to ensure that engineering was even more secure, although he couldn't believe anyone could have got in.

Sabotage?

No. Couldn't be… Who in their right mind would want that and what would it gain them? The questions racing through the chief's mind were unsettling.

In Cabin C2001 there was a frustrated passenger who couldn't understand why her mission had failed…

#

Cherice Diary entry extra:

"Hi Danny, did you miss my messages? I'm now going to be a nurse or a doctor as they are really great and so kind and always want to help you. I asked Dr Sreisse the other day if I could visit the medical bay and as it was quiet then he said yes. I'd been there a couple of hours and they showed me the scanners, I went under one and they made a full 3D model of me and everything inside but all in a clear sort of material.

Ugh, I didn't realise how ugly we are inside under the skin. But then they had an emergency and I had to leave. Dr Sreisse has told me they saved three of the crew who had tried to repair something in the engine bay but were made very sick. I don't know what it was, but later I asked Chief Engineer Coaraskk about it and the chief just said that it had been a drill, not an actual real emergency and not to worry.

The Last Voyage of the StarVista 4

On to other things, whilst we had our long gap between systems the captain allowed for another series of shuttle flights and Delieezas took me out flying again. I can't decide on what I want to be when I get older: pilot, engineer, archaeologist, astrophysicist, doctor or nurse. They are all important I guess but I do like the flying bit! We will be coming up on a series of quick stops as the next star systems are close to each other so I'll be in touch after those stopovers.

Must go now as it's mealtime.
Byee!"

#

"Passengers of the StarVista 4 we have a special event to celebrate this evening. It has come to light that one of you is about to celebrate a very special birthday. Yes, *Xanalorer tric-al-pascer*, it is indeed your good self I am addressing. By arrangement with your home planet authorities, we will be hosting a live-link up with your planet's chief elder along with your family that are with you on this voyage.

The captain cordially invites you to attend her cabin for pre celebratory drinks at 18:30 ship standard time. This will be followed by a special banquet in your honour."

Graylor finished and Xaoping Shoo was pleased as she turned to Carson.

"Are the link-up preparations going to be smooth Carson? I don't want it to be spoiled due to interstellar static or whatever it is you usually give as an excuse for poor connections."

"Why Captain, you do me a disservice, when have I let you down before?" Carson looked a little downhearted to say the least. After all, he had a reputation to defend.

"Two seasons ago, Vitriac coronation, ring any bells?"

"Now Captain, that is a little harsh. There was a major solar flare just at the wrong time, Carson couldn't have done a thing about it." Graylor stood firm next to Carson who smiled appreciatively at the support.

"Very well, just keeping you on your toes Carson. Triple check everything and then do it again just to make sure there is no problem later. If it all goes to plan, then I'll give you a bonus myself in appreciation."

Now that offer made Carson smile and nod to the captain.

"I won't let you or the passenger down Captain, promise."

"Good, I'll hold you to that."

#

The celebrations were in full swing and Carson kept his side of the bargain as the chief elder on the planet T'pc spoke eloquently via hyperlink about how proud his people were on Xanalorer tric-al-pascer reaching four hundred and eighteen orbital periods.

Only three other T'pcians had reached into their four hundreds and she was the first in two hundred years to do so and still be in amazing health.

Xanalorer was given the hyper comm and addressed them all.

The Last Voyage of the StarVista 4

"Thank you, Chief Elder, T'pc grand council and the many millions of good will messages I have received for my birthday. I am often asked how I have done it. Blah, I have no idea as I love my food and especially a little, or should I say a large, tipple of trianquer wine and I do like to indulge in my favourite Squilt fish delicacies. So, I have no answer except to enjoy life, your friends, family, especially family as I have so many now.

Who would have thought I could be a great great great great and yet again great grandmother to so many T'pcians! I thank our wonderful captain and marvellous crew who have made my voyage so enjoyable. Now let us do something very special. You, yes you dear, come up here to me."

Everyone looked to see who she was pointing to; Cherice stood petrified as she realised it was she in the spotlight. Natalie bent down and whispered in her ear.

"Go on dear, just think about it and enjoy the moment."

Cherice stepped forward hesitatingly then picked up her courage and walked up to stand with Xanalorer who spoke.

"Here we are, is this not wonderful and a marvellous sign of our wonderful Galactic Arm Association. Everyone on T'pc, this is Cherice, she is the youngest to be allowed on such a voyage with her parents. So here we are, the youngest and oldest passengers at the same time. How wonderful it is. Thank you for coming along and joining me here tonight Cherice and I hope you have many years ahead of you - take my advice, enjoy them all to the fullest!"

The Last Voyage of the StarVista 4

She raised her glass and took a long swig of the black fluid as everyone joined in with cheers and laughter.

Day 133
Diary entry

Hi Danny, we had a party on the ship as one of our passengers is four hundred and eighteen! She is called Xanalorer tric-al-pascer and she is from one of the minor and newer worlds to join the GAA. Her world is called T'pc so we often say 'topic' but she doesn't mind. For her species it is very unusual to reach three hundred and fifty and even rarer to reach four hundred so to get to be four hundred and eighteen is very special for them so her world treated her to this voyage.

Daddy thinks it is wonderful too, but did then tell me that a year on T'pc is shorter than ours and so she is actually the same as a one hundred- and fifty-seven-year-old human. If you ask me, she is still old! I was part of the celebrations too, I bet Mummy and Daddy have already sent you the holo recording of me with her as she seems to like me and we're the oldest and youngest on board so we're very special.

I always told you I was the special one! Next stop is Elac V so I'll be in touch after that.

Byeee.

Stra-k'er 3
A remote, inhospitable planet in the Scorron system.

The human agent landed his small, but high-speed, long-distance transport at the designated coordinates on a small and quite plain looking flat area of the plateau. Immediately the flat section began to descend, but the agent was not surprised at all.

This was the nerve centre for the Galactic Arm Association Security Service and very few outside the service knew this facility existed. The reason for that involved a dummy facility located on the Ziancan home world acting as the 'public' face of the GAA Security service and allowing for the actual work of the service to go barely noticed from Stra-k'er 3.

The platform came to rest, and his ship's sensors indicated the atmosphere was now breathable, so he exited his ship and used his nav tracker to head purposefully in the direction indicated for the door.

It opened silently for him, and he walked deeper into the facility, before coming to a halt outside the elevator door. Again, due to his biosensor activating it, the door slid open; he stepped inside and briefly waited before it began to descend even further into the heavily protected facility.

Once it stopped and the door opened, he stepped out into a brightly lit corridor and strode

The Last Voyage of the StarVista 4

along it until a blue illuminated door lay before him; it too opened at noting his biosensor presence.

"Good. Quick work there Malin, Zepf here thought it would take you another day to arrive."

Malin looked at the five seated and one standing occupant, the latter had addressed him and Malin recognised her as Traic-sen Flr, a Gu-Alt. He knew all of them but knew only to address the one in charge unless any of the others spoke to him directly.

"I was always taught not to keep anyone waiting, especially when there is an urgent matter at hand." Malin said matter of factly, as he looked about the small group. Alteran, Ziancan, Scorran, Bilastronon, Gu-Alt and Krelti, the six oldest and primary GAA member civilisations.

"We have a delicate mission for you under your civilian guise and human nature. You served the GAA Security service very well on your mission to infiltrate the StarVisa 1 a few years ago, so you are familiar with their ships of leisure and in particular the StarVista class ships.

What I am about to disclose is highly classified and only ourselves and a small handful of vital workers know of the seriousness of what we suspect.

We have intelligence to indicate that there is a potential threat to the GAA building up on a remote system at the farthest reaches of our interstellar boundary. Have you heard of the star system Cantrara?"

Malin thought for a moment as something tingled deep inside his subconscious and drifted up to enlighten him.

"Barely, very remote, similar star type to the Anchi system star, but hardly explored. One thing of potential note is that it has a gas giant planet with an unusual rings system, but I can't recall its name..."

"Tianca." offered the Billastronon and Malin nodded appreciatively at the representative.

"Correct, Tianca." added Traic-sen Flr. "The unusual and rather odd circumstance is that normally interesting systems are thoroughly explored before our more general populace are allowed to venture to such newly discovered systems. However, despite the initial reports of, as you say, an unusual ring system surrounding the largest planet, no other official explorations have taken place."

"Seems very lax, why not if it is that interesting?" mused Malin and now Zepf, the Ziancan representative spoke up.

"Exactly. It is as if someone or something is deflecting any requests. Except we have accidentally discovered that for some reason, the StarVista corporation has been given approval for their StarVista 4 cruise ship to venture to Tianca at the end of their current voyage."

Traic-sen Flr moved several tentacles and Zepf acquiesced and fell silent.

"This however gives us our chance to find out what is going on, both with the StarVista 4 and this odd ringed planet. We are arranging an unusual passage for you, as you will not be able to use your own ship for the final part of your journey. You will be taken to star port Falaise-c-puc and there use your renowned skills to become part of the passenger list.

The Last Voyage of the StarVista 4

We are aware that forty two originally booked passengers were unable to take up their places on the voyage so I am quite sure you will have no problem securing a cabin. I also assume you will use the same persona you used for the StarVista 1 voyage which will at least help provide a back story to your character. Have you any questions?"

Malin looked thoughtful for a moment.

"I will be operating on my own with little in the way of support?"

"Actually, no, the newly appointed ambassadors from Terra to Zianca will also be on the voyage and they are very trustworthy. They are now aware someone will be joining the ship and there will be an addition to the itinerary, but you are not to make contact unless absolutely necessary.

They have also been sworn to secrecy so unless something happens that compromises your mission then remain anonymous whilst you try to discover why the StarVista 4 is going to Tianca. That is all."

Malin nodded politely and turned, leaving the room in deep thought as to the nature of the possible threat to the GAA and why Tianca was so important, considering its remoteness…

Day 135: Elac V, Pallasadine and Pol

"Elac system ahead Captain, fifty-two hours before orbital rendezvous with Elac V. It will be tight, but we should make it in time just before the event occurs."

"Good, nice work there Deli. Looks like we're on a northern approach vector?"

"Yes, this system is inclined at thirty-two degrees to the galactic plane; twelve planets, eleven in their systems equatorial plane with one retrograde, presumed captured, planet eighth out from their sun. Elac II, III, IV and V are in the habitable zone, but what makes Elac V special is its orbital resonance with Elac VIII.

Elac VIII makes regular close passes of Elac V, every twenty-six of their years, giving rise to violent tectonic activity on the surface facing Elac VIII. At the closest point to each other the volcanic eruptions can throw material out into space looking much like solar activity, but lava instead. The material is usually caught up between the gravity wells of the two planets and becomes strung out as a new series of planetoids, which are fortunately mostly flung outwards away from the inner populated planets.

According to local data, since the first telescopes were pointed at Elac V from Elac II, the first planet to develop intelligent life, there has never been a failure of the eruptions. There are several safely positioned orbital complexes around Elac V which will be monitoring the event and due to its nature we are only allowed to take the SV4 in to a million chaks.

The Last Voyage of the StarVista 4

However, we can send in up to two remotely piloted shuttles to give our passengers close up views on the observation decks screens.

"Excellent. Good to see you are up to speed, I assume you will be the one remotely piloting the shuttles?"

"Yes Captain, unless you wish otherwise."

"No, continue, Carson can take the helm of the SV4. You are up to the job are you not Carson?"

"Indeed captain, Delieezas has thoroughly briefed me and everything is in place once we get to one million chaks."

"Very well, we're in good hands. Graylor, brief the passengers as usual please."

#

Diary entry

Silly me, I thought it wasn't recording! Hi Danny!

On to our recent stop. It was amazing. The good news is that this time they got the timing right! What am I talking about? Well, it was the rare eruption of a super, super geyser on Elac V.

Every twenty-six years, because of some other oddball planet in the wrong orbit, it erupts and sends a huge splurge of lava, water and stuff that actually escapes the planet and then becomes trapped in orbit forming a giant temporary ring system, until it slowly spreads out and fades away.

Some of it even escapes into their outer solar system. We got there with just a few hours to spare and watched it from a distant and safe orbit.

The Last Voyage of the StarVista 4

The Captain had worked everything out so a shuttle had gone on ahead and showed live coverage from close in. They have to be at least ten thousand km away for safety and as this time it erupted just before dawn it formed a spectacular rainbow effect as the spray shot up into the light.

You know how much I love rainbows! I'll not forget that one in a hurry, but I don't think the pics I've attached really do it justice.

Then we headed off at high speed and three days later were at the planet Pallasadine, the fifth planet of a nineteen planet system called Sadine. All the planet names of this system end in 'sadine', apparently. However, it wasn't the planet we were there to see but a huge tri annual exodus of what I can only describe as space bats, creatures that are almost half a mile large!

They migrate from Pallasadine to the sixth planet, Xsosadine for several of our years then head back again. No one knows why they do it, but Mummy said it doesn't seem to be for you know what!

We'll be coming up on our next stop in the next few days, called Pol. Something to do with a dead species that no one knows much about, so I'm not sure what to expect.

I'll call you with pictures after it. Did your new 'date' go OK? You haven't said anything yet about her so it makes me think you maybe don't want to tell me about it.

Guess you are still annoyed with Carrie for seeing someone else? Like Mummy says, there are plenty of others out there who will love you for who you are.

I'll be in touch soon again.
Byeee!

The Last Voyage of the StarVista 4

Day 141

Lariq stood with Cherice as they gazed out into space from the port observation deck C.

"So, we have been given permission to fly alongside the main approach hyperway to the Pol system and I thought it would be fun to spot and count ships."

"Ooh yes, but I thought we had to stay in the main hyperways for most of our voyage. Is it not wrong for us to be just outside them?" Cherice was a little confused as to what was and was not allowed.

"Normally commercial ships travel via the hyperways between star systems so there is no chance of collision and as a passenger ship we normally follow such routes. But we also have special dispensation where possible to fly just outside them if it is deemed necessary and safe.

The Captain arranged for us to do this last part of the trip to Pol a few hundred thousand chaks away from the hyperway so passengers could enjoy the unusual view, watching the ships who are travelling along it.

We did something similar a few months back when I showed you that freighter, remember?"

"Yes, seems like a long time ago now."

"Look over there at that bright green 'star'." Lariq touched the observation view screen lightly and zoomed into it. "That's a marine transport. Have you studied the 'Nlie' culture yet?"

"No, I don't know them."

"They are an aquatic culture and their ships act like giant, I think you would call them, 'fish tankers'?

"Ahh, I see, so they can't breathe our normal air?"

"No, they would die in a very short space of time. As they are such a specialised culture, they have their own special 'cruise ships'.

That appears to be one of them. They struggle with interstellar hyperflight so for most of their journeys they are held in suspension."

"I wonder if they dream?" Cherice asked as she watched the green 'star' slowly drop behind them.

Lariq was not paying attention however as he had noticed something leave the hyperway. He tapped on the screen for info and nodded his head thoughtfully.

"I am not surprised. See that 'star' getting brighter? It was in the hyperway but has changed course and is looking like it is checking us out. It will be a GAA Defence ship so they will just be doing their job. I bet the captain will be pleased."

Lariq zoomed the screen in and tapped to lock onto the view as they watched the ship get closer so that they could see more and more detail on it. A formidable ship indeed.

On the command centre bridge it had also been noticed.

"Captain, I have incoming message from the GAA Defence Ship Ziqfel requesting our flight clearance and itinerary" Carson reported as Xaoping Shoo looked at the approaching ship on their view screen.

"Very well, send the details over to them. Just doing their job, we have official clearance so I can't see there being a problem."

The Last Voyage of the StarVista 4

They watched as the Ziqfel matched heading and position just over a chak away, still close enough to see the larger ship's structure.

Carson listened in then smiled.

"All clear, everything in order and they hope we have a good trip.

Their captain, Ilerik, notes we will be heading to Falaise-c-puc Starport and requests us to say hello to the GAA Defense Ship 'Cazalee'. They suggest that we tell them not to have too much fun on holiday whilst others in the fleet have to work hard."

Captain Xaoping Shoo smiled as she realised, she knew the captain of the Cazalee. "Inform them it will be my pleasure to tell Captain Rii what Captain Ilerik says."

Carson turned back to his station and began to speak to the Ziqfel as it began to pull away from them, leaving them to continue on their course.

Soon, the StarVista 4 felt the gravitational tug of star system Pol and with the skilful guidance of Delieezas, it approached and entered orbit around the only rocky planet in the system, technically Pol IV. Even from orbit it was a desolate looking world, primarily desert; yet dried up mighty riverbeds, estuaries and signs of depressed areas suggesting that major seas and oceans had once been present.

That and what looked like the signs of a vanished civilisation were as mere parchment marks on an ancient scroll.

Astro-archeologists had almost two hundred excavations going on, dotted around the planet, yet little was known of the species that had lived there and there was not even a clear sense of how long ago it was that they had disappeared.

Only one enduring monument could be found, the Pol 'spire' a twenty km high column of unknown origin and composition, with the last few metres of the tip a dull brown colour compared with the sand-coloured rest of the spire.

With no obvious signs of an entrance and the material defying any form of examination it was now a huge tourist destination. No building works were allowed by the overseeing civilisation charged with looking after Pol, the Nelz, so visitors could only sightsee by landing at the designated sites via shuttle and by local Nelz transports.

The StarVista 4 orbited, giving everyone superb views of the planetary features. When the Pol spire came into view the fleet of shuttles ferried passengers down to explore for themselves.

A mystery that not everyone thought was interesting…

#

Diary entry

Hi Danny, we've reached a planet called Pol. It was boring for me as the highlight was exploring some really ancient ruins, again of some people that no one knows anything about. The only interesting thing for me was it does have a huge column that stretches twenty km into the sky, but there is no entrance to it and no one can scratch the surface.

The Last Voyage of the StarVista 4

The really odd thing is that the tip is a different colour and no one knows why or what purpose it served. It's a mystery. It seems I was one of the few that wasn't that impressed with Pol, perhaps I'm turning into a Scorion!!!

Byee until next time!

The Last Voyage of the StarVista 4

Day 143: Detour and a high note.

Comms Officer Carson listened carefully then sent a signal to the captain who entered hurriedly from her side quarters. Seeing Graylor next to Delieezas she motioned for her to join them.

"Run that by me again Carson."

"Official request from Cep'll, confirmation from headquarters too. We are close enough to that system to do a detour as the long-standing head of state has passed away suddenly and our on-board ambassadors are to attend the funeral on behalf of Terra and Zianca. To show a mark of respect, there are to be no passenger stopover visits whilst there. I've passed on the schedule details to Mr Delieezas."

"Well Deli, how does this impact our normal itinerary?" asked Xaoping Shoo. Delieezas was already busy examining the data.

"I can adjust speed as we've been given special permission so we can do the detour with only two days loss to the schedule. According to this we only need less than a day in orbit at Cep'll. The ambassadors and you can go ahead of us with Shuttle Trallaac, so you can be rested up and in position for the funeral procession. It is a steady walk of about two standard hours from the central palace to their ceremonial centre for the commemoration, after which you will be free to return to the ship."

"Ahh, the Trallaac, your favourite and I'm guessing you wish to fly us too?" asked the captain smiling, knowing what the answer would be.

"It would be my honour, Captain."

"Very well. I assume the ambassadors have also received a communiqué about this, Carson?"

"Yes Captain."

"Good, inform them of our arrangements to leave. It looks like you have the ship for a couple of days Graylor. Don't lose it will you!"

Graylor zXanders was mildly amused at her captain but knew she would make up for it another time. Xaoping looked over towards Delieezas.

"Am I correct in thinking they're adapting a captured asteroid to become their main star port rather than building a usual station?"

"Yes Captain, it will be stationed at the forward stable orbital point and I believe it is twelve chaks long and eight wide, so plenty of space to excavate and build inside it. I was hoping to visit it on my next leave as I'm fascinated with it.

It will have an entrance and exit either side of it and can take even the largest GAA ship, so they are being quite ambitious. Mind you it's expected to take another ten Terran years to complete but on our way out of the system I could perform a flyby as long as the Cep'll authorities are in agreement."

"Very good, might have known you'd be interested in that. Yes, let's make it another special addition for our passengers, and at no extra cost too. They will love that."

Delieezas smiled and turned back to his console pleased as a Flaraina fly swan!

#

"You are to represent both the Ziancan and Terran civilisations at this sad time of passing of the Head of the Cep'll civilisation, 'Pallr tsk Pinolver XIX'.

We have to take part in the funeral procession and once the ceremony ends we can leave." Natalie Richmond read the holo screen out loud as Carl stepped back into the room from the bathroom facilities.

"So don't we have to stay for the new head of state to be sworn in?" he asked.

"I was just coming to that. Seems the new head walks alongside the funeral carriage of the old head, then once inside they sit next to each other. I assume they must have a way of holding the dead person up. They then ceremoniously swap the state gown from the deceased to the new head and that's it. They are then the official head of their civilisation."

"Sounds quick and neat. All over and done with then in a short space of time."

"Yes, then there are three months of celebration both of the past head and looking forward to the new one's time in office. We're not needed for the rest, otherwise our voyage would be over."

"Cep'll, that seems to ring a bell with me…" Carl knew there was something in the back of his mind that was familiar about the planet.

"Ahh, I think you mean that as Pallr tsk Pinolver XIX was quite elderly, she'd begun to make official statements suggesting the GAA was being infiltrated. They were dismissed as no one could produce evidence proving it. She was, after all three hundred and twelve of our years old, and some do say she was losing her marbles so to speak."

"Guess we'll have to ask Lariq to stay with Cherice, she'll be happy with that as they do enjoy playing games together. I got to know a bit about his family and he says they live to quite a long age compared with us. He has a very young niece who is also called Lariq and he's been telling his niece all about Cherice's adventures. Isn't that sweet?"

"Guess so. Perhaps once we're settled in at Zianca we'll have to see if they can come and visit between his cruises."

"Oh, what a good idea. Cherice will love that. We'd best let her know we've got a change of plans for the next few days when she comes back from one of her little explorations.

"Little?" She knows more about this ship than most of the crew, I'd wager!" Carl chuckled as he and Natalie headed towards the door to meet up with Captain Xaoping Shoo for a briefing on what to expect.

Day 143
Cep'll Detour

"Wow, that's a lot of ships!" Carson looked on with the command crew as they entered orbit at the designated coordinates given to them by the Cep'll orbital authorities. Ships of a huge range of sizes and from almost all of the GAA civilisations were now in attendance as a mark of respect.

"Cep'll was the eighth civilisation at the founding of the GAA so I'm not surprised so many are here.

They may be a relatively small civilisation by Ziancan, Scorran and Alteran standards but they are highly respected elders, so it is befitting that so many send their delegates." Xaoping commented then turned to Carson. "Have we received confirmation of details of where we fit into the ceremony and when we should head down to the capitol?"

"Yes Captain, I have informed the ambassadors to meet you and Delieezas at shuttle bay one in an hour's time ready for departure."

"Very well, let us go get prepared with our ceremonial garments. Deli and I'll meet you at the shuttle bay. Graylor, take command and Carson, the helm is yours, don't wreck the ship whilst we're gone!"

Xaoping Shoo and Delieezas left them; Carson looked at Graylor then at Calsohn, the science officer, with a glum face.

"Will she ever trust me? I only mixed up the orbital coordinates once and she's never let me forget!"

"Now, Carson, can't you tell it was in jest? Mind you, you humans do struggle interpreting Gu-alt expressions, so don't worry. I'll be keeping all eyes on you."

Carson turned back to his station as Calsohn smiled at them both and the banter.

#

Cherice stood next to Lariq as they watched the start of the ceremony taking place on the planet below them.

The Last Voyage of the StarVista 4

She knew it was important as most of the passengers were on the various observation decks where the screens were showing aerial and space borne views of the event taking place. A couple of times she had even spotted her parents and the captain as they sombrely walked the ceremonial walkway. They were a long way back in the entourage and she felt pride that her mother and father were so important as to be asked to attend such an event.

But she was getting bored. All the views showed the very long procession. It seemed like they were taking forever to reach the official sanctity where the body would be placed in a sitting position next to the Cep'llian who was to succeed them.

Cherice carefully tapped Lariq's left leg and he turned and looked down at her with a puzzled expression.

"Yes, Cherice?"

"I'm bored. Can we do something else now?"

"Well, this is important but… not everyone is watching the funeral procession and you have been good and watched some of it, enough to spot our party amongst the attendees. So, I believe we can say we have done our duty. What would you like to do?"

"How about 'hide and seek'?"

Lariq looked at her, blinked, slower than usual as if he was thinking very hard about the possible consequences of anything going wrong, then tilted his head slightly, a gesture he was slowly picking up from her.

"Very well. However, I have to impose conditions.

The Last Voyage of the StarVista 4

No areas of the ship that are in the crew quarters or zones, only areas you have been allowed access to by the captain when she gave you the freedom of the ship.

Also, due to the time and the size of the ship, we must limit ourselves to the first four passenger decks and no further back than one third of the ship. Is that understood?"

He brought out his holo display and activated it to show an overall plan of the ship. Quickly he marked out the areas she could and couldn't use and then transferred the info to her own holo recorder display.

"Now, so we are not too late and will be back at your quarters in time for your bedtime, I'm imposing a time limit of two of your hours."

Cherice looked at it and nodded enthusiastically. "Oh thank you Lariq, now you'd better get going."

Lariq looked at her perplexed and she continued.

"Not me to hide, I want to find you. Shall we say ten Terran minutes for you to hide somewhere then I'll start to look."

She closed her eyes and put her hands over them as Lariq chuckled, then looked around and headed off down the nearest corridor knowing full well Cherice would be safe. After all she had explored most of the accessible sections of the ship since being given the ship's freedom.

Everybody seemed to love her and it was certainly true that the crew felt protective towards 'the special one' as she had been called by a few of them in good humour.

Once she felt Lariq had enough time to get far enough away and was no longer on the observation deck Cherice opened her eyes and watched the time tick away on the screen as it counted down the minutes, then seconds.

Finally, it reached zero. "Ready, I'm coming to find you." she said to herself and briskly set off skipping along the corridor, much to the amusement of a couple of Scorans who were late to view the funeral procession.

She wondered where Lariq would go and cheekily asked several passing passengers and even crew members if they had seen him, but to no avail.

Half the time was gone when she stopped and had a brief flash of inspiration. It was naughty and would take several minutes but she knew where she could go to find out Lariq's hiding place.

Meanwhile Lariq felt pleased with himself. She'd spend ages looking for him and if he was correct, he was in the one place she wouldn't consider. He settled down, brought out his holoscreen and began to watch the most recent messages from his family and especially his favourite niece, also called Lariq.

She had not long turned female from being neutral so was getting used to the change. He smiled as he knew that the eventual change to male would then make her, his nephew! He wondered how long it would be before Cherice became bored…

#

The door slid open.

"And what can I do for you little humarling? Are you feeling ill? Where are your parents, oh, yes of course, they will be down on the planet. So, are you exploring or at a loose end?"

"I'm feeling very well Dr Sreisse but I wonder if you can help me. I've been trying to find Mr Lariq as he got called away whilst we were on the observation deck watching this slow procession for the funeral that my parents have to be at. I know it's probably not right to ask but I remembered we all have bioscan chips implanted in us, so I wondered if you could locate him for me?" She smiled at the doctor sweetly, but his interest was piqued.

"Well in that case, can I go a step better than that and just call him?"

"Oh no, don't do that, I want to…surprise him to show how good I am at finding him if needed."

Dr Sreisse looked at her a little suspiciously. "Now little humarling, what if he is with someone important or helping one of the other passengers under his care? Are you sure this is what you want to do? Is there something else perhaps?" He looked at her with his piercing eyes, yet they didn't look menacing, more inquisitive. She looked down at her feet then back up at him sheepishly.

"We're playing hide and seek and he has to hide from me." she said quietly.

Dr Sreisse burst out in the loudest laugh she had ever heard and he turned to look at his display then tapped a few times and nodded. He tilted it to show her and her eyes widened with glee…

Twelve minutes later she entered the room and shouted 'gotcha' as she surprised Lariq, quietly sitting in the lounge of her parents quarters minding his own business, thinking it was the last place he thought Cherice would check.

#

"But that is unfair of you miss Cherice." Lariq was clearly upset that she had cheated, and she felt a surge of guilt overcome her.

"I, I thought I was being clever…" she whispered.

Lariq looked at her and tilted his head to the left, a gesture guaranteed to make her smile.

Cherice however looked back down at her shoes and began to tremble. Lariq carefully took her in his arms and rocked her gently as her parents had shown him shortly after their arrival on the StarVista 4.

"It was indeed clever, but you must always play within the spirit of the game. Now, do you want to have another go?"

"Oh yes please. Can I hide this time?"

"Indeed, and I will not be asking the medical team how to find you. But as time is catching up on us, don't go too far."

He swiped the air and a holo player appeared before them. He marked out where she could go and the decks she could use and she looked at it and smiled. He transferred it to her own holo player and pointed to the door.. "One, two, three, four, five…"

She was out the door before he could reach six.

The Last Voyage of the StarVista 4

Almost an hour later Lariq crept along the passage leading to the original docking entry point where Cherice and her parents had first entered the vast ship and his hunch paid off. The ornamental flowering shrubs that faced anyone on first entering the ship looked a little suspicious and slightly out of place. Either the robotic cleaners had miscalculated, unlikely, or a certain person was trying to hide behind them. He carefully walked past looking this way and then that.

His heightened sense of hearing caught a stifled giggle behind the shrubs and he spun round behind them and tapped Cherice on the shoulder as she burst into fits of giggles, stumbling out into the open.

"That was hard, you did well Miss Cherice!" Lariq smiled at her and she did a little curtsey, something Lariq had not actually seen and was instantly amused by. He tried in his ungainly way to mimic her but almost fell in doing so. She laughed then helped him up.

"Can we just go to the observation deck and let me count a few stars before we have to go back to my room? Please?"

"Very well, but not too long."

They headed off and soon stood looking out but the glare of the lights hampered the view. Lariq looked around to make sure there was no one in that section who would be affected then he looked up.

"Ship, dim lights in this section by eighty percent."

The lights dimmed just as Cherice looked up at him. "Why did you look up when you asked?"

The Last Voyage of the StarVista 4

"I don't know, just felt natural to look up as if the ship is above us. Which of course it is but also all around us, otherwise we wouldn't last long would we!"

Cherice nodded then began to count the multitude of stars she could see. Lariq wandered a little further on from her position and admired the view. He was used to it, after all much of his life had been spent on one ship or another but there were few actual moments when he looked out at the stars.

Usually he was much too busy. But Cherice had been a breath of fresh air as he had started to view the voyage through her eyes and he was rediscovering his own sense of wonder. He was deep in his own thoughts and memories when he noticed the sound. A gentle tune and song he was unfamiliar with and he turned in wonderment as he realised Cherice was singing under her breath.

He carefully watched her as she continued and stood impressed and amazed as she began to hit what he could only think of as high notes for her species.

Then she did something extraordinary. Her range took her higher and he tingled all over as he realised, she was singing in tones that were especially significant for Alteran and Ziancan ears. Beautiful to his own ears, even though she needed a little voice training for the highest notes.

He approached, an idea forming, a crazy idea indeed.

"Cherice, did you know you can sing very high and in particular in a range that is most pleasing to some species on board?"

She looked at him a little puzzled.

"That's funny you should say that. Mummy and Daddy always say I can sing some songs at high notes for an extended time - you mean you can hear them too?"

"Can you?"

"Yes, to me it seems normal, but I don't like to tell people because I don't know anyone who like me singing like this. Until now."

"I can help you get the upper notes clearer if you like but perhaps, we should do it alone as I have an idea if you are willing to listen?"

"Ohh, yes, shall we go back now and you can tell me what it is."

"Very good. I think we can make your parents very proud of you if I am right but we don't have much time."

With that Lariq took her by the hand and they headed back to the ambassadors' quarters, Lariq thinking about how he could coach Cherice to sing in high Alteran…

…in time for the gala.

#

"Captain, I have been in communication with the Cep'll authorities and we have been given permission not just to perform a slow fly past of the new station but we can also have a surprise quick visit inside."

Xaoping Shoo looked at Delieezas and shook her head, a human trait that she had picked up, although sometimes she found it hurt a little. She knew she should make an effort not to do it again.

The Last Voyage of the StarVista 4

"No, we haven't time to allow even a few passengers the chance to go inside, we ca…" Delieezas cut her off carefully.

"Sorry Captain, I meant we can take *the ship* inside for a short fly through. They've completed the initial entrance and exit points and we can actually fly right through it which will show everyone the immense work that is being done to turn it into a state-of-the-art space station."

Before Xaoping could react, there was a low whistle from Carson.

"Now that would be neat!" he stated then realised he'd pre-empted the captain. Graylor looked sternly at him then back at her captain who just smiled.

"I agree Carson, nice work Deli. Graylor, kindly inform the passengers they are in for a treat and tell them if they want to get the best views to head up to the observation decks. Time to the fly through, Deli?"

"Four Terran hours."

"Oh, good, time then for something to eat, I'm hungry after all that walking yesterday!

Join me Graylor?"

Guess who didn't need asking twice…

#

The mighty StarVista 4 left the orbit of Cep'll and with perfect timing and precision approached the station asteroid. Right up until they were just a few chaks away it looked like a tiny pinprick to the naked eye.

The Last Voyage of the StarVista 4

A little magnification showed its roughly ovoid shape and as they closed in, the nearside of the asteroid showed a large crater with a 'hole' at its centre.

The entranceway to the station. For the time being the entrance bay door was permanently kept open as so many other smaller transport and specialised machinery ships were entering and leaving. Most bringing materials and workers, heavy machinery and part-built structures to the construction zone. At a pre-arranged moment, the flow of ships stopped and moved to one side as the StarVista 4 approached.

"Passengers of the StarVista 4, we are on the approach and looking forward. Helmspilot Delieezas has us perfectly lined up to enter the asteroidal star port under construction. We are the *only, I repeat, only,* commercial passenger cruiser to be allowed a first look many years before it becomes fully operational.

So do take a moment to marvel at the engineering skills and colossal work that has already been done to create such a large entrance portal. Graylor out."

The ship slowed to a quarter manoeuvring thrust and slowly the StarVista 4 moved into and through the larger cavernous interior.

The extensive works showed the hugely complex task of tunnelling out and excavating the asteroid's interior ready for the multitude of facilities required in any star port. Graylor's voice once again came over the internal comms.

"For your information, we have been informed that the star port, once completed and operational, will be officially called Star Port *Pallr tsk Pinolver XIX* to honour the recently deceased and beloved head of state of Cep'll, although I think we all suspect it will probably be shortened to Star Port Pinolver!

The current, much smaller star port will then be decommissioned but plans are in place to use it for other purposes as yet to be defined. Enjoy the flight and once we exit, we will resume our original course for our next stop over at *P'rlaac.*"

After just thirty minutes most passengers had become bored but those that stayed enjoyed the exit as Delieezas was given permission to speed up out of the exit dock in an unusual fun manoeuvre. He enjoyed doing it too!

Day 149
Diary entry

Hi Danny, I can't believe we've already been on board almost five earth months! We had a change to our schedule and Mummy and Daddy had to attend a funeral now that they are official ambassadors. Something to do with us being the closest so easiest to send in time for the ceremony.

I was able to be with Lariq and we played 'hide and seek' but we had strict instructions where not to go. Even so we had a lot of fun and a few of the passengers also joined in by helping me find Lariq. I must admit, I cheated by asking Dr Sreisse if the bioscan would show where Lariq had got to.

The Last Voyage of the StarVista 4

He said that was an unfair advantage using my celebrity status but as I said, I was trying to be clever. Anyhow, once Mummy and Daddy and the captain got back we did a fly through of the new star port being made out of an asteroid. Then we headed at high speed to our latest stopover which was to see the four hundred mile high cliffs of P'rlaac.

I have to admit I thought it was amazing. You can't imagine the scale of it and the captain took the ship in close. P'rlaac is a very large rocky moon and at some stage it has been hit by something large and it was broken up. Then the bits came back together all higgldy piggldy, but part of it slumped, at least that is what Chief Geophysicist Raskaert said. I want to be a geologist like her now!

Oh, sounds like Mummy is calling so best go.
Byee!

Day 157
Diary entry

Oh, Danny! I'm so excited that you will be coming to greet us at the end of our voyage at Viliak. It would have been more fun if you had been able to come with us in the first place but, I know, the studies had to come first. I know Mummy and Daddy are also happy at the news.

Two days ago we had our stopover at Nempiuq Three star port but it wasn't the actual touristy stop. That was yesterday when we explored the Cazliq Nebula with its twisted, towering columns of gas and dust. I thought the captain had said we would not be going to any more nebulae but this time it was OK.

The Last Voyage of the StarVista 4

It's funny really that from a long way away they look very thick, then as we flew through them they were almost see through! Stars are being born there but we were not allowed to get too close but had to view the protoplanetary disks from a safe distance. Something to do with how our flight into the Qrianlairing Nebula went with its unusual flashes that disturbed me and some of the other passengers. This is how our solar system might have been born apparently.

I was allowed to visit the astrophysics and navigation centre and I met up again with astrophysicist Crayt and it was amazing. So now I want to be an astrophysicist when I grow up!

It won't be long now brother until we see each other and don't have to do these recordings. It's almost a week until we get to the Falaise-c-puc Starport so guess I'll be in touch sometime then.

Oh, I have a secret but can't tell you what, so don't tell Mummy and Daddy. I shouldn't have said anything should I!

Byee!

The Last Voyage of the StarVista 4

Day 169: Falaise-c-puc starport

"Attention passengers, we are now on final approach to Falaise-c-puc Starport and Science observatory. We will be here for three days allowing you the chance to get close up to a pair of merging singularities. Current estimates mean they will merge in the next four years and the habitable planets nearby have already begun evacuation procedures.

Meanwhile Falaise-c-puc Starport remains operational and for now we are of the understanding that our trip is the last of the tourist cruises. After we depart, the starport will become the prime evacuation centre for the system, whilst continuing to monitor the natural phenomena. If you wish to know more then our on-board Astrophysicist Crayt is more than happy to help with your enquiries. Graylor zXanders, out."

Graylor turned as Captain Xaoping Shoo entered the command centre and took her seat.

"Captain, Falaise-c-puc confirms our approach, docking port 91. Delieezas is just waiting for final confirmation before taking us in, as we speak."

"Very good. Crayt assures me the merger won't take place for a long while yet and that they have it calculated to a high degree of accuracy, so I put my trust in science."

Delieezas turned with a smile on his face.

The Last Voyage of the StarVista 4

"They had better be right, I've noted fifty-eight passengers and transport ships currently docked and a steady stream of ships heading out to Falaise five to pick up the first evacuees.

We're lucky they've allowed us to approach. There is also the GAA defence cruiser Cazalee docked at port 87 on a diplomatic mission to ensure the evacuation is orderly." He paused, studying something on his console. "That's odd…"

Something had caught Delieezas attention.

"Hmm, guess they've been cleared…"

"Something wrong Deli?" asked Graylor as she moved over and began looking at Delieezas console.

"That small ship that just passed us off on the port side. You know I like to know who's around or near us at all times and the initial registry scan came up as a privateer, one that was on the wanted list. But it's now classed as a legitimate small transport. They must have done something *really* good to have pulled that off."

"Or they're on a con…" Graylor offered.

"What, right under the noses of the Cazalee? That'd be suicide."

Captain Xaoping Shoo turned to Comms Officer Carson. "Put me through to the Cazalee, tell their comms it's Shoozy for their captain."

That was news to the rest. They'd never ever thought of the captain having a nickname…

The view screen flickered briefly, then a Scorion stood next to an Alteran, the captain and comms officers of the Cazalee.

The Last Voyage of the StarVista 4

"Well, well, Shoozy. Long time no comms. You are apologising then?" said the captain of the Cazalee.

"Fall into the singularity you rascal. Everyone, meet Captain Rii. Hah, of course not. Never. Should be you bowing to me for saving your skin that time. Anyway, more important business, the privatee…"

"Yes, we saw them. The ship is called the Lucky Seven and the captain, for want of a better word, is a Scorron by the name of Screoria. They arrived all brazen, flew straight towards Falaise-c-puc; we were about undock and apprehend them when orders came through they had been granted amnesty.

They're now a legitimate private courier, or so our new records say. We've cleared it with the authorities and although they too are puzzled, it's all been cleared at a much higher level than you or I will ever aspire to. Apparently, they have someone of high importance to bring to the space port on diplomatic credentials, but they are not permitted to say who it is. Very odd but as they are now legitimate there is not a lot we can do.

Shame too as we've had a couple of run-ins with them before and they were sneaky, got away by their necks so it would have been good to take them in. But someone up top likes them - a lot. Not right at all in our books. Orders are orders however, so our hands are tied. You here long? Fancy looking ship you have there."

The Last Voyage of the StarVista 4

"The finest of the fleet is the *'Four'*. We're here for three terran days so once docked and I'm happy we're secured, I'll call you over for a brief tour."

"Very good. I'll await your call. Cazalee out."

#

"So, Shoozy, great ship, get any excitement though?" Xaoping glanced over at Captain Rii half expecting such a comment from her long-standing friend.

They'd both entered service at the same time and had immediately struck up a bond. The rivalry was gentle and always good humoured, but they knew each had the other's back. It had been a strained time however when at the end of the fourth year of training Xaoping had chosen the civilian space service instead of a military career.

Rii was always aiming to get his own ship in the military and made no one doubt his ultimate goal. They had gone their separate ways but somehow, across the myriad light years of space, they had stayed in touch with a gentle, often cheeky rivalry, but also with a deep respect for each other.

"Trust me, dealing with the huge variety of species as passengers would have cracked your sturdy case long ago. I see you keep it highly polished. I can see my reflection!"

"Cheeky. Don't crack it with your ugly sight. I spent a lot of time getting it this good. So, you're happy then? Is Graylor good for you or shouldn't I ask?"

"My love life is not open for discussion. Yes, she is! Better than old Scranny, remember him?"

The Last Voyage of the StarVista 4

"Oh dear, yes, did 25 years good service then went over to your lot and if I remember right, is still the captain of the SV1."

The travelator slowed to a halt before the command centre door and Xaoping Shoo swiped the air to open it. They stepped onto the command centre bridge as the officers stood to attention.

"At ease everyone, Captain Rii is after all off duty." They began to walk round as Xaoping introduced her crew to Rii.

"Deputy, first officer and second in command, Graylor zXanders."

"Ahh, good to meet you after all Shoozy has said about you. Hoping you are making sure she doesn't get into trouble?"

Graylor stifled a smirk and just nodded politely. Xaoping moved them on to a group of officers standing in line.

"This is our science/engineering officer, Calsohn, primary helm, Delieezas and comms/backup helm, Carson."

"Ahh, Carson, a human officer, not many as yet in the service but hoping to see more of your kind represented in the military fleet. How are you finding Shoozy here as captain?"

Carson looked shocked and a little lost for words but finally found his tongue. "Er, Captain Xaoping Shoo is an excellent and a very fair captain, Sir."

Rii turned to Xaoping. "Paid him well to say that - never mind, only being humorous. Good to meet you all and if I may say a fine command crew indeed.

The Last Voyage of the StarVista 4

Any of you ever think of coming over to the military, let me know first and I'll put in a good word for you. Your captain here is one of the best in civilian circles and she or the StarVista company wouldn't have chosen just anyone, I can assure you.

Well, time is running short Shoozy. A drink perhaps before I leave?"

Xaoping nodded and ushered Rii out of the command centre into her briefing room, much to the remaining officer's relief.

Inside, she indicated to a row of brightly coloured decorative flasks and Rii chose the orange one, much to Xaopings delight.

"Knew you would. Always was fond of a little drop of Ziancan brandy." She poured two small glasses and they toasted each other silently.

"Tell me Rii, what's the Cazalee really doing out here? Your class of ship is heavyweight, normally checking on the border worlds and keeping an eye on the few systems not embracing the GAA way of life."

Rii eyed Xaoping and put on his serious face.

"Now, now Xaoping, you know I can't divulge what the GAA military gets up to. But to be fair we're simply on a diplomatic assignment. Keeping an eye on the evacuation proceedings and here to offer assistance if needed. So far it's been quite boring, I can tell you."

"Guess it would have livened things up if that privateer was up to no good?"

"Yes, I was really disappointed we couldn't 'say hello' to them so to speak. Very odd if you ask me.

They're wanted across the GAA interior systems or at least *were* wanted until a matter of two days ago. Something is wrong but my hands are tied. If you happen to see them again, keep an eye on them and drop me a line.

Oh, duty calls. I see my comms is pinging me to return, so with your permission Captain I will take my leave of you. It's been really good to see you again, let's not leave it too long before the next time, Shoozy!"

"I agree, I'll keep an eye out for the Lucky Seven just in case and will let you know. I'll let you in on a secret but you must not divulge anything yet until you hear it officially from me. Graylor and I are entering a formal arrangement and I was going to ask you if you would honour me by being there at the ceremony?"

"Oh of course I would, excellent. Not a word then and get in touch with enough advance warning as you know what it is like in the military. Very pleased for you and I like Graylor, a good match for you and I know you'll be very happy."

"Thank you Rii, now let's get you back to your ship".

#

Diary entry

"Hi Danny. They have lost my toys and games luggage again and no one seems to know where it is. I thought I'd got over it being missing but I cried a lot, although I have been having lots of fun with the other passengers and especially the crew as I explore the ship.

The Last Voyage of the StarVista 4

I do miss my toys and games when we are between destinations. I really hope they turn up. Lariq enjoys coming over and looking after me when Mummy and Daddy have one of their special meetings now they are officially ambassadors and he tells me they are very important on the ship even though it is not part of their official duties yet.

We have just visited Falaise-c-puc starport and science station. It's close to, and monitoring, the site of a twin black hole thingy but we couldn't get too close. It is two really strange black stars that are very dense and so are spinning closer and closer before they stick together and do something like merge according to Astrophysicist Crayt.

As there are something called intense X-rays and gamma rays, the ship couldn't get close but they sent a special probe close in and beamed back images. I actually found it a bit boring as I was hoping they would suddenly go bang.

I know, you can't hear anything in space, but you know what I mean. Not long now until we see you at Viliak so I'm counting down the days as I now feel like this trip is taking ages!

Byee for now, love you Bro!
Byeeee"

The Last Voyage of the StarVista 4

Day 178
Diary entry

"Hi Danny, we reached our next special site a couple of days ago and it looks really odd. It is a gas giant planet that spins so fast it is very oval in shape, so that its polar size is a third of its equator. It looks really weird! It's called Braylon Seven and Astrophysicist Crayt says it could break up any time in the next few hundred years, so there is a big science station orbiting from a safe distance to keep an eye on it.

It also has bands and zones just like our Jupiter but the winds at the equator are the fastest known in the GAA! To be fair, I wasn't that impressed, it was just another gas giant planet that's all and for once most of us seemed to agree it wasn't that special. Perhaps we are all turning Scorran!

So, you want to try again with Carrie, huh? Are you mad? Sounds like me and Mummy will have to talk to you at Viliak when we meet up! Still, if that is what you really want, and she says she misses you then it really is up to you. Love you always Bro!

Byeee!"

Day 180

Carl and Natalie sat relaxing in their quarters after looking through the pile of paperwork they'd had printed out. Done so they could each go over their duties and be up to speed once the voyage was over. It was hard to imagine that it was already coming to an end in the next few weeks and that in just over two months they would be travelling to Zianca to take up their duties as the Terran ambassadors.

The Last Voyage of the StarVista 4

"Carl, have you noticed that Cherice and Lariq are spending a lot more time together? You don't think we should be worried do you?"

"What, of Lariq? Seriously?"

"Carl, something is going on and, well, I thought I was alright with them seeing each other as it helped us when we were busy, and the captain gave him the freedom to keep an eye on her for us. But don't you think it a bit strange that she's now off with him yet again and she won't say what they get up to?"

"Well, now, I had noticed and I have already put feelers out and it seems they are working on something to surprise us. I don't think we should worry otherwise it might spoil the surprise and she's clearly having a lot of fun and it is all above board."

"I hope so, for your sake…" Natalie sighed as she leafed through the formal arrangement documents yet again.

#

Meanwhile, 18,723 light years away, on the other side of the Galactic Arm Association on a small planet hardly anyone ever bothered about…

The messenger nervously waited outside the heavily fortified building as the security guard checked the small metal slip for the messengers' credentials and clearance rank. They grunted approval and held up an appendage to indicate the messenger should wait as the guard passed on the details via the secure link.

The guard turned back to her and pointed towards the entrance which now opened up to reveal a long corridor, poorly lit.

The messenger headed along until she reached a bend where she came to a stop before a new person. Someone so high up in rank she had to bow in deference to show she was unworthy to be in their presence. They in turn indicated to her to follow and another door slid open as she was ushered inside.

It was far brighter in there and she realised there was a seated group of the highest ranking officers. The one at the head made her three hearts pause in their work for a brief moment and she thought she was about to die.

Not yet.

Not this time…

"Speak!" The order came from the one standing at the head and she trembled, knowing they were likely to silence her permanently after she had given them the information she now possessed.

She dried up and just stood there shaking.

"Well? What news is so important that you have to come directly to me?" demanded the head of the group.

She found her voice.

"Excellency, I have news of an unfortunate turn of events that may expose our mighty endeavours to the Galactic Arm Association."

Now that got his attention and he gestured for her to continue.

"We have discovered that a tourist cruiser has been given permission to visit, er, to visit the Cantrara system…"

The Last Voyage of the StarVista 4

"WHAT!"

"Someone in the StarVista corporation gained permission to add the system to the end of the itinerary of one of their voyages. The ship is called the StarVista 4 and it is well into its voyage."

"BUT! How can this be? We infiltrated the GAA hierarchy at the highest possible level and made sure no one would be able to travel out that far, so we could hide our point of entry until we were ready to strike. How did this happen?"

"We do not know your excellency, there is no indication that the GAA security council know of us or our plans. It is a mystery."

His excellency turned to the fourth person sitting on his left. "Tragx, discover if we have a traitor in our midst.

Most of their kind have short life spans compared with ours and in their terms it will take us one hundred of their Terran years for us to have constructed and deployed our fleet. Nothing must interfere with our plans. We need to place someone on board that vessel to discover what they know and why they are going to Cantrara."

"Yes, your excellency. It will be done. I have already in mind someone who was due to go back to home world with the intelligence gathered so far. She is already on board that very ship because it would take her most of the way to Star Port Viliak where the original plan was to commandeer or steal a ship that could take her to the Cantrara system and the planet Tianca.

I will inform them, codenamed Sicanrinka Tavaska, of the change of plan and make arrangements immediately."

Tragx stood up, bowed slightly and left. The messenger stood quietly and awaited her fate.

"You. What is your name?"

She hadn't expected this and hesitated a moment.

"Excellency, Corafa, first of Arana."

"Very well Corafa, first of Arana. You have done well and I thank you for bringing this straight to me. Go back to your station and monitor the situation, answer only to me with any further news.

Understood?"

"Yes, your excellency."

"Now go."

Corafa, first of Arana turned and left, stunned to be walking out alive considering the seriousness of her news…

Day 182:
The surprise and Graylacq Twenty Nine

"Beloved passengers of the StarVista 4, we are delighted to hold our once a voyage Gala entertainment night. My talent scouts have scoured the ship and we can bring you amazing members of both crew and passengers, who will perform for you tonight their specialities for all tastes and species. Given that we do have a special young guest on this voyage, we have made allowance and so there will be no adult performances, but I assure you, you will not be disappointed. I am your host for this gala extraordinare, Trionice -pkci."

She took a bow to thunderous applause in the ships main amphitheatre whilst a little girl sat nervously with her friend backstage and wondered why she had agreed to the event. Lariq sensed her worry.

"My dear Cherice. You have a rare talent, an ability to reach high notes at the limit of normal human capabilities and together we have honed your singing to perfect them. There is no one else in this show that has such an amazing talent, one unexpected in both a human and one so young. Your parents will be immensely proud. And Trionice -pkci is completely in awe of you."

Cherice chuckled at the name. "Sounds like Tricycle Pixie to me every time you say it. I have to stop myself from laughing when she was teaching me how to do those high Alteran notes."

Lariq tilted his head to one side and looked at her sideways making her grin. "I still don't understand what a pixie is, but never mind."

In the audience, Natalie and Carl sat next to Captain Xaoping Shoo in the prime seating zone and watched the gala as many acts took their turns. Both parents nervously waited for Cherice's moment. Xaoping turned to Natalie.

"When did you find out?"

"It was an accidental slip by Lariq that gave the game away. To be fair, we were a little concerned as they seemed to be spending a lot of time away from us. Well, it was worrying as we didn't know why and neither of them were saying, except it was a surprise.

Lariq and Cherice came back just a few days ago and were so excited that Lariq blurted out she was ready to perform, so that was it. We invoked ambassadorial privilege and they both told us about the gala and her singing spot in it." Carl tapped Natalie lightly on the shoulder as Trionice -pkci came back onto the central stage of the ships amphitheatre.

Natalie and Carl knew this was the moment and felt nervous for their little girl about to come on stage.

"Dearest passengers and crew, my how we have been entertained tonight and it has been a wonderful and moving evening for us all. Now for our final act.

She is the most endearing little humarling I have ever had the good luck to know. She shines like the Rainbow Star of Anchi, but until recently I did not realise she had an amazing singing talent.

May I introduce to you, our own little starlet, to sing a cross over song featuring both human and High Alteran vocals: 'The Stars they are a Wandering High' sung by Miss Cherice Richmond!"

Trionice -pkci stepped back and swung her three right arms around in a sweeping gesture towards the back of the stage as a gentle spotlight formed on a small figure.

The audience applauded enthusiastically then the applause died down as the music began. Cherice stood silently looking around at them nervously, a frightened look about her. She looked up towards where she knew her parents were supposed to be sitting, trembling sightly, but then she spotted her mother and father nodding at her and smiling broadly, encouraging her.

The music faltered, stopped, then started again from the beginning as the audience waited patiently, nervously wondering if stage fright had taken hold.

Then from somewhere inside her, a little voice began to sing:

> *The stars they are a wandering high*
> *Far and away, way up in the sky.*
> *Never to fall, only to shine.*
>
> *The stars they are a wandering high*
> *Travelling between dark and light*
> *For you and I, beyond the sky.*
>
> *We see them shine eternally*
> *Far and away, way up in the sky*
> *A beacon of light in a milky night*

The Last Voyage of the StarVista 4

Far and away, way up in the sky
Linking us to places unseen
Giving us hope to dream
Spreading their varied beams
Lighting up our Uni-verse
For it to be seen.

The stars they are a wandering high
Far and away, way up in the sky.
Never to fall, only to shine.

The stars they are a wandering high
Travelling between dark and light
  For you and I, beyond the sky
For you and I, beyond the sky.

The stars they are a wandering high
Travelling between dark and light
  For you and I, beyond the sky
For you and I,
beyond the sky.

Cherice repeated the last verse then shifted into a higher key pushing her vocal chords to their limit. Natalie turned to Carl.

"Oh, the poor love, she did well to get this fa…"

Captain Xaoping glanced at Natalie in amazement.

"She's incredible, who would have known?"

Natalie and Carl looked at her, puzzled.

"Known what?" Natalie asked. Xaoping leaned over and whispered to them.

"She can sing in High Alteran, I have never ever heard a human sing so beautifully in our audio range. All who have tried from your species have failed yet, yet she is singing beautifully!"

As the captain spoke the vast majority of non-humans in the audience were getting to their feet, cheering Cherice on and clapping excitedly. Cherice launched into a final repeat of the last chorus before she spun round, finished the song and dropped to the floor in dramatic fashion. As she did so she bowed her head to the upstanding and almost delirious audience.

The thunderous applause continued for several minutes as Trionice -pkci came back on stage, in tears and carefully embraced Cherice. She turned and gestured to the side where Lariq gingerly stepped out and walked over to them, embraced both, then gently hugged Cherice, tears streaming down his face.

Cherice covered the tiny microphone looking concernedly at Lariq. "I didn't mean for you to cry. I didn't know you could!"

"Oh Cherice, it is indeed a rare thing for us Alterans, but they are tears of joy for you. You are an amazing little humarling indeed and a credit to your parents."

By this time Captain Xaoping Shoo had brought Natalie and Carl down onto the stage and her parents hugged her as cheers continued to ring out around the auditorium.

It was an occasion never to forget and one to tell Danny about once she was back in their quarters.

The Last Voyage of the StarVista 4

Day 183
Diary entry

Hi Danny, I can sing in High Alteran! Lariq first heard me sing by accident. When I hit high notes apparently, it's in the range of the Alteran and Ziancan species that is special to them, known as High Alteran. We worked on a surprise for Mummy and Daddy as I was the last act on the voyage's Gala night and everyone was surprised and loved it. Perhaps I should think about being a singer now?

Anyhow we've had some odd, but exciting, news. It seems we have been given extra special permission to go to a world that hasn't been fully explored yet; apparently it is famous as it has many strangely inclined rings around it. It's a gas giant that is almost a star and we will be the first passenger ship to go to it, so everyone is excited. Daddy says that this extra extension of the voyage is free on the company so we have nothing to pay.

I'm not happy however. I was really looking forward to seeing you at Viliak. It's going to be a short stop in case there are passengers who don't wish to carry on and they also say that no one is allowed to board. If we choose to stay for the extended voyage then we can't get off either, even Daddy can't sway the authorities as it is a very tight turnaround for us to leave Viliak.

Mummy says that if anyone gets off then they must be mad as this will be an historic occasion, but I have a bad feeling about it, don't know why, just a funny feeling in my tummy. I saw Dr Sreisse about it but the good doctor couldn't find anything wrong with me. I still can't get over the sight of my insides displayed holographically in front of me!

The Last Voyage of the StarVista 4

In the meantime we are approaching Graylacq Twenty Nine, it is a small, molten rocky world that orbits its star so closely that the surface is always liquid. Sounds dangerous to me, but Captain Xaoping has told me we are quite safe and that the StarVista 4 could actually fly into the outer corona of a massive star if it needed.

She told me though that they won't need to do that, which is a relief I can tell you. She has also asked if I would sing to the passengers on the final day of our voyage as many have been asking for me to sing again. I must admit this voyage has been amazing, even without my toys!

One thing I do think is a bit odd, but no one else seems to have noticed. I think one of the passengers has changed as one of the humans like us doesn't look familiar. During our trip I thought I'd got to know everyone on board so there can't be someone else on board now as we are all monitored from the medical facility and I'm sure they would have said something to the captain. It might just be me but I have a strange feeling about him. He also seems to spend a lot of time at the bar, not that I'm allowed to go near one but I've often spotted him at the main bar from a distance.

Must go as Daddy is calling for me.
Byee.

#

18,757 light years away...

Corafa, first of Arana, looked at the message she had just decoded and trembled. This was very bad news and completely unexpected but nonetheless she had to report it to his excellency.

She hurriedly headed down the connecting corridors that took her to the central command area and was allowed into the chamber. Tragx was nowhere to be seen but his excellency sat and motioned for her to approach.

"You have news?"

He saw her trembling.

"Speak!"

"Your Excellency, terrible news from the Cantrara system. Our link ship with home world was discovered by a small GAA ship and they were about to destroy it when…when they were devastated by it exploding. They cannot travel back to home world now and have limited manoeuvring ability with little chance of repair."

"How, how has this happened? No one, no one was supposed to go to that system and now we have TWO unscheduled ships from the GAA there! Order them to try to effect what repairs may be possible and intercept the cruise ship and destroy it before all our plans are exposed."

He saw her hesitate.

"Do as I order, on pain of death!"

"Your Excellency, I can't… We have lost all communications with the ship. Our intelligence believes it has been destroyed." She bowed her head and waited to be executed but it didn't come.

"Find Tragx and get him to order his agent aboard that cruise ship to do whatever is needed to compromise that ship. Their lives are now expendable and we need to provide a reason why the cruise ship was destroyed at Cantrara.

Don't just stand there. GO!"

Corafa, first of Arana rushed out of the chamber still shocked that she had once again escaped death!

#

StarVista 4

"On approach to Graylacq Twenty-Nine, orbital insertion at a safe distance will be in twelve minutes." Delieezas stated as the captain stood close by looking at a holo display of the upcoming fiery world they were about to visit.

"After everyone's apparent disappointment with Braylon Seven, hopefully this one will make up for it. Already looks impressive - see there..." She pointed to the view screen and Delieezas boosted the magnification. A column of molten lava was being thrown several tens of kilometres high, not enough to reach escape velocity, but nonetheless impressive as it began to collapse back on itself and cool at the same time.

"A few like that will work very nicely I imagine." Delieezas added as he spotted another spout being thrust up. Smaller, so less detailed but the views were improving rapidly as they closed the distance.

"Time for the official announcement Graylor, looks like the passengers will be in for a treat."

"Indeed. Carson, open up the passenger channel for the captain's announcement."

"Passengers of the StarVista 4, we are almost in orbit around Graylacq Twenty Nine and we are already seeing plenty of volcanic activity.

The Last Voyage of the StarVista 4

Usual facilities will be available on the observation decks and information about this molten planet can be found in the joint infocast by Astrophysicist Crayt and Geophysicist Raskaert.

Look out for the sudden outburst of a new lava column that can occur anywhere on the planet and in particular note how some are influenced by the strong magnetic field of the planet. We shall remain here for one standard day, so enjoy the view."

Carson saw Graylor give the usual signal and he cut the comms. They were almost in orbit as Delieezas manipulated the controls and confirmed with the navigation AI they were at a safe distance.

"Orbit achieved Captain."

"Excellent. Let's hope for a few more interesting displays like that one to keep our passengers happy." Xaoping happened to glance over towards comms and noted Carson looked puzzled, almost even straining, as he tilted his head oddly. "Carson, are you well or do you need to see Dr Sreisse?"

"Oh, sorry Captain. Had a strange blip for a few moments, seemed like a comms signal at first but I think it was more likely the effects of the magnetic field on our comms. I'll do a full system check if that is acceptable?"

"Yes, indeed, no one else out here so clear it up and make sure we have no problems with the comms.

Don't want a complaint from our youngest passenger that she can't send her usual diary messages to her brother now, do we!"

The Last Voyage of the StarVista 4

Day 186: Finality of Communication...

Diary entry.

"Hi again Danny. Wow! Graylacq Twenty Nine really was something! There were really big spouts of lava shooting into space and the surface has no solids on it at all - it was like a glowing hot red and orange boiling ball! We didn't get too close but the captain did send on an unmanned shuttle to view one of the eruptions up close. They lost the shuttle!

A second eruption of lava surprised even helmsman Delieezas so I'm glad he wasn't in it, but flying it remotely. He was so calm about it that I still want to be a pilot like him when I grow up.

I'm sad that you won't now be at Viliak when we get there in a few days time but if we can't get off and you can't get on then I can understand why you've decided to stay back at Alteran. I hope you can come out to Viliak when we finally get to the end of the voyage and come back to Viliak, but I seem to remember you had exams and I know how important they are to you.

I'll be in touch about this ringed planet, Tianca, when we start to head back so love you bro and can't wait to see you when we get back.

Byee!"

Final transmission entry for Cherice Richmond, StarVista 4.
All transmissions completed and received by recipient.
Indications of no further transmissions sent.
Communications terminated.

Part 2

The StarVista 4 at Tianca
Days are numbers…
(Count the Stars)

Tianca approach and orbit

"Attention everyone, passengers of the StarVista 4 this is Captain Xaoping Shoo and I am delighted to inform you that we are now entering the Cantrara system.

In a little under six hours we will enter into orbit around the famed, yet little researched, gas giant planet known as Tianca. Please remember that we are privileged in being the first ever commercial passenger ship to be allowed to visit the system.

Under normal circumstances, newly discovered worlds orbiting stars on the very edge of the Galactic Arm Association are surveyed extensively before public contact is granted. However, we have been given special permission due to the wondrous nature of the ring system of Tianca, which if you have consulted the, admittedly limited details available in your cabins, you will know are in a unique state of flux.

Therefore, I appreciate some of our more, let's say fortunate clients, may wish to take out or hire our fleet of shuttles to explore closer. Please be advised that this is *still* forbidden under the terms of our contract of operation and so please do not attempt to hire a shuttle for your party as this will be refused and the passengers making the enquiry may well find themselves heavily fined and censured.

However, I am confident no one will break the rules as this is such a marvellous opportunity and I am sure that in the near future the StarVista Corporation will be granted full access on a regular basis, once all safety factors have been assessed.

The Last Voyage of the StarVista 4

On our approach Tianca will initially be ahead of us and so the forward observation decks will be fully prepared to accommodate all of you. I expect you will want to get your first glimpses of this stunning world as we are on our approach. We will then take up an orbital synchronous parking position and the planet and its majestic rings will lie on the port side. Our orbit will ensure that the planet and rings will be at half phase which we have been assured is the most stunning view with the night side of the planet to the right and its star, Cantrara, off to the left hand side.

Please ensure you are fully aware of our safety protocols in case of an emergency and familiarise yourselves with the paths to the appropriate lifeboat shuttles, although I am confident we should not be in any danger. We are only allowed to venture to two hundred and fifty thousand kilometres from the ring's closest edge.

That equates to a distance of fifteen chaks for our Alteran passengers, four million quintatias for our Scorion passengers and twenty two thousand plicks, the universal distance for the Ziancans and majority of the Galactic Arm Association cultures. If you have any further queries, then do ask our many information booths and crew who will be only to happy to help you. Thank you for your attention and enjoy the approach and rendezvous with Tianca and its rings."

Captain Xaoping sat down heavily in her command seat and sighed. She liked an easy life and had been captain of the StarVista 4 for seven years now and was normally quite content with her lot in life.

The Last Voyage of the StarVista 4

The StarVista 4 was a fine ship but Xaoping had not been happy at the last minute addition of the Cantrara system to their latest voyage. New planetary systems were always fully explored and cleared for commercial passenger ships after extensive and exhaustive surveys, yet this seemed to have been rushed through. Someone high up at head office had pushed this, despite seemingly breaking all the usual protocols.

That made her uneasy. It also didn't help that she had been informed she was to provide a full report on the death of the young Ziancan because of the prank that went horribly wrong back at Etel Six and she knew that there was a chance her career could be over. Well, to use a Terran phrase, she would cross that bridge when she had to.

Graylor zXanders smiled at her and nodded in agreement as if she were a mind reader. She too had been a little puzzled as they had been three quarters into their seven month star cruise when the orders had come through. Still, they both agreed that this was a unique possibility and that they had the good fortune to be the first commercial passenger star liner to visit the system, which would ensure their names would go down in the history books. Not forgetting of course, the large bonuses the crew would receive for this unusual addition, according to company rules.

Xaoping smiled and looked around the command centre bridge at the efficient officers who always made her job far easier than it should be. Most ships systems were automatic and could be monitored and controlled from anywhere on the ship.

But helm, communications and engineering/science stations were the exception. A hark back to a time a couple of centuries earlier when the advancing AIs grew too clever and instigated a revolt, which was awful and bloody but fortunately short lived.

Sentient AIs were now seriously limited and could not have access to a ship's full systems. Indeed, they were effectively outlawed throughout the GAA but rumours persisted that some worlds still did research on the subject.

Xaoping's mind came back to the present.

"Delieezas, how long before we enter orbit at our chosen position?"

Delieezas did a quick assessment then turned to face Captain Xaoping.

"Five hours and twelve Terran standard minutes, Captain."

"Very good. Graylor, I am going to have a short meal break then head off to the forward observation decks and mix with the passengers. I'm sure they will appreciate the captain giving her time for them as we approach this historic moment. You have the bridge but signal me when we are an hour out from final orbital position."

"Yes Captain."

Captain Xaoping briefly smiled at Graylor then headed for the side antechamber before making her way out to the passenger section of the ship.

#

The Last Voyage of the StarVista 4

Carson sat in his quarters, having a rest period between duties but as a comms specialist he also couldn't help but tap into the main comms of the ship and scan for unusual frequencies. It was a hobby of sorts as sometimes unusual astronomical phenomenon produced comms noise that could be interesting to monitor.

He liked to sometimes mix various spurious signals to form music, although those who had heard his compositions usually just said it sounded like static!

He sat listening and musing about how little radio static there actually was when a faint oddly broken up signal caught his attention. He tuned his system as best he could, but it stayed just too faint for him to clearly make out its origin. His own recorders duly took a copy and he thought about it, then tapped for a link to the helm.

"Delieezas, have we been close to anything artificial in the last few moments?"

Delieezas' face appeared on the monitor and he did the equivalent of a human shrug.

"Here? Of course not. There's nothing out here but us. We've just done a fly past of the largest moon, Zospher and we have another three hours, ten before we reach the orbital coordinates. Why?"

"Odd, but I could have sworn I picked up some form of signal just now."

"Got to be static as the last official probe to visit here was a decade or so ago and it was a flyby.

Most of our info comes from that mission and Cantrara is so far off the mainstream hyperways there can't be anyone else out here.

Come to think of it, that probe did disperse small recon probes to the various other worlds in the system so perhaps one of those could still be active, perhaps damaged?"

"Yes, it didn't seem to be a distress call so perhaps I'm making too much of it. I'll ask the captain if we can maybe take a look when we leave - use it as an excuse to explore the moon to get more data on it to cover us. A bonus to add to the bonus of this detour for the passengers."

"Good idea. For now, you will be needed on the command deck in twenty minutes time ready for our arrival so don't be late!"

"As if!" The comms went dead, and Carson was left still a little puzzled by the short but faint signal. He continued to analyse it and make notes.

#

She knew there was a chance and, sure enough after speaking to what seemed like hundreds of excited passengers, she came across the one who wasn't excited at all at the prospect of seeing something completely new and being part of history.

"CAPTAIN! Captain, I am *so* glad to see you, perhaps now I might get my complaint taken seriously." The middle-aged human looked sternly at her and she had no trouble recalling the bursars report.

"Well Mr Roberts, I gather from my chief bursar that you have already made a formal complaint and that of course is your right.

The Last Voyage of the StarVista 4

I fully understand how you feel but on a ship this size, with two thousand passengers, I'm afraid I can't divert this historic voyage just for one person."

"That is not the point Captain. This is an additional stop to the original voyage and one I did not sign up for, nor have the finances to pay."

"But my dear Mr Roberts, you are *not* being billed at all for this part of the voyage. Indeed, you are getting it completely for free as a thank you for your continued custom. What is more, everyone was given the chance to disembark at Viliak, Spaceport Shalaiq, our original final tourist stop eight days ago. So, if they had other plans after our voyage they could continue on to their home worlds, again at the expense of the StarVista Corporation. So why did you choose to stay on board?"

Roberts looked flustered as several passengers passed by them heading for the port observation decks. Several of them were aware of his complaint and gave him a withering look as they passed by. This infuriated him even more.

"That is not the point, I did not ask to be kept on board for this farcical extra and I should have been given a shuttle to fly back so I could keep to my own schedule. That was the least you should have done for someone not wishing to continue like the rest of the sheep here on this ship."

That latter comment drew angry looks from the passing passengers and two came over, an Alteran and a Ziancan.

"Captain, may we be of assistance?" inquired the Alteran.

The Last Voyage of the StarVista 4

Captain Xaoping smiled at them both but shook her head as she put her tentacle up to Roberts to hold his tongue. For the moment, he realised that he should keep quiet.

"I'm fine and *Mister* Roberts here has a good and interesting point which we of course will look into, *after* we arrive back at our original final port of call back at Viliak."

Roberts scowled, shook his head angrily and stormed off to wallow in his own misery knowing he could only watch and wait until they finished the voyage. After that, he was sure his sister-in-law would be able to represent him and win compensation. At least that is what he had told the captain in his earlier official complaint and for now he had to stick to his story and stay in character...

Captain Xaoping turned and pointed a six fingered tentacle towards the left-hand side of the forward observation deck they were on.

"Ahh, I see we are turning. I had best return to the command centre, and I suggest you two kind people head to the port observation deck for our rendezvous with Tianca. Thank you for coming to my aid but I think a mere human is no match for a mildly angered member of my species."

The Alteran turned to go but his Ziancan colleague was curious.

"Why did the human stay on board when he could have disembarked at Viliak, if I may be so bold?"

"Let us just say that if you spend the previous twelve hours propping up the bar, then sleep through the five alarm calls we sent to his cabin, he really doesn't have a leg to stand on.

The Last Voyage of the StarVista 4

Oh, I believe I have just made a human joke, leg to stand on, when he was apparently legless!

His own fault and I am totally confident that if he does indeed complain officially then the company will fully back me. I must leave you now so enjoy the next forty-six hours as they are pretty much unique and we shouldn't let him spoil it for us all."

With that, Captain Xaoping turned on her six spindle like legs and gracefully left the pair as they in turn headed towards the exit gantry for the deck to return to their respective quarters. Xaoping didn't get very far however, as suddenly she was approached by the one person, other than the annoying human, who she had successfully evaded for most of the walkabout.

Almost.

Sicanrinka smiled, ensured the tiny hand recorder was operating and checked the sound volume.

"Why Captain, I thought you were *avoiding me*. So glad I found you before things get interesting."

"Now why would I avoid one of the official, sorry, *only*, official reporter on the ship when there are so many excited passengers to interview?" Xaoping attempted to walk away but Sicanrinka was not having it.

"Well now we are almost at our final exceptional destination, can I simply have a few words with the one captain who has been allowed to bring their passenger ship to the Cantrara system, in particular Tianca?"

"If you must, however we are now close to our rendezvous point and I can only give you a moment as I should be back on the command centre bridge any time now."

"Perfect! Why *was* a system that has hardly been explored, let alone checked for safety, been added at such short notice to the itinerary?"

"Well I am sure my superiors can give you an answer as I am simply the captain and follow my instructions. Those instructions came as quite the surprise to myself and the crew but we are professionals and we have been given a job to do I intend for us to complete this voyage with every success it deserves.

Now, I really do need to be back in the command centre, so I hope you get some great passenger reactions to the wonder we are about to view and make sure I, the crew and the corporation, get a good mention in your report."

With that, Xaoping purposefully strode off towards a travelator leaving Sicanrinka a little bemused.

"Well there you are, a captain with little time to discuss this historic encounter with the multi ringed plant Tianca with you, the viewers. What with passenger discord regarding the sudden addition of this final planetary encounter and a Captain unwilling to engage with us on what this voyage means to the Galactic Arm Association, only time will tell.

We'll surely get to the bottom of this once we finally arrive back at our final official port of call at Viliak.

The Last Voyage of the StarVista 4

This is Sicanrinka Tavaska of the Havaerian news guild reporting from the StarVista 4 on the final approach to our extra *unscheduled* destination of Tianca and its famed ring system."

Well, she had to keep up appearances for the time being, she mused…

#

"On final approach, systems stable and 100 percent. Full scans ahead complete with nothing to report, the orbital position is clear of anything that may cause us any harm or damage.

I can give all clear for final orbital insertion, Captain."

"Thank you Delieezas, well done. Graylor, patch me into the ship wide system please and stand at my side." Graylor smiled and moved close to Xaoping, looking at Delieezas with immense pride as he, in turn, placed them spot on target at the correct coordinates they had been given from the StarVista Corporation.

"Attention everyone. It is with distinct pride and pleasure that I can announce we have officially arrived at our rendezvous position with the giant planet Tianca and now, on the port side, you can all enjoy the magnificence of the multitude of rings of this wonderful gas giant planet. It is an honour and a privilege to have brought you here on this historic occasion.

Celebratory drinks, on the corporation of course, are now being distributed to everyone on the passenger manifest.

The Last Voyage of the StarVista 4

There are also many forms of interstellar cuisine that have been prepared for this moment for you to enjoy from our many waiters as they pass amongst you, again complimentary.

We of the StarVista Corporation thank you for your patience at this extension to our original voyage itinerary. For your information we have been granted a minimum of six hours here and a maximum, at my discretion, of up to two Terran day periods before we will have to take our leave and head for our original final port ready for disembarkation.

Any queries and we shall do our best to help wherever we can. Now enjoy the spectacle that is Tianca and its rings."

Xaoping indicated with her right first tentacle to cut transmission and once more she looked about her command centre bridge with pride. "Graylor, private crew channels please." The second in command nodded at Comms Officer Carson who indicated the channel was open for only the crew to hear.

"Attention crew. As this is such a privilege and honour extended to the StarVista Corporation, the corporation has given me additional leave to allow the crew to have time to also enjoy this unique occasion.

Officer zXanders has drawn up a rosta for you all to have some time to enjoy the view and capture your own memories of this event.

The rosta is being implemented as I speak so please enjoy this unusually kind gesture from our company, as they don't come often."

The Last Voyage of the StarVista 4

Graylor cut the transmission as Captain Xaoping handed over the bridge to Delieezas and together they headed out for the captain's quarters.

#

Cabin C2001

She sat in shock as the message was decoded. How could this be? Her rendezvous and return home was compromised. She was unable to get back to give the reports her spies had already gathered. In theory, the Azline plans could still go ahead as they didn't depend on any single being or for that matter, ship, but she had spent too long in this wretched form and wanted to get back to normal.

Plans would have to change, but on thinking it over she suspected she could use the adapted pod for a direct return now that the return support ship had been compromised. Pity the poor fool who would be piloting the pod, Zalokq, he'd never be allowed to live once she'd got back and would likely be interrogated, not that he would be of much use to them, small scale fodder.

She would persevere.

Things afoot

"Mummy, do I have to do this?"

"Yes dear, I've already explained to you, this is really historic and in the years to come you will look back at this moment and say '*I was there*'." Natalie knew full well that Cherice was a little young at eight years old to have been granted permission to be on such a voyage, but she had proven everyone wrong and was now a star as far as the passengers and crew were concerned.

It still puzzled her however why Carl had pulled a few strings before he and Natalie had been promoted to full ambassadorial status. This trip had been a reward for their many years of hard work but something had not felt quite right ever since they had embarked on the voyage. She kept thinking about the strange message they had received whilst in flight on the voyage and shuddered. Her attention was swiftly brought back to her charming little star.

"*Harumph!*"

"Now Cherice, that is very unkind of you. Have you not enjoyed this voyage of discovery?"

"I suppose so, but there was no one to play with of my age, they are all adults and they lost my games and toys case! Only Lariq made this trip special." Cherice pouted her lips and her mother could sympathise with her. The lowest age limit for such commercial passenger voyages was fifteen but for some reason her husband, seemed insistent on taking the voyage and bringing the family.

It was a shame their son Daniel had elected to remain at his university to continue with his studies and so was not with them. It was only when everyone was given the choice of disembarking or taking advantage of the extension to go to Tianca that Carl had admitted he had been privy to inside information from the Alterans about the extension to the voyage, *right at the start of their cruise!*

Not that she minded. The thought of actually seeing the unusual rings of Tianca thrilled her and so now all she had to do was keep Cherice happy for another few days. After that, they would be off the ship and heading off to get used to living on Zianca in the splendour of the ambassador's residence.

"Mummy, can't I stay in our room and watch on the holoplayer? I could meet up with Lariq instead?"

"Good grief Cherice, we come all the way here only for you to stay inside the room and miss seeing it with your own eyes. Whatever next! Your father would be aghast. Come along, time for us to meet him as his meeting should be finished and we are expected to catch up with him in the upper port observation deck, with the other dignitaries."

"If you say so." Cherice said in a resigned tone and she took hold of Natalie's hand as they headed for the door.

#

"You do realise that in Terran culture we would be looked down upon for having a relationship whilst being command staff."

Graylor said as she slid over to one side of the large bed and faced Xaoping, smiling after the exertions of the last ten minutes.

"Gryitz col tan-flr yantz, or as the Terrans would say, tough excrement to that!" Xaoping turned over and faced the large bulbous porthole; she gently dimmed the lights and admired the rings of Tianca stretched out before them. Towards the front of the view and almost out of sight, a small 'star' suddenly appeared then winked out. Perhaps a small meteoroid had struck the rings, wondered Xaoping idly.

"I think they actually say tough sh.."

"Yes, yes, I was being polite. This is not a Terran owned ship nor is it run by a Terran corporation, and it is not against GAA regulations either. Graylor, be open with me, are you concerned about our conduct and how the crew sees us and our fitness for command?"

Graylor chuckled and snuggled back up to Xaoping.

"No, it was a simple observation of how a more primitive culture sees us. The crew don't care at all as long as it doesn't interfere with our jobs. I'm sure you also know that the corporation has a similar view otherwise we'd have been grounded years ago."

"True, I did have this discussion with my superiors a while back and they wondered why it was so important to me. Now if something happened to go wrong on our watch, then I expect it would be a different matter.

The Last Voyage of the StarVista 4

And I guess with the incident involving the Ziancans back at Etel Six, that may well happen. As for the humans, let us not stakle, sorry, tar them with the same brush after our experience with Roberts. In my experience this trip has been especially enjoyable with the other two hundred and nine humans. Especially little Cherice. She is such a sweetie."

"Yes she is. As for Roberts, ahh, he is a strange example of a human. I did some background research and discovered he had also flown on the StarVista One around five Terran years ago. He was just as much of a nuisance to its captain and crew as he is with us now. Yet I am puzzled why he's only started to get annoying on the final leg of our voyage. Something feels wrong and I can't put my mind at ease."

Xaoping had not really been listening to the last part.

"Oh, that would have been Captain Scranatkatcha on the StarVista One, nice but could be quite stern at times. It is a wonder Roberts has been allowed to fly with the corporation again if he annoyed Scranny."

"Scranny?"

"Yes, let me just say it was before your time, before we met. Way back when I was barely a junior officer we had a, call it minor, fling at the StarVista training academy. Underneath that hard exterior he was quite soft really if you know what I mean."

Xaoping closed her eyes in a seductive and sexy way and Graylor was about to respond when a soft chiming bell interrupted them. Xaoping slid over and grabbed the comm.

"Xaoping, go ahead."

The Last Voyage of the StarVista 4

"Delieezas here. Captain, I'm sorry to bother you both but we have, well, we've got something odd occurring approximately ten degrees ahead and three chaks closer in towards the closest ring's edge."

"Clarify, something odd?"

"Well, as best as we can make out, gravi-magnetic ripples on a small scale of just a tenth of a chak wide at most, but quite unusual."

"We're on our way. Hold station for now but keep monitoring." She cut the link.

Graylor looked at Xaoping, puzzled, then they both dressed and headed to the command centre.

Delieezas turned to them as they entered and Xaoping took her command chair as Graylor stood to one side of Delieezas.

"Any change?" Xaoping asked.

"No Captain, just small intermittent and quite irregular ripples."

"Graylor, thoughts?" Graylor went over to the science station and along with Officer Calsohn, studied the data. They briefly whispered to each other in consultation, then Graylor nodded and turned to the captain.

"Captain, the phenomenon is highly localised but does not seem to have any origin or anything that could be creating it. We advise continued monitoring and at the first sign of any change suggest we move the ship further out to ensure the safety of the passengers, and of course, crew."

"Agreed. Calsohn, this is not that unusual, that gravity and magnetic fields can be in flux is well known, so why is this one an oddity?"

The Last Voyage of the StarVista 4

"All known examples, of which there are indeed many, have a source, something that is causing the event or disturbance. But in this case we can find nothing that is causing or producing the effect. But then again, we're not a fully equipped research ship."

"I can find nothing like a ship at the centre of the ripples as that was the first thing I thought of, perhaps a ship in trouble, but scans show no sign of anything artificial at the centre or indeed within twenty-eight light years of us as we are so far off the beaten track", offered Delieezas and Xaoping nodded.

"My thoughts exactly Delieezas, there won't be anyone else out here under the circumstances. Well, it is not often we get a chance to possibly make a discovery of our own and the corporation could benefit from the extra good publicity. Let us give it another ten minutes and if nothing changes then Delieezas, I want you to slowly drift us in to around a chak from it.

If we move slowly then the chances are the passengers won't notice we have moved and we can study it whilst they continue to enjoy the views of the rings until we have to leave. All agreed?"

Graylor looked thoughtful.

"You don't concur Graylor?"

"Perhaps it would be wiser, as this is a relatively unexplored system, to move away and for now keep our distance from whatever it is we are detecting?"

Xaoping nodded as well as a Gu-alt could.

"Understood, but so far there is no indication of any potential danger, so for now I think we should continue to explore, but carefully. If we move away that will alert the passengers that something may not be well and could cause alarm and I wish to avoid that. Agreed?"

There was general agreement from the command crew, Graylor nodded in agreement after a little more thought.

"Good. Carson, request Astrophysicist Crayt and Geophysicist Raskaert to perform extra studies of the planet and its rings and come up with possible explanations of what we're seeing. No doubt it will make their careers if this really is something never before seen.

I gather they are not the best of friends, but they must put that aside." Captain Xaoping sat back in her command chair, pondering what they might find over the next hour or so.

#

Cherice looked up at her mother. "It does look pretty."

"There you go, see, I was right, wasn't I?"

"Yes Mummy." Cherice turned to her dad. "Daddy, can I go back to our room please?" she asked in her special daddy winning over voice.

"Now poppet, this is a very special occasion and very important for Daddy and Mummy so stay a little longer? Tell me how many rings you can count?"

Cherice might be eight years old, but she wasn't stupid. Everyone knew the rings were probably countless if you looked more closely.

"Seventy-two main rings have been identified in the five major ring planes based on the last flyby probe. However, on a finer scale they are probably uncountable. According to Astrophysicist Crayt."

"Atta girl, now is that not amazing?"

"I guess so, but I'm bored..." she replied looking down at her feet as both Natalie and Carl looked on in dismay. Natalie took her hand.

"Stay with us and when it is over, we can go back to the room before lunchtime, OK?"

Tears began to form and Cherice looked so downhearted that Carl's heart broke and he relented, as any father probably would have done.

"OK poppet. Listen, tell you what, we've had a great trip so far. So, as you have at least seen Tianca's rings with us, you can go back to the room. Head back now but if you get into any difficulties, you know what to do don't you?"

"Yes Daddy, clench my palm really tightly and an alert to security will tell them where I am and they will alert you and come to my aid. Not that anything can happen on this ship anyway, everyone likes me so I'll be OK. I'm a celebrity, even more so since the gala night."

"Good girl. Off you go then and we will be there soon, I promise. About an hour or perhaps a little more as we do have to mingle with some special people."

Cherice brightened up and so, as she left, she waved at them for several metres, then walked away. Rounding a corner, she started skipping along the vacant corridor.

She didn't notice that someone had spotted her leaving but was keeping well back, out of sight. It was good that everyone was on the observation decks and it struck Cherice that for a short while, she could explore the starboard side of the ship as everyone seemed to be on the port side for the planet with rings.

Hah! Ringed planet. She had not really been that impressed with Tianca. A bit messy with all those inclined rings. Now a good nice clean cut ringed planet had to be her favourite. But she couldn't decide between the rings of Jalthor or Saturn in her own home system. Still on this voyage she had gasped in wonder at the four hundred miles high cliffs of P'rlaac. She knew the GAA geologist had explained how they could stay as they did, but she kept imagining how incredible it would be if they suddenly collapsed.

Now that would be something spectacular!

She found the travelator and hovered her hand over it which immediately brought a segment to a halt. She stepped on and it carefully manoeuvred itself back into the ever-moving flow. She loved the ride as the air rushed through her hair and as she passed a few of the crew they recognised her and waved, some with their multiple limbs much to her enjoyment.

The Last Voyage of the StarVista 4

As the youngest on the ship she had gathered a bit of a fan base amongst the crew and indeed the passengers too. But it was the crew that had taken her under their collective wing and made sure she didn't come to harm. Cherice still couldn't believe she'd been allowed to see how some of the important professions worked and chuckled to herself at the thoughts of her being an engineer, a pilot, doctor, archaeologist, geologist, the list seemed endless.

She knew she would have a hard job when she grew up on deciding what to be when she finally left school, not to mention university, like her brother.

Ahh, Danny. It was a real shame he wasn't with them to experience this and to be with her too.

As the travelator slowed she wondered if she would have what was needed to be a captain and for a brief moment she thought of herself as captain of the StarVista 4 then chuckled again to herself.

"Captain Cherice Richmond at your service." she said out loud and giggled at the thought of being so important.

She arrived close to her room, then had a sudden impulse. She knew that the travelator could take her quickly to the starboard observation decks. Changing her mind, she decided to go count the stars from the second level observation deck, just as she and Lariq had done several times during the voyage.

Three minutes later she was there. Basically, the same as the port sided, except this had one very important difference.

There was no one else around.

The Last Voyage of the StarVista 4

Cherice had the deck to herself, much to her pleasure. With that in mind, she ran to the huge clear wall that looked out into space and had a thought.

"Ship? Lights dim?" She called out, remembering how Lariq had done it on several occasions.

As she was the only one there, the intelligent system calculated there was no harm and that the passenger wanted to view the stars. With the lights on, it was almost impossible to see any except the few brightest ones, but it calculated she wanted to see them *all*.

The ship obliged as the deck lighting dimmed and she looked on in awe at the vast span of the galaxy's spiral arm strung out before her. The galactic bulge lay off to the right and she smiled. She knew she wouldn't be able to see Sol from the Cantrara system, but she still looked over in its direction.

She was glad Daddy had pointed out the patch of the Milky Way in which Sol lay just a few days before they arrived at this, out of the way, extra destination.

She started counting, knowing full well she wouldn't be able to count them all, there had to be tens of thousands visible at any moment. She started at the left side and worked her way up and down but reached less than a third of the way across the vast view when she had to start again. She tried three more times, each time she managed a few more and was thrilled she made it to nine hundred and eighty-three when, once again, she lost count.

The Last Voyage of the StarVista 4

She knew that for her age she was doing well so started again on the left. A few brief flashes high up across the sky caught her attention for a split second but she figured they were probably due to the rings, so she started her counting again.

She got up to eleven when something struck her. She again started counting but then noticed it.

There had been a lovely bright orange, supergiant star she remembered Astrophysicist Crayt calling them, it was the first one on the lower left.

But now there were an extra three fainter whiter stars to the orange star's left. She started again and this time hit a thousand and four stars before a small coughing fit put her off.

So, start again.

'Oh', she thought.

There were now five stars to the left of the orange star so she now started watching intently as a sixth slowly drifted into view.

She blinked, then thought about it. They were moving, very slowly, but still, they were moving the ship slowly. Perhaps the captain had a better spot for the passengers and for a second she thought about heading back to her parents on the second observation deck, port side.

Cherice shook her head, it was probably nothing, and decided to carry on counting. This time she began on the right but decided to skip round the main bulge of the galaxy - too many even for her to count!

She became lost in the task at hand and forgot about the extra stars...

#

Half hour earlier...

"Back here again I see?" bartender first class Anatonyp noted as the human wandered into the bar on the port observation-second level deck.

"My credits are as good as anybodys on this dump of a ship. Usual please, the free stuff actually as they are giving it away."

"Yes, *Mr* Roberts." Anatonyp turned away shaking his head but duly obliged as was his duty. "Any further word on your case?"

"Ha! No chance, they're too busy buttering up the elite at the moment to care about a legitimate complaint."

Roberts sipped at his drink, grimaced at the taste and looked for somewhere to tip it out, but Anatonyp gave him a vicious look and he just put the glass down and pushed it away instead.

"Usual?" Roberts asked hesitantly and Anatonyp nodded and started preparing the, in his opinion, obnoxious concoction.

"Mr Anaturnip or whatever it is, answer me this. Why are we here? This system has not been properly explored so how is it we've been able to come out here?"

Anatonyp ignored the deliberate mispronunciation of his name , finished preparing the drink and turned to face Roberts.

"I have no idea. We go wherever the StarVista corporation sends us, we just do our duty and job. Why are you so against this extra and free addition to the ship's itinerary?"

"It may be free, but it's not right. No one ever goes to a new system until the GAA have fully explored and cleared it. That's not been done to this system at all, so I smell a rat."

"Is it something of a delicacy? I thought I knew the various Terran aspects of cuisine and that one is not familiar to me."

"Don't get clever Mr barman. You know the GAA rules just as well as I do. Something is not right."

A slightly shrill voice piped up behind him and he turned around then frowned. "Blooming reporters, get everywhere! I've said my piece Sicanrinka."

"Well that is a nice welcome I must say. What is it you drink?"

"Alteran brandy, Ziancan so called tonic water, whiskey and a dash of Jamacan rum."

"Looks and indeed smells obnoxious! Well pretty much all of those except the Alteran brandy would kill me so no thanks. Not enjoying the festivities then?"

"Well you're here so I guess neither are you, so they can't be that spectacular!"

"I think you humans say something like, *touché*. It is actually quite magnificent, but I see you are still wallowing in the bar and happy to be the odd one out."

"Listen you clap happy freak of wherever it is you are from, we shouldn't be here! I tell you again what I overheard a few nights ago but no, not into conspiracy theories you say.

YOU! You are the one who should be asking the captain why we are here. Thought you were a top reporter? Blooming freak that you are!"

Anatonyp stood up as tall as his frame would allow and leaned over the bar menacingly.

"Roberts, OUT, NOW! You don't talk to me, my customers or fellow passengers like that under any circumstances. GET OUT!" He reached over but Roberts quickly stood up, wavering a little as he did so, quickly downed the rest of his drink, then put the glass down hard on the bar's surface.

On star cruisers fortunately they did not carry normal glass items and so it didn't shatter, but Roberts didn't care and staggered out, cursing.

Anatonyp calmed down and tuned to an intercom on the wall behind him.

"Security, port obs second level, bar station one, Yes, you've guessed right, human Roberts has had too much once again and was rude to one of the clients without provocation, so please do the necessary."

He turned away to face Sicanrinka and did what his race would consider a fair impression of a human shrug. "Sorry about that but he seems to get on everyone's nerves. Can I get you anything?"

Sicanrinka shook her small head and stood up. "No, I had best get to see what the passengers are making of our extra special stopover. He's right though, even though I detest him, we shouldn't be here so why are we? No, I'm not expecting you to answer but it does make me wonder what is going on. Thanks for the help though."

With a small flourish of her cerebral markings she headed out as Anatonyp watched her go then reached for the internal comms again.

"Message for the captain, message is: Sicanrinka and Roberts have been nosing around again. Over." He closed the link but then an Alteran triple group came in for a brief break and refreshment once they had spotted Sicanrinka leave. They had been accosted by her several times already and were getting fed up with her continually asking if they agreed or not with the decision to add this additional stop to the itinerary.

Anatonyp sighed, back to normal business, he figured and put on a smile.

Outside, just a dozen metres away, security wandered over and took charge of Roberts as Sicanrinka watched from a distance, slightly bemused.

Now whilst security were a little preoccupied with Roberts, it was time to put her plan into action…

However, something had caught her attention. She noticed in the distance across the observation deck, that Cherice Richmond seemed to be up to something so, discreetly, Sicanrinka decided to investigate.

#

Cherice sighed as once again just at around one thousand and forty-eight, she lost count. She looked at the mass of stars straddling across the view spread out before her and thought about giving up.

The Last Voyage of the StarVista 4

Then something caught her attention; looking to the left which she realised was almost looking forwards. She noticed a few more extra stars then, something twinkled and caught her attention.

Puzzled, she fished out her personal holovid flicked it on and held it in front of the view.

"Zoom please"

The holovid responded: *what level do you require?*

"Half max."

It zoomed in on the twinkle and she frowned. The largest moon of Tianca, Zospher, was an almost full phase but something seemed to be off to one side of it.

"Full max."

It obeyed and she started, then gasped with glee. Cherice air swiped to capture a quick selection of still images then switched to video record and looked in fascination at the view before ending the recording, folding the screen away and starting towards the exit.

She'd never discovered anything before today on her own and she could barely contain her excitement as she imagined announcing her discovery to the captain. She didn't get to the exit however, as just then someone approached...

#

Sicanrinka walked away smugly, quite pleased. Worryingly her initial plans now had to adapt yet again after seeing what Cherice had inadvertently discovered. But at least her back up plan was in place.

The Last Voyage of the StarVista 4

It had begun almost as soon as the ship had set off from Alteran star port *Atrica*. Always worth having a back up in place, she had figured.

It was quite easy really. Watch the crew go about their work, figure out who was both potentially important *and* had a weakness that could be exploited. Throughout the GAA there were many things, including vices, that each member civilisation had in common, drugs and gambling in particular. Both were allowed, but in moderation and via strict rigidly enforced rules so no one could get out of their depth.

That didn't mean it was impossible….

Sicanrinka had done her homework then she had been given information that the StarVista 4 would not end its voyage at the Viliak star port. Instead, they would be going to the relatively unexplored, or for that matter non vetted world, Tianca. That suited her perfectly now her assignment was over. She didn't have to find a way to get to the system on her own to return to home world.

Even with her original rendezvous ship compromised and probably destroyed, she knew as long as she could get to a certain, almost hidden, way point in the ring system of Tianca, then she could still get back.

She redoubled her efforts and unfortunately for him, it was ensign Zalokq that had come to her attention…

…and was now in debt to her to the tune of five hundred and forty-seven thousand Ziancan credits. Of course, it had been her own doing, setting up the illegal gambling ring on deck 73 in the first place.

The Last Voyage of the StarVista 4

But it had been a cinch snaring the unsuspecting and rather naive Zalokq. He was relatively young and more importantly, unattached, no relatives back on Zianca colony Aztra and above all, he felt lonely.

Perfect... Even the bioscans had been fooled into thinking they were elsewhere on the ship to prevent them being discovered.

So, there are you have it, Zalokq fell under her 'charm', was enticed into visiting and then partaking of, the gambling ring. At first, like all stings, he won; not large sums, but enough to keep him coming back for more.

She ensured he had a new account that would not be monitored by the ship's security and he was under no illusion that he could spend his winnings on the ship.

They were going to accrue enough so that they could elope and he would be able to leave the employ of the StarVista Corporation and naturally they would settle down on one of the farthest Ziancan colonies to start a new life together.

Oh, Zalokq was so, so gullible. Sicanrinka at times did feel a little sorry about using him. But this was a cut-throat business, and she knew that as the Havaerian news guild had effectively given her a full pass and clearance to do whatever was needed to get her story, then she had plenty of options. Well, at least that was her cover story.

It gave her the chance to get back home and she wasn't going to miss the opportunity, news guild or not. By the time her superiors had finished, there was probably going to be no news guild or even GAA left anyway.

The Last Voyage of the StarVista 4

She could only assume that someone higher up the ranks had pulled the strings which meant their long term plans were on track.

Apart from the unsettling setback of her transport home being disabled with no explanation and the fact his Excellency seemed to think she was no expendable and that was not going to happen as far as she was concerned. She'd deal with the fall out if needed at a latter time.

The GAA was quite open when dealing with external threats but there was nothing to suggest they knew the real secret of Tianca.

Yet.

Yet, someone had somehow arranged for the StarVista 4 to visit the planet against all usual protocols and procedures. Either her masters were extremely good, or it was a sign someone in the GAA had stumbled upon information that they needed someone else to investigate. She did suspect Mr Roberts was not all he seemed, although to be fair he was quite obnoxious as a human.

But he did seem to always be asking about why the ship had been given an extra stop and clear pass to voyage to the Cantrara system and orbit Tianca.

That's life, or at least that's how the humans put it. She smiled at Zalokq in a reassuring sort of way as they approached the pod and her mind turned to more immediate matters.

The Last Voyage of the StarVista 4

"Don't worry, we'll be back before they find out. Now remember, sweetheart, I've been promised a very lucrative retirement from my news sponsors and together we will make that new life out on the edge where few will know us and we can live a life of luxury." Sicanrinka smiled as she said this knowing full well that she had other plans.

They didn't include Zalokq, or the GAA for that matter.

Zalokq accessed the panel and they entered the pod. He took his place at the controls and with a deep breath in turn from each of his four gills he rechecked the overall system status.

"Very well my love, systems check out. I've bypassed the pod and dock safety checks to read as if nothing has changed and the sensors on the release doors have also been rigged to mask our departure."

He turned and looked sideways at Sicanrinka strapped in the seat on his left. "You, you have everything set up? The biochips have been adapted to give a wrong position for us? We can leave once the StarVista 4 gets back to Viliak? No one will know about this trip?"

"Oh questions, questions, have a little, what is it the humans say? Faith! Have faith in me. If you've done your part right then I have everything else sorted. As long as we get back to the ship safely undetected. Otherwise…" She trailed off and Zalokq shuddered inside but held his nerve.

He depressed several pads in sequence and the pod bay doors opened. Their modified pod slid out and detached from the ship leaving the pod bay doors to automatically close again as if nothing had happened, with no record of the event whatsoever.

The Last Voyage of the StarVista 4

Zalokq took a wide berth of the ship and headed astern, dipping under where he knew there would be sensors so that they would not be visible from the observation decks. It had been risky but strangely exhilarating to modify the escape pod for a longer flight and he was a little excited at seeing the strange rings close up.

Compared with the StarVista 4 the pod was almost unimaginably tiny and he was counting on that as he angled the pod in towards the gap between the two closest of the inclined rings of Tianca.

The view was admittedly breathtaking and even Sicanrinka marvelled at the sight. They moved closer to a point almost midway between the two largest ring planes. She knew the access point was getting closer.

"Take us down to the lower ring, let's see what they look like close up" she effectively ordered Zalokq, but he didn't mind as he was just as mesmerised by the sheer beauty of it all.

They headed down and levelled out just a few hundred metres above the rings, then skimmed over them slowly as Zalokq rotated the pod round so they could look directly at the chunks of irregular ice.

Except they were not irregular at all.

Each chunk was a symmetrical shape, all the same size. Each was orientated in the same direction.

Each one shimmered slightly for no reason.

Zalokq felt uneasy.

"This is not right. Nothing here looks natural…"

He turned to face Sicanrinka and ducked just in time as she attempted to use an immobiliser on him.

Training kicked in and he instinctively lashed out sending her sprawling back into a bulkhead, cracking her neck as she slumped to the floor, lifeless. She shimmered, then he gasped in astonishment as her true form was revealed.

He felt nauseous, whatever 'she' was, she wasn't part of the GAA and he knew he'd been used but also knew they were all in grave danger. He tried the communications but there was only static. She or 'it' had sabotaged the communications systems, how or when he did not have time to fathom.

He had to get back and warn everyone…

Zalokq gunned the engines and the pod began to speed up out of the plane of the rings, four chaks away from the ship, three chaks…Two…

Then something powerful seized the pod and pulled it violently back. Zalokq didn't feel a thing as the pod was enveloped in a strange phenomenon, putting him into a form of suspended animation as the pod was hurtled across a vast distance of space. In a fraction of a second it was gone from Tianca…

The shockwave set off a series of undulations in the gravity/magnetic field of the nearest rings, rippling outwards like the surface of a disturbed pond, taking with it a part of the strange phenomenon that had formed where the pod was. But there had been a miscalculation…

The perpetrators of the transport beam had expected it to be a much larger ship…

Entrapped

"No passengers reporting noticing our slow movement so far captain. I have informed the crew attending them to just comment that we are making slight adjustments to our orbit with the planet to give the best view."

"Very good Graylor." Xaoping noticed something about her second in command. "Something is bothering you, care to share?"

Graylor looked a little uncertain. "Some of the passengers and crew have noticed flashes of light emanating from several of the inclined rings. It may be an electromagnetic effect as Tianca does have a strong ionic flux with it's largest moon, Zospher, so it may well be nothing at all."

"Very well. Calsohn, keep an eye out for these flashes with the port sensor array just to be on the safe side. I have to admit there was nothing about flashes or gravitational ripples mentioned about this system, so perhaps we might be witnessing a new phenomenon.

It would certainly make this an even more historic voyage and give a boost to the corporation." Xaoping turned to face her trusty helmspilot.

"Delieezas, how long until we reach our new position nearer to the anomaly?"

"Just under two Terran minutes Captain."

"Very good, Calsohn, any change in the ripples?"

"No Captain, exactly the same as our first sighting."

Carson looked disturbed and Xaoping indicated for him to speak.

The Last Voyage of the StarVista 4

"May I say something Captain?"

"Yes of course, go ahead."

"I may be letting my imagination run away with me but, well, it reminds me of a fishing line as it touches the surface of a lake."

"Ahh yes, your species does have a strange idea of capturing live creatures swimming about in di hydrogen monoxide. I'm glad you saw sense and started to use artificial fish instead…"

Xaoping frowned, thought for a moment then a deep seated instinct took over. "Delieezas full stop and pull us back a little, around a chak should be enough."

"Aye Captain."

The ship slowed to a halt then started to back away just as a small object headed towards them, suddenly stopped and was pulled out of sight before they could notice it. The ripples suddenly expanded at the same instant. Enhancing the weaker outer ripples, they combined, ensnaring the ship with the strange phenomenon.

Everyone momentarily felt space and time shimmer then settle down to normal as if nothing had happened, but warning klaxons sprang to life in response to the brief event.

"Graylor, check with the crew as to any effects and I'll reassure the passengers, Carson, kill the klaxons and patch me into the comms, ship wide, passengers and crew." Carson nodded then gestured that the captain was live.

"Attention ladies and gentlemen this is Captain Xaoping Shoo. There is no cause for alarm. We experienced a slight gravitational anomaly and, as you can see, we are now back to normal.

The Last Voyage of the StarVista 4

However just as a precaution we will be moving the StarVista 4 to a wider orbit which in turn will give you a slightly different view of the multi ringed planet Tianca as a bonus.

Please do feel free to ask the crew anything if you have any concerns, but for now please continue to enjoy the view and our complimentary service."

Xaoping indicated to cut the comms and Carson did so.

"Everyone, report!"

Delieezas: "All flight and control systems normal Captain."

Graylor: "Medical bay reports no casualties amongst passengers or crew. All systems reporting in as normal, Captain."

Calsohn: "Science station appears to be functional…"

Xaoping shot him a sharp glance.

"What do you mean, it either *is* or *is not*, which?"

"Everything appears to be working, however according to the ships systems sensors, we haven't moved at all. We are instead inside something I can only call an anomaly, based on the readings if they can be trusted."

Silence.

"It expanded?" Xaoping asked incredulously.

"It would appear that way, but everything is stable, and we don't appear to be seeing ripples anymore." Calsohn offered.

The Last Voyage of the StarVista 4

Delieezas looked up. "Captain, our controls appear to be working but I've rechecked and as Officer Calsohn says, we are not moving despite the engines being set at one tenth above station keeping velocity."

"Bring them up gently to a quarter…" Xaoping ordered and Delieezas complied but then looked concerned.

"Nothing, no change in our position. Shall I go to full manoeuvring thrust?"

"No, I don't think it will make a difference and if it did and we suddenly moved, the passengers might start to wonder what's happening. So, for now we are stuck here, well, in this orbital location at least. I want full systems triple checked and close monitoring of our position. Inform me if anything, no matter how slight, changes. I will be in engineering. Graylor, you have command until I return."

"Yes Captain." Graylor replied as Xaoping got up and left knowing full well there was going to be an inquiry if the corporation found out she had ordered them closer to the anomaly against Graylor's recommendation.

She would face that another time. As long as the passengers were calm then they were bound to sort out why they couldn't move.

Meanwhile Calsohn looked a little glum and deep in thought.

"Spit it out Officer Calsohn, what is it?" barked Graylor.

"I just get the feeling Carson is right and we've been hooked…" was his reply.

#

The Last Voyage of the StarVista 4

Engrossed, Cherice felt the strange ripple passing through the ship and for a second she was frightened as the klaxons sounded. She looked about now, fully conscious that she was alone and a sliver of fear began to take hold.

Not only that, but she was also not where her parents thought she was and she turned and looked back towards the deck exit when Captain Xaoping Shoo's calming tone filled the air...

"Attention ladies and gentleman this is Captain Xaoping Shoo. There is no cause for alarm as we experienced a slight gravitational anomaly and as you can see we are back to normal. However just as a precaution we will be moving the StarVista 4 to a wider orbit which in turn will give you a slightly different aspect of the multi ringed planet Tianca as a bonus.

Please do feel free to ask the crew anything if you have any concerns but for now please continue to enjoy the view and our complimentary service."

Reassured, nonetheless Cherice decided to head back to their room. She had one last look at the stars then set off, completely forgetting about what she had discovered and who had approached her.

#

"Carl, CHERICE! She's on her own."

Natalie looked at her husband, worry spreading across her face. Everyone had just experienced the ripple sensation, accompanied by the klaxons, then fortunately the calming voice of the captain. But that did not stop Natalie worrying about her little girl.

"Right, you go to our room and make sure she is all right and I'll see what I can find out. That was no simple gravitational effect. For a second or so I could have sworn I was displaced a little. I'm still puzzled about those flashes above the ring system; I'm sure there was nothing in the info briefs they gave us a couple of days ago."

Beings of all kinds from across the Galactic Arm Association were no longer looking at the, admittedly fabulous, rings of Tianca, instead looking around, anxiously. Some were already having animated discussions with the crew that were present.

Ambassador Richmond made a beeline for a beleaguered waiter surrounded by a dozen or more concerned passengers; many Alterans, some Ziancans, three humans including one he vaguely recognised who looked a little drunk and a Scorion who hovered at the outer fringe of the group.

"Excuse me dear colleagues but I am Ambassador Richmond. May I try to get to the bottom of this occurrence?" The noise from the group he had approached died a little and several of the passengers nodded and muttered that an ambassador would be better to argue with the crewman. Carl turned to the poor chap, an Alteran.

"As Terran Ambassador to Zianca I wish to have an explanation from the captain in person as is my right under the GAA Intersystem charter."

"Sir, the captain has assured us that all is well and it was a minor incident that was unforeseeable, but has passed. I can send on your request to her shortly but as…"

The Last Voyage of the StarVista 4

The waiter was cut short by a new announcement from second in command officer Graylor.

"Passengers and crew of the StarVista 4 we would like to once again assure you that everything is all right and that we experienced a minor anomaly as we were station keeping giving you the best view of the majestic rings of Tianca.

There are no reports of damage or casualties but to confirm the captain's decision, we are, as a precaution, moving the ship soon to a higher orbit which in turn will give you an additional splendid view of Tianca.

We thank you for your patience and understanding and trust you will continue to admire the rings until we prepare to depart the system tomorrow. Thank you for your attention and cooperation."

The waiter looked round the group and, in the Alteran way, gave a shrug.

"There we are, no need for concern and I have been instructed to ensure you have plenty of refreshments and condiments whilst we enjoy our stay here at Tianca."

The various groups around the crew started to disperse and head back closer to the observation screens, whilst some took advantage of the refreshments that had appeared from a lower deck via a flurry of waiters. Ambassador Richmond stood for a few moments as his group melted away and the waiter carried on with his duties but then one of the humans approached him.

He now realised it was the awkward Mr Roberts who seemed a little inebriated, as per usual, Carl couldn't help but think.

Carl turned to leave intending to head back to the family's room to check on Cherice and Natalie but Roberts took him by the arm, surprising him with the firmness of the grip.

"Walk with me Mr Ambassador."

"Now look Mr Roberts I do think that is not called for, I…"

Roberts held up his other hand and an identi-card caught the ambassador's attention. Plus the fact that Mr Roberts now seemed completely sober.

"Good grief…" Carl muttered, a little shocked.

"Come with me to your suite, it's very important." replied the now enigmatic Mr Roberts.

Carl nodded. They left the stunning views of the Tianca rings behind for the other passengers to enjoy.

There was more to Mr Roberts than anyone could have guessed.

#

Cherice was lucky. She had arrived at their suite just a few moments before her mother, but she couldn't contain her excitement. Natalie on the other hand was both pleased to see Cherice perfectly well and in their room, but then in consternation at discovering Cherice had been at the starboard observation deck rather than where she had said she would be.

Cherice wanted to show her mother what she had discovered, but Natalie was having none of it as Cherice scrolled through the images captured on her holo recorder. Frustratingly, none showed what she had spotted.

Had she imagined taking the other pictures? she wondered as she frantically scrolled through what pictures there were left. She couldn't help thinking her memory was a little off.

"Sweetheart, I'm sorry but that isn't important. What is, is that you disobeyed your father and I and didn't come to the room like you said you would. What would have happened if there had been a genuine emergency? Can you imagine how we would have felt if something awful had happened to you? You must promise me you will not do anything like this again, *promise*?"

"Yes Mummy. But Mum, I want to show you what I found when I was counting the stars outside but it's not here anymore, I think she..." Cherice went to activate the holovid again but Natalie took it off her and placed it in the cabinet drawer.

"No darling, enough excitement for now. Daddy will be here soon when he has found out more about what happened. Now are you sure you are all right? No feeling sick or giddy?" Cherice shook her head and was about to try to explain again when the door chime piped up.

"Open." stated Natalie and the door slid open to reveal not just Carl, but the annoying person she had seen a few times at the bars dotted around the ship. She shot a questioning glance at her husband.

"Natalie, could you do me a favour and take Cherice back to the observations deck. If you see Lariq then ask him to look after Cherice and come back here as soon as you can, OK love? I would like a quiet word with Mr Roberts here. It's official business so has to be private, you understand."

The Last Voyage of the StarVista 4

Natalie always knew when Carl was up to something. She looked at Roberts, shook her head, then took Cherice by the hand and they left the two men in the room alone.

Carl Richmond was still a little in shock.

"OK, tell me everything…" he said as he turned to face Mr Roberts.

#

Captain Xaoping made her way back to the command centre, every so often fending off questions from the few passengers and indeed crew who were not up on the port observation decks.

Chief Engineer Coaraskk and his team could give no answers as to why the ship did not appear to be moving. All systems checked out, all appeared to be functioning yet with no actual effect.

Xaoping was worried. She knew that once they did manage to get underway again there would have to be questions answered as to her complicity in taking the ship closer to an unusual phenomenon. Pretty much every regulation stated that passenger ships were not to investigate but simply report on what they found if anything unusual occurred on a voyage. A science vessel would then be dispatched to do the real research.

Suddenly she experienced a ripple pass through her and realised that the ship had undergone a second anomaly. The klaxons sounded once again. Quickly Graylor's voice came over the universal tannoy reassuring everyone not to panic and that the situation was under control.

The Last Voyage of the StarVista 4

Xaoping felt a sense of foreboding wash over her and she was just about to call Graylor when her comms pinged. She waved a tentacle to open the channel.

"Captain here."

"Captain, Graylor here. I've had an urgent request from Ambassador Richmond to see both of us immediately. I have tried to assuage him of any fears he may have about everyone's safety but he continues to insist. What do you wish me to do?"

"Very well, I'll meet him in the briefing room of the forward observation deck in say half a Terran hour. I'm on my way to you, so join me in my anteroom in about ten minutes. If we can put his mind at ease then he will be of help with the rest of the passengers if we remain stuck here for a while."

"Yes Captain." The comms went quiet and Xaoping shook her head as best a Gu-Alt could do. She took stock of where she was before continuing down her present route hoping that no one else would ask for an audience…for now.

The Last Voyage of the StarVista 4

The Cazalee
8 days earlier...

Falaise-c-puc star port

Captain Rii was just finishing his inspection of the starboard launch bays when his comms buzzed for attention.

"Yes?"

"Captain, Felick here Sir. I've received a priority coded message for you marked urgent and for your immediate attention."

"Send it to my quarters and I'll head there now. Out."

It only took six minutes to get to his quarters despite the size of the GAA Defence ship Cazalee. He was proud to be the captain of it and the crew were loyal and trustworthy but in all his years of service he'd never had such a priority message before.

Intriguing.

He sat down and tapped his comms to bring up the holoscreen and swiped to decode the message.

It began to play. He sat shocked as he realised the commander in chief of the GAA Defence force was sitting there looking annoyed - and it was a live broadcast, not recorded.

"I know that even with hyper messaging there is a delay, but I don't expect to be kept waiting this long Captain Rii when it was a priority alert."

"Commander Xial, my apologies, I was not told it was a live message, just a priority message

The Last Voyage of the StarVista 4

that needed privacy, hence I came back to my quarters."

"I figured as much, inform Comms Officer Felick to take extra training to distinguish between the two, otherwise she may be finding work as a civilian. Understood?"

"Yes Commander."

"Good, what I am about to tell you is classified for now and I expect you and your crew to maintain secrecy and discipline. This information is on a need-to-know basis.

We have been given information that for some reason the commercial passenger cruiser, StarVista 4, has been given permission to extend their latest voyage to a world on the very edge of the GAA. I believe you are familiar with the ship's captain?"

"Yes sir, Captain Xaoping Shoo and I were at the first stage academy before going our separate ways but have stayed in touch intermittently. I saw the StarVista 4 and Captain Xaoping when they were here recently at Falaise-c-puc star port. Are they involved in illegal activity?"

"Not as far as we are aware but that is where you come in. They have been granted permission to visit the multi ringed planet Tianca in the Cantrara system although under current guidelines and rules no civilian or commercial ship is allowed to any of the more recently discovered new systems until they have been thoroughly charted, examined and vetted to be safe.

Yet somehow, someone has managed to pull strings and they are going to Tianca. We find it very strange and so, as you are the nearest ship, I want you to go to Tianca and keep an eye on things from afar. Do not engage with them unless you feel there is a threat or they are in danger. Ensure you are not seen. Do you understand?"

"Yes sir."

"Good. Keep this to yourself and only contact me or the Defence Ministry as a last resort. It may all be innocent and we're getting concerned over nothing. Many commercial concerns often try to push the boundaries of the rules, but this seems to be flagging up more concerns than most, so take care.

Incidentally, it may be a coincidence, but we've also noted that the privateer ship Lucky Seven has for some reason been granted clemency and cleared of all wrongdoing. Very odd, as you and I have been after Captain Screoria for a long time now, so someone has also been pulling strings for them."

"Indeed, we were about to intercept and capture them at Falaise-c-puc star port when they turned up all brazen on approach then we received the urgent communiqué that they were no longer on the wanted list." remarked Rii.

Commander Xial nodded. "What's more, they have disappeared not long after leaving Viliak, Spaceport Shalaiq. For them to first be at Falaise-c-puc star port, then turn up at Viliak, Spaceport Shalaiq is interesting as the direction is also towards the edge of GAA space and in the general direction of the Cantrara system. Coincidence? Not likely. They are also up to something but what, no one seems, or wants us, to know.

By my calculations, even at top speed, if you set off now on a direct maximum hyperspeed course you'd get there less than a day after the StarVista 4,

The Last Voyage of the StarVista 4

so make haste Captain, get out there and bring me some answers.

Out."

Rii sat there looking at the now blank screen and ran through what he'd just been told. He turned and swiped for a connection to the command deck.

"Felick, don't EVER forget to inform me when a message is a real time priority call. Understood? Good. Patch me through to navigation. We have a new task and we need to get underway immediately. After that put me through to the chief of operations on Falaise-c-puc star port." He waited until he was through to navigation and set things in motion before having to explain to the star port why they were unexpectedly leaving. A little white lie would have to suffice for now and hope it would be enough.

A short while later, the GAA Defence ship Cazalee slipped silently out of docking port 87 and headed out into deep space.

#

7 days later

"On approach Captain, Cantrara system ahead, shall I begin stealth scanning for other ships?" Nav officer Jalik turned to face her captain as she spoke.

"Yes, I expect two contacts if our intelligence is correct, one should be the StarVista 4, the other a smaller ship, in fact our old friends, the Lucky Seven.

"Beginning scans now, we are a long way off still but should at least pick up the larger passenger cruiser pretty soon by my estimates." Jalik replied as she turned back and studied her system scans.

Captain Rii nodded and absent mindedly began to polish a part of his uniform that had a slight speck on it. Very annoying, he thought.

"Felick, any comms at all from the Cantrara system?"

"I have intercepted several hundred personal messages both from passengers and crew from the expected location of the StarVista 4 and the usual engineering data as per standard on commercial ships. Nothing out of the ordinary to report however."

Jalik turned to Rii.

"I have contact sir. Definitely the StarVista 4 but..." Jalik's voice trailed off as if she were in deep thought.

"And?" prompted Captain Rii.

"Well, I do have something as a secondary contact. Close to the large moon Zosper, it appears to be slowly closing in on the StarVista 4's location. It's, it's much bigger than what I'd expect from the 'Lucky Seven'. Its motion is also quite slow, almost like it is creeping up on the StarVista 4..."

"That can't be right; no one else is supposed to be out there. Sound general quarters and put the squadron on standby for immediate deployment at my command when we are in range. I don't like this. Now I know why our superiors were suspicious of the addition to the StarVista 4 schedule. Someone knew there was something else out at Cantrara. If it's not the Lucky Seven then who and what are they? And, where is the Lucky Seven?

Felick, can we contact the StarVista 4 on a tight beam from this distance?"

Felick shook his head. "No, they don't have our sophistication and use civilian bandwidths so we'd have to transmit on a wider frequency which could tip off the other ship."

"This is not good." Rii thought out loud as Jalik interjected.

"Captain, this is very odd. I can now theoretically pick up anything the size of the Lucky Seven but instead I've picked up one of the StarVista 4 pods leaving the ship and heading into the ring system."

"Well, any of the premium passengers could well have hired a shuttle to take them in for a closer look", Rii suggested, but Jalik shook her head.

"No, much too small for a shuttle, it has to be an escape pod, but it's illegal to use them for anything other than an emergency. The pod is five times smaller than the Lucky Seven, so I should have picked them up as well by now, but there is no sign of the former privateer."

"What is Xaoping up to I wonder? She wouldn't do that. If there is an emergency why is there no distress call? Why just one pod? This doesn't make any sense."

"I don't get this; the pod has reached the lower set of inclined rings but after a short pause it has suddenly turned around and starte...WHAT?" Jalik exclaimed suddenly.

"Captain, some form of beam shot out from the rings and snatched the pod. It's gone, but, but, something else is happening...so, so has the StarVista 4!"

Before Rii or the rest of the command crew could ask...

The Last Voyage of the StarVista 4

"Now the other contact has also vanished!"

"Jalik, nothing vanishes. Is something interfering with our systems? Report status everyone." Rii ordered but could see his team were already running checks.

"All report that systems are operating perfectly. But as we're closing in, I can confirm Jalik's observations. The StarVista 4, its pod and the other contact are no longer there."

Captain Rii stared at the view screen lost for words as the Cazalee raced ever closer to the Cantrara system.

StarVista 4: No answers but a surprise

"Graylor, when it comes to the inevitable court proceedings, you must be truthful regardless of your feelings for me. It is your duty, and I won't hold it against you."

They were in the captain's briefing room next to the command centre bridge. Graylor had been expecting the conversation.

"Captain. We were not to know, we should face whatever comes our way with dignity and fortitude."

"Indeed. Now report on our current status."

"We have now been in this position and unable to find a way to move for twelve Terran minutes. We have experienced two of the ripple effects but apart from a few reports of brief symptoms of dizziness and a little nausea there appear to be no other health detriments. The ship *appears* to be fully functional but simply cannot move and until engineering can solve this we could well be stranded here for a few hours or possibly even days, hopefully not longer.

I was going to seek permission to send a classified signal to the GAA security ministry on Zianca asking for their advice, but I didn't want to inform them of our predicament due to the potential adverse publicity it may generate. Also, I wondered about us informing the company of our predicament, but again it might be a little hasty."

"You were right to hold back, for now at least. If we can solve this and get the passengers back safely then we stand a chance of keeping the corporation out of trouble."

"We do have Ambassador Richmond asking to urgently speak with you and he is still waiting in the briefing room on the upper forward observation deck. He has someone else with him who I think you should also see, despite my deep reservations."

Captain Xaoping looked inquisitively at Graylor who continued.

"Roberts."

The look on Xaopings face was enough. She motioned to Graylor and they set off in silence to meet the ambassador and his 'guest'.

#

"Ahh, Captain, about time, I have urgent business with you, and it concerns Mr Roberts here as well. I think you need to hear what he has to say."

Ambassador Richmond was not used to being kept waiting but as another of the unusual ripples had passed through the ship before the captain had found time to see them, Carl Richmond had managed to assuage Mr Roberts for the time being knowing the captain probably had a lot on her plate.

Xaoping turned to Graylor and muttered something.

She in turn nodded and stood to one side as Xaoping waved for the ambassador and Mr Roberts to take a seat. Richmond turned to Roberts and he in turn now spoke up.

"Captain, I have to inform you that I have not been open and honest with you and your crew and for that I apologise. As we seem to be having difficulties with the ship, I believe it is time to come clean." He showed his identi-card to the Captain who took in a sharp intake of breath.

Roberts continued.

"As you can see, I am in fact, Isaac Robert Malin, Ministry of Security, GAA. I joined under cover when you were at Falaise-c-puc Starport. One of my little skills is to infiltrate systems and ships to, let's just say, make it look like I have always been on the voyage. I took the place of a passenger who has a passing resemblance to myself, and I expect is now enjoying a new life on another world. In the meantime, I altered the bioscanners to accept my readings as his.

My mission was to discover why the StarVista 4 had suddenly been given permission to add the Cantrara system to the end of your latest voyage. Considering that it was barely explored and had not yet been given clearance for public or commercial exploration it puzzled my superiors. I am sorry if I have had to come over as rude, but I wanted to prise out of you what your orders were and why you were sent here. With my somewhat offbeat methods I felt I was almost there until we had the unusual gravity ripples affect us.

Have you an explanation for what has been going on and for that matter, what were your actual orders?"

Roberts sat back awaiting a reply.

"I'm afraid I have to disappoint you Mr Roberts, I am no wiser than you as I have patiently explained ever since you began to harass my chief officers and me. We received the orders from the corporation a few days before we arrived at Falaise-c-puc, before we headed out to the Falaise Singularities.

The crew and I were informed it was an historic occasion and that we would be given a large bonus and additional holiday if we did not object to the addition of the Cantrara system. I was informed that it had been cleared at the highest level, so I assumed the system had been cleared for public exploration whilst we were already underway on our current voyage.

Naturally none of us refused and we have done as we were instructed. So, as Graylor here will attest, we were just as surprised as yourself at the late addition. As far as we and the rest of the crew were concerned it was just going to be a minor inconvenience for a few extra days with a very handsome bonus at the end of it. No one was going to refuse that."

Roberts shook his head.

"But none of you wondered why?"

"Why should we? The company is pretty good to us overall and I know that over the last few years it has been requested by various factions. So, as far as I was concerned it was only a matter of time before the corporation, or one of their rivals was given permission. Something like this doesn't come along very often Mr Roberts, so who am I to refuse such an historic chance?"

Ambassador Richmond sat down and looked up at the three with a puzzled expression.

"It still doesn't make sense, however. You only found out a few stops back, but I was informed *before the voyage even set off*. Indeed, I was made aware a month or so before you left Alteran Star Port

The Last Voyage of the StarVista 4

Atrica. I was however told to keep it quiet until an official announcement had been made. Like you and your crew I was told it was an historic occasion and a short historic visit."

Roberts nodded. "According to what the ambassador has told me, someone quite high up in the Ziancan administration let the ambassador know as he and his wife were going to be confirmed as the new Terran ambassadors.

Ambassador Moore stated she was stepping down and taking early retirement providing the opening for a new ambassador. That begs the question of what would they gain from letting Carl know, but then swearing him to secrecy? We at GAA security had suspected something might happen as the StarVista 4 was the only peaceful ship that had the potential to be diverted this far out due to its design and long flight capability."

Carl Richmond was a little confused however and Captain Xaoping explained.

"By Interstellar treaty 4907, sub section eighteen, any star going passenger ship has to be able to support its passengers for a minimum of one Alteran year, the equivalent of almost two of your Terran years, in case of emergencies such as the failure of the propulsion systems or a quarantine situation. All in the StarVista fleet have such capabilities, but there has never, ever, been an incident so it's often thought of as a bit old fashioned and obsolete in this modern age of ours. With the current voyage we have just under a Terran year's supplies left but of course we are not expecting to use a fraction of that.

The Last Voyage of the StarVista 4

As you know we are quite self-sustaining so theoretically we could actually remain in space for several years but, again, it's never been done and never been required."

Roberts stood up and nodded as he looked round the small group.

"Well, you may have noticed, the GAA defence ship Cazalee just happened to be at Falaise-c-puc star port and that wasn't a coincidence. Such ships can also stay in space for years at a time, much longer than a StarVista vessel. I'm sure that if anything is amiss then it won't be long before it also comes to Tianca.

Well, I don't think we are going to learn any more from this and so I expect captain you have more important matters to attend to. As I understand it the ship can't move independently for the time being, so I believe we should keep what we know to ourselves for now and hopefully it won't be long before your engineer sorts out the problem and we can head back."

He was interrupted by Captain Xaoping.

"How did you know we had problems with the engines? We've not made any public announcement so as to avoid panic."

"Well, I am a GAA operative after all and I have my ways Captain. Don't worry, I understand the importance of keeping this under wraps for the time being and hopefully it won't be long before we are able to leave the system, before anyone becomes suspicious.

I do think that we should keep an eye on the reporter, Sicanrinka, as we have no information about her prior to just a few months before you began your latest voyage. She defies any attempt at trying to strike up a normal conversation with her. I don't like it or for that matter her, one bit.

What still intrigues me is what would be gained from coming here? The only thing, apart from the admittedly amazing view of the ring system, is the occasional flashes some passengers and crew have reported, but that could be nothing. On the other hand... the ripples may be the reason we are really here, so was it part of the plan for us to be caught up in them?

A risky plan using a civilian ship but then, who'd expect a StarVista cruiser of anything untoward? I don't know but there is a lot to think about whilst we remain stuck here."

Xaoping looked thoughtful as she took in what he'd said.

"If that is all then I believe Mr Roberts you should remain in your guise of a rather annoying passenger, no offence of course, and meanwhile Graylor and I will hopefully get answers from Chief Coaraskk as to when we can get back under way.

Ambassador Richmond, naturally I assume there will be discretion and no talk of what we know with anyone else, including your daughter, as the last thing we need is wild speculation and possible panic amongst our passengers. I'm reasonably confident the crew will remain professional whilst we are stuck here and none of them need know anything more unless it affects the ship and our safety.

Feel free to contact myself or Graylor however if you notice anything unusual. I expect you will brief your wife however, as I do think as the only other ambassador onboard, she ought to be included."

Carl nodded in agreement, and they all cordially shook hands, in Xaopings case her third tentacle as was customary in the Gu-Alt culture and they left the room going their separate ways, with a lot on their minds.

#

"Officer Zaclin, may I have a moment?" The duty officer for the maintenance crew hesitantly asked as she stood in front of Zaclin's systems desk. Zaclin looked up and quickly searched his memory before recognising the Scoron before him.

"Yes, Yahniz-lq-yin is it? Something wrong? I can't ever recall you making a personal visit before in all my years on the StarVista 4." Yahniz shuffled a little but realised that even with a crew of seven hundred, it was no real surprise that the security chief would recognise her. He was known to be thorough.

"I have lost a member of my section crew."

Zaclin looked at her and stopped himself being sarcastic. "Well, it is a big ship and there is nowhere to go to, so please explain how you can actually lose someone from an SV class cruise ship out in the depths of space?"

"That's just it. It is completely out of character. It's Ensign Zalokq, he should have reported to maintenance bay five, an hour ago. He is usually spot on time and more often as not, early. No one has seen him. I've tried knocking on his room door but there is no answer and only security have clearance to enter without permission. I worry that something has happened to him. Perhaps he is unwell and has collapsed with no one to know?"

"Well, firstly the medi-centre would have picked up on any illness and I can soon tell you where he is via his biosensor." Zaclin swiped on his holoscreen and flicked at a few icons then his face changed expression to one of incredibility. "When was the last time anyone saw him?"

"Well yesterday, as he finished his last shift. Why?"

"As you know, ship wide sensors are linked in to the bioscans of the crew and passengers as company policy. The system doesn't show him at all."

"Sorry?"

"He doesn't appear to be on board the SV4!"

Yahniz looked stunned.

"But how is that possible?" she asked as Zaclin quickly brought up and checked more data streams.

"I don't know, simplest explanation is that the biosensor has failed, at least I hope that's what this is. I don't need another instance of someone messing with their biosensors to fool us! Come with me and we'll check his quarters. I'll ask Dr Sreisse to join us in case there is a medical emergency that can explain this."

Yahniz followed and they hurried out as Zaclin called the medical bay.

Several minutes later as they arrived at Zalokq's quarters, Yahniz gestured to the door as the doctor joined them, looking puzzled.

"Most odd Chief Zaclin, I've checked the medical logs and ensign Zalokq has not reported any illness for more than two flight seasons. I can't think what could affect his bio sensor to stop it completely. I'm puzzled as to why our systems didn't alert me or my team if there was a problem."

"Indeed. Here we go." The door opened and Zaclin entered followed by Dr Sreisse then Yahniz.

"Ensign Zalokq, report immediately. Ensign Zalokq?"

The room was empty yet neat and tidy except for the bed which was was a little disturbed but not unduly messy. Zaclin scouted round and into the private facilities but returned shaking his head.

"This is strange. Yahniz, I'll assign a couple of security crew to come down to the maintenance bay and ask around as to when the last time anyone saw Zalokq.

I'm sorry to have wasted your time Doctor, but at least there isn't a body here for you to examine so I take that as a possible good sign. I'm heading back to my station as I want to do further ship wide checks but keep a lookout in case anyone else disappears."

They parted company, all of them none the wiser as to the whereabouts of Ensign Zalokq.

The Last Voyage of the StarVista 4

The Cazalee incident

The Cazalee dived into the system entering into orbit about Tianca and quickly began search efforts, deploying all fighters to cover as large an area of the orbital zone as the StarVista 4 should have been likely to be in.

No debris, no emergency life pods.
Nothing.
No secondary contact either.
It was as if no one had ever been there.
Or existed.
Captain Rii was puzzled and now highly suspicious.

"Felick, get me a direct link with the commander in chief and put it through to my briefing room."

"Yes Sir."
"AND DON'T MESS IT UP THIS TIME!"
"No Sir!"

A few moments later the comms chimed and the wall screen lit up, but not with the expected face of the commander in chief of the GAA Defence service.

"Sorry to disappoint you Captain Rii but the C 'n C has been replaced by me. I've only just found out about your little escapade. It was a ruse to get your ship away from Falaise-c-puc starport. There was no passenger ship at Tianca, nor a privateer either. Not your fault as you were only following orders. Maintain secrecy so as to not give away to the public how easy it is to mislead our forces.

You are to head straight to the Qrianlairing nebula and join a crack force we are assembling as we have reason to believe there are hostile forces gathering towards the galactic centre across from the Scorran territories. I expect you to arrive in about fourteen days' time and the other ships will be informed you will be joining them but each doesn't know the exact positions or timings of each other to help with the surprise element of the simulation.

You will conduct war drills but with ships armaments in simulation mode and once the drills are completed you will be given your new assignment.

This is a dangerous time for us and quite unexpected, but maintain secrecy at all times so we don't panic our citizens. Hopefully we can keep things under control and deal with any possible threat without the public needing to know.

Understood?"

"Yes Sir. We'll head straight there at maximum speed and in silent mode. Cazalee, out."

Rii watched as the screen went dark but was troubled.

He knew that he and his officers had seen and identified the StarVista 4 and an unidentified contact too at Tianca. There was something more going on and he knew they were in the thick of it. Rii stepped out onto the command deck.

"Listen up people. We have been ordered to the Qrianlairing nebula to join a crack force for simulated war games and we are to go to silent running. We are not to discuss what we saw at Tianca, as it is now classified. Recall all fighters from the search and inform me once they are all accounted for.

The Last Voyage of the StarVista 4

Nav Officer Jalik, once that is accomplished set course at maximum hypervelocity for the Qrianlairing nebula. Felick, keep monitoring all channels and alert me to anything unusual whilst we are still in range of Tianca. I'll be in my quarters. Let's move, people."

Captain Rii left for his quarters deeply dissatisfied with the turn of events and couldn't help but wonder what had happened to Shoozy and all aboard the StarVista 4. What was the significance of the unidentified contact and how could they all just disappear like that? Above all, why was the GAA commander in chief suddenly replaced with no explanation?

Using his own private channel to the nav station Rii made an unusual request. Jalik understood and complied.

All fighters retrieved, two hours later the Cazalee left the Cantrara system and headed off in silent mode.

#

Fourteen days later...

"On approach to the Qrianlairing nebula Captain, twenty thousand chaks out from the outer edge and closing."

"Very good Jalik. Maintain silent, simulation mode. Weapons on sim mode. Shields down. As we're joining a training task force it's possible they may use us as an approaching target for a bit of practise so keep sharp people and make sure we give as good as we get, simulated of course. Best not damage any of our own out there! Any contacts yet Jalik?"

"Yes sir, seven contacts giving us their brief credentials but have now gone off grid and silent. They are doing a good job of staying hidden now."

"Well that is the whole point. What ships?"

"Tlpfer, Anmastol, Cheik, Rhoster, Charger, Zahnck and Pristohrohnian." Rii felt something stir in the back of his consciousness but couldn't quite bring it to the fore.

"Anmastol..?" Rii muttered out to no one in particular and the others just looked and kept quiet.
"Any comms traffic Felick?"

"No sir, static due to the electromagnetic fields intertwined throughout the nebula."

"Yes, that's why they would choose this region for a test but… Anmastol. That's Captain Parlonz and her crew, but I thought they're normally out patrolling the far side of the GAA, it would take them at least four months at maximum speed to get here. Odd, very odd. You are sure it was their comm signal ident?"

"Yes Captain, perfect match for all the idents." replied Felick.

"Very well, bring up the idents to the right and link so that once we identify them their position is highlighted on the tactical display." Rii turned to face the nav officer.

"Jalik, summary of the Qrianlairing nebula?"

"There are numerous proto stars here with strong and in many cases violent bi-polar winds which are stirring up the dust and gas around them, so this is a good test of any ship's systems. It's er, it's also renowned for the ghost ship sightings too."

The Last Voyage of the StarVista 4

"Indeed, ghost ship, stuff and nonsense, I hope you don't fall in with that rubbish. If I were to hide then it would be as close to the densest cluster of them I could find. Jalik, what do you think, how many dense clusters are there in here?"

"Over fifteen, with up to twenty or more stars forming in each, we do have a particularly dense region nearby that could mask a ship, so definitely a good place for simulated war games."

The Cazalee continued in but skirted around a denser knot of gas and dust keeping engines at low thrust to minimise their energy transmissions.

Felick spotted something.

"There, lower left corner, a fleeting glimpse of a dark shape." The rest shook their heads.

"You're jumpy Felick, no one else saw it. Now don't go spotting ghost ships, we have a job to do." replied Rii.

"Contact to upper quadrant 3a, brief contact with ident Anmastol." reported Jalik.

"Hold course but simulate their possible course and form an intercept path with them on my mark..." ordered Captain Rii as he keenly watched the screens.

On the command bridge Helmspilot Gilespicq arrived and saluting the captain, moved over to take up his station. He couldn't help note the tactical display and stood still, staring at it. Captain Rii noticed.

"Gilespicq, take up your post."

"Yes sir, but..."

"What is it? Spit it out!"

"Well, it's odd, the Anmastol, that can't be correct!"

The Last Voyage of the StarVista 4

Capatin Rii's senses were tingling but not in a good way. "Explain?"

"Well, I have a relation on board as nav officer, Cal Rool See, and we were in touch via hypermessage yesterday and they were across on the other side of the arm, they can't be here..."

Gilespicq was interrupted by Felick.

"Got something. Seemed like an accidental transmission quickly cut short, a mistake by someone. Ahead, three chaks, X 23, Y at 289, they've gone silent again but if they manoeuvre then we should have them!"

Rii's attention was briefly diverted but he was now seriously troubled as Gilespicq's comments reinforced his own thoughts.

"This is very odd. Something is not right here. Zee minus forty for fifteen seconds then zee plus forty five. They'll probably expect us to go in on the level so let's duck under and come up from underneath. That'll surprise them whoever it is!"

The ship dropped under a denser bank of dust and gas then rapidly rose into a clearing.

"Good work team. Make it look like we're sticking to our course before we..." Captain Rii didn't finish as seven large ships cut them off, surrounding them.

"CAPTAIN, THEY'RE NOTHING LIKE ANYTHING I'VE EVER SEEN BEFORE. THEY'RE NOT GAA!" Gilespicq shouted out what everyone was thinking.

They didn't stand a chance as all seven opened fire blasting the Cazelee, battering it, punching holes straight through the hull like it was butter.

The Last Voyage of the StarVista 4

On the bridge it was mayhem.

"WE'RE DOWN SIR, ALL BATTERIES, LAUNCH BAYS, LIFE SUPPORT, ALL FAILING!"

"WHAT... Abandon ship, aban..." Rii's last words as the command bridge was taken out. The few escape pods launched were picked off one by one...no survivors.

A small automatic distress pod launched but in silent mode as per the Cazalee standard emergency procedure and so the attacking ships didn't pick it up. It headed away missing the attackers, but unfortunately deeper into the Qrianlairing nebula to become lost. Three of the attacking ships manipulated their magnetic fields to entrap the battered hulk of the Cazalee, corralling it and the surrounding debris field, guiding them towards the nearest proto star to be engulfed and lost forever.

The command ship launched a falsified distress pod giving an entirely different view of events before they moved back deeper into the nebula out of sight.

The only ship able to confirm the strange disappearance of the StarVista 4 and an unknown contact nearby had been silenced...

#

GAA all systems newscast reports.

'It was announced today that the StarVista 4 passenger cruise ship may have encountered difficulties whilst visiting the outer arm border

The Last Voyage of the StarVista 4

world Tianca in the Cantrara system. Rescue ships have been dispatched from Viliak StarPort Shalaiq but ships at high speed will still take several Terran days to reach the scene.

No more communications have been received from the StarVista 4 but as one expert explained, that may be the problem in its own right with an equipment malfunction.

In other news, reports are coming in that in a freak accident the GAA defence cruiser 'Cazalee' has been destroyed whilst trying to navigate the hazardous Qrianlairing nebula. Little is known about the accident and family and friends are being informed as we broadcast.

We will keep you posted as more news comes in.'

The Last Voyage of the StarVista 4

The mystery deepens

Captain's Report: Cantrara system, Tianca orbit, extended stay. Thirty six hours since our arrival.

'In consultation with my second in command, Graylor zXanders, we have had to announce to the passengers and crew that we have a minor problem with our systems and will be staying for a few days in orbit round Tianca to effect repairs.

We have hopefully deflected growing unease that we have not left the Cantrara system for Viliak Spaceport Shalaiq although we are both uneasy at having to lie and cover up what could be a serious situation developing. So far, Chief Coaraskk cannot explain why we are unable to move the ship and are stuck in orbit about the multi ringed giant planet.

This is most unusual, the chief is amongst the best in the fleet and I have never seen Coaraskk at such a loss as this. The ship is the chief's pride and joy and often tells me in no uncertain terms. I have kept ambassadors Carl and Natalie Richmond and GAA Security Officer Roberts informed and arranged for the latter and my own Security Chief, Zaclin, to meet so that at least Zaclin is in the know regarding Roberts' true identity.

I have a deep unease with the situation we find ourselves in at present, a trait amongst my kind and a throwback to a time when we were still a superstitious species. Yet, I have often followed..." The chimes rang gently, sounding an alert that someone wanted to see her. She paused the recorder and checked the security screen. "Yes, enter."

Security Chief Zaclin and GAA Security Officer Roberts came through the door and then made sure it shut tight behind them.

"Captain, I need a word, it is serious and I'm afraid may well be connected to our current situation." Xaoping stood, intrigued and yet again a sense of deep unease swept over her as several of her tentacles quivered unexpectedly. She indicated for Zaclin to speak.

"I didn't come straight away and report as I felt at the time it was something quite trivial and not something to disturb my captain with. However, my discoveries have changed everything. Six hours after we arrived at Tianca and felt the first ripple effect, a maintenance ensign, Zalokq failed to turn up for his shift. He has an exemplary record and so his immediate superior, Yahniz-lq-yin tried his quarters but naturally didn't have clearance to force entry. She came to me and, on entering his quarters along with Dr Sreisse, we found no sign of him. We..."

"Just hold it there please Zaclin. His bioscan readings would clearly ind..."

"Yes sir, but that was the point, I could not find any sensor readings of him *on the ship. None.* It was as if he had simply vanished. The sensor logs last show him in his quarters but then nothing. What's more there was no alert issued that his bioscans had stopped. Someone must have tampered with them.

His room was quite neat, and he had slept in his bed, but otherwise there was nothing. I did check his personal holorecorder but again there was nothing on it to suggest how or why he is missing.

The Last Voyage of the StarVista 4

So Yahniz and I systematically checked our systems for unauthorized shuttle or pod launches, airlocks being opened and cargo/baggage docks but there was no indication of anything out of the ordinary. I was at a loss, but then a breakthrough, a short while ago one of my teams physically checking the status of the escape pods discovered that one was indeed missing. However, the inventory shows it as present and correctly docked in its bay. There are no logs showing it launching."

Zaclin stopped to let the captain take in the news. Xaoping briefly looked at Roberts who nodded and she looked back at Zaclin, square on.

"So, what would possess someone like him to falsify the system and take a pod without authorisation? Where would he go? It doesn't make sense, we're too far from the nearest starport for a pod to make the journey. It might make it to the outer edge of this system at a push but what would it gain him?" she muttered.

"There is more to the puzzle Captain and you won't like it one bit. Who is the one person you would have expected to be covering, questioning and getting under our skins about the delay in heading back to Viliak? Apart of course from our Mr Roberts here whom we now know was acting. No offence Roberts."

"None taken." Roberts replied.

It didn't take a genius to work it out.

"Sicanrinka." said Xaoping in a quiet tone. More of a statement rather than a question. Xaoping took in a deep breath and exhaled slowly as she continued to listen, her mind beginning to go into overdrive as Zaclin continued.

"The one and only. We've been doing a lot of delving into both of them. Her bioscan is also absent from the ship. Stopped at the same time as Zalokq's. I have discovered she had set up illegal gambling sessions which were cleverly concealed, and I am sorry to report that I failed to discover it until events overtook us today.

My officers have now questioned three other crew members and two passengers who took part in the sessions, and all say that Zalokq ended up heavily in debt which was covered by an account I have discovered in Sicanrinka's company name. I believe therefore Ensign Zalokq may well have been blackmailed, as he would not dare risk coming out in the open and being discovered. May I have access to your holoscreen captain so I can show you something?"

"Indeed, here…" Xaoping activated it then entered the security pass allowing Zaclin access. He quickly linked into the security systems.

"I've just received word that my team have found something. Watch the screens for what they are about to show."

They looked on as four multi screens appeared, each with a view of the outside of the ship.

"These are our maintenance systems, and they show nothing out of the ordinary. They have been tampered with and Zalokq does possess the skills to achieve that. Now watch."

A new screen came to life in full screen and showed a slightly different angle of the side and rear of the ship. Suddenly a small dot raced away and round the stern of the ship out of sight.

The Last Voyage of the StarVista 4

The view changed and showed the side of the ship towards the stern, but on the side facing the ringed planet of Tianca.

The small dot appeared and streaked away from the ship heading towards the rings vanishing into the distance due to its size. Captain Xaoping looked at Zaclin, but he gestured to look back at the holoscreen. He manipulated a control and the view zoomed in closer to where the pod appeared to disappear.

"It doesn't vanish but comes to a stop close to the ring particles themselves though we can barely resolve the pod and certainly not the constituents of the rings. Then the pod suddenly appears to be racing back towards us when..." he stopped talking to let the captain see for herself.

The small pod rushed back almost directly towards the ship, but then an incredibly thin pencil of faint light leapt out from near the rings and the pod was yanked back and vanished. Xaoping began to speak but was hushed by Roberts. As they watched, a ripple in space extended outwards and engulfed the StarVista 4. Xaoping watched with fascination and sheer horror.

"That was when we were caught?"

"Yes Captain. That wasn't the first of the ripples but they were small until the pod was snatched out of view. We then found the StarVista 4 immobilised and have remained so ever since. The question that worries me is..."

"Why whatever grabbed the pod hasn't grabbed us and taken us to who knows where?"

"...*Yet*..." added Roberts and Zaclin nodded uncomfortably in agreement.

"I do have a thought, if I may? Perhaps we are too large a ship?" offered Roberts.

Captain Xaoping Shoo felt stunned and mortified but Zaclin was not finished.

"Dr Sreisse and I took a team to study Sicanrinka's room and it's not good. It had been deliberately cleaned to an incredibly high level. It's so spotless that we've not found a shred of organic matter from her. Dr Sreisse says the cleaning has been done to a better than surgical standard. However, we then examined Zalokq's quarters in greater detail and stuck in the disposal unit almost out of reach was a small bag of equipment that could have enabled him to bypass our security measures. We're not sure at the moment."

"Why not, Chief Coaraskk would know what it's for?"

Mr Roberts spoke up with a worried expression about his face.

"I'm afraid not, this equipment is like nothing we've seen before, indeed apart from a clear modification to connect to the ship, the items look… alien…"

Captain Xaoping Shoo looked at both of them in shock.

"But, but are you saying they are from one of the newer sentient species to join the GAA or…"

"…from outside the GAA." Roberts finished for her.

Zaclin wasn't done yet, however.

The Last Voyage of the StarVista 4

"One final thing for now Captain. I have done some background research into Sicanrinka, along with Mr Roberts' help and we can't find any record of her until she suddenly appeared at the Havaerian news guild two Terran years ago, based on what our onboard library informs us.

Also, as you are aware, our systems are normally directly linked to any number of GAA facilities as a commercial passenger ship and those records are always constantly updated.

We've had no contact from the rest of the GAA and they may not have had any further information from us since we became stuck in whatever it is holding us. If the latter, then with luck there may soon be a number of ships coming to find out why we have fallen silent, so that could be the one item of good news.

As far as we can ascertain Sicanrinka is a mystery and her actions along with Zalokq's may well have endangered us all. We fear there is more to this system than any of us ever thought possible and I have to now agree with Mr Roberts, someone knew something was not right at Tianca and somehow had enough influence to have us diverted to explore unofficially."

Roberts spoke up now with sombre tone.

"The fact that the GAA security ministry went to the trouble of implanting me on the StarVista 4 via a wanted privateer means they must have had a suspicion or been tipped off. However, I doubt anyone there could have suspected we'd become trapped like this and it is possible that it is simply an accident or coincidence."

"Or.." joined in Xaoping, "Someone needed an excuse to send us in deliberately to see what would happen. If that's the case, then they'll have almost three thousand of us wanting their head or heads and I'll be leading the charge."

"If we can escape…" Zaclin added ominously and the three stood silently as they contemplated that thought.

The Last Voyage of the StarVista

A new guest

"Mummy, why are we still here? I'm fed up and want to get back to Viliak to see my brother. I'm sure Danny can't wait very long for us as he said he'd have to be back at the university."

Cherice looked sullen and downcast.

"I know, sweetie, but as the captain said a few hours ago, they have a problem with the ship and need to fix things before we can head back to the starport. You wouldn't want us to leave orbit with something wrong with the ship now would you?"

"No, I guess not but it doesn't feel right."

"What love? What doesn't feel right?"

"The ship, I think it needs a doctor to look at it."

"What makes you say that, it's just some silly fault and I think the chief engineer, you know, Chief Engineer Coaraskk, is working on it.

"Oo I wonder if he wants me to help as he did say I would make a good engineer when I grew up."

"Now sweetie, I think you'll find he has enough on his plate without having to keep an eye on a little one roaming around in engineering. But tell you what, I'll send him a message and see what he says, how's that?"

"Oh, goody, I'm sure I can help him. Thanks Mummy."

Natalie tucked Cherice up in bed and turned the light down to one notch above complete darkness, kissing Cherice on the forehead before leaving the room and closing the door behind her.

Carl was sitting looking at an update Mr Roberts had sent to him and looked up.

"Cherice. OK love?"

"Bearing up but getting bored. What's going on Carl? You've become quite pally with that odd chap Mr Roberts and you seem to be getting lots of messages from him and the captain in the last few hours."

"Oh, I'm just keeping up with the latest reports on our status. It appears to have fallen to me to liaise between the captain and a few select people on board."

"And Mr Roberts?"

Carl Richmond hesitated before answering, something that Natalie noted quietly with a little unease.

"Listen, I am in an awkward situation here, let's say that Mr Roberts is not the uncouth, miserable person he makes himself out to be, but an important person and you have to accept that I trust him now. When the time is right, I can hopefully explain what's going on. OK?"

Natalie frowned. "No Carl, we're joint ambassadors to Zianca and I have every right to know if something is afoot that may affect us all and in particular our little girl. SPILL!"

Carl looked at her and knew she was right. He began to fill her in on what he knew.

#

"So, this is the plan." Captain Xaoping addressed the small group in her briefing room.

The Last Voyage of the StarVista 4

"Delieezas, you pilot shuttle Trallaac, that's the most recently overhauled, plus I know you like that particular shuttle, it handles well under your control I expect.

Officer Zaclin will accompany you. I have to stress this could be very dangerous as we have no idea what happened to the pod that Zalokq stole so please confirm one more time to reassure me that you are willing to proceed?"

"Yes Captain." they both chimed in unison. Once again Captain Xaoping Shoo felt pride in her fellow crew members, especially knowing there was a chance they might not be able to get back.

"Thank you. As Chief Engineer Coaraskk has noted, we don't know if the shuttle is large enough not to be pulled into whatever it was that the pod encountered. For one thing, we don't know if it was a natural phenomenon or if somehow something or someone was in control.

If we are to understand what is preventing the ship from leaving orbit then we have to take a chance; I appreciate your loyalty and dedication to the StarVista 4 and the corporation. Dr Sreisse will be monitoring your status and the instant you feel anything is wrong you get out of there and head back, do I make myself clear?"

They both nodded again as Dr Sreisse ran his sensor over them, satisfied they were healthy and the data streams were clear and in sync with the ship's medical bay' He gave them the all-clear.

"Very well, you leave in twenty Terran minutes. We'll also be following you from the command centre so all I can say is good luck and let us hope we can get to the bottom of this. That is all."

The Last Voyage of the StarVista 4

They all stood and saluted the captain before heading out. Xaoping sat down for a moment hoping she was doing the right thing and not sending two of her most trusted crew mates, and indeed friends, into danger.

#

"All systems check. Captain, this is Delieezas, we're all set. Please give final clearance for Bonnie, sorry, shuttle Trallaac to proceed…"

"Clearance granted, good luck and don't make a sight seeing tour of the rings whilst you are out there!"

"But Captain, that was the reason I volunteered for this. OK, so it wasn't but we understand. We are now initiating hanger door sequence and launch. Hanger bay doors are opening and.. .that's odd…"

"Shuttle Trallaac, repeat that last bit?"

"Captain, readings suggest that the hanger atmosphere has not evacuated as the doors opened."

"Yes, we concur, That's unheard of. Do you wish to proceed?"

Delieezas turned to Zaclin and looked at him for a final decision.

"Affirmative Captain, I'm sure Mr Delieezas can fly this shuttle even if there is an atmosphere present. They are designed for atmospheric flight after all."

Delieezas looked a little smugly at his colleague and gently operated the controls. The shuttle lifted delicately then crept forward building speed as it reached the open hanger bay.

The Last Voyage of the StarVista 4

Then dramatically slowed to a halt as it was halfway out.

Delieezas and Zaclin looked at each other and Delieezas steadily opened up the engines.

Nothing. Then they noticed the view of the stars, or rather the way the outside universe appeared to gently wobble like some humongous jelly. An anxious voice came over the intercom.

"Delieezas report. Why haven't you left the hanger bay? We're not picking you up outside yet?"

"Erm, Captain? We can't seem to get out. We're sort of just stuck here. I'm going to increase to half thrust."

"Negative, Deliezas. Not in my hanger you won't! You'll incinerate the insides with an atmosphere still present." Chief Engineer Coaraskk interjected. Delieezas shook his head, exasperated at the situation.

"Very well, returning to the docking platform." He deftly operated the controls then Zaclin looked over at him.

"Well? Are we landing then?"

"Doesn't look like it. We can't turn or reverse."

He flicked the intercom on. "Chief, we have no control. Can't move the shuttle in any direction at all! We're, well the only way I can describe it is we're stuck in some form of jellified space."

Coaraskk watched from the hanger bay control monitors and shook his head as he linked into the command centre comms. "Captain, we have a problem…" Then he addressed the shuttle.

"Delieezas, cut power in increments and keep watching to see what happens."

"Now at eighty percent, sixty-five, fifty, no effect, it is as if we are simply glued in place. Do I cut power completely to the engines?" Delieezas asked.

"Yes, I'm monitoring your level from here but as you say, there has been no change to the shuttle whatsoever." Coaraskk replied, worried.

"Forty, thirty-two, twenty-six, fifteen, five, zero. No change at all. Still stuck in position. Orders and suggestions welcome from anyone?"

"We are monitoring no escape of the atmosphere at all. Delieezas, you and Zaclin exit the shuttle via the escape hatch on the rear port side whilst there is still an atmosphere. Don't hang around either as we don't know if the atmosphere will suddenly evacuate. I've deployed a service sentry to assist with your evac. Confirm?"

"Confirmed Chief, we're not waiting around here to find out what happens." replied Delieezas and they both made their way to the rear left escape hatch. Its safety caps blew and it blasted away from the shuttle smashing into the wall but there was little choice in the matter. Within a few moments Delieezas and Zaclin were safely standing in the hanger control room with Chief Coaraskk, looking over at the stricken shuttle.

"So now what Chief?" Zaclin asked as he stared out, noticing a slight shimmer in the view of space beyond it.

"We try to manually drag it back in so we can close the hanger doors."

It took sixteen crew members to manually haul the shuttle back, then just as it was fully inside the hanger, it dropped like a stone on to the deck injuring several of them.

The Last Voyage of the StarVista 4

They didn't try to fly out again with a shuttle.

A remotely controlled pod fared no better and it was clear there was no escape from the StarVista 4...

#

Captains Report addendum: Cantrara system extended stay.

It has now been five Terran weeks since we became stranded at the Cantrara system in orbit around the so called wonderful ringed planet of Tianca.

Understandably the wonder has worn off amongst the passengers and crew of the StarVista 4 as our situation has developed and we are unable to find answers as to why we are stuck in orbit around the giant planet. We've been continuously transmitting a distress call now for five weeks but for some strange reason we cannot receive anything from the usual GAA comms traffic. I'm afraid that must also mean our transmissions may well not be getting out.

Despite this, and at the suggestion of Natalie Richmond, Cherice has restarted her diary messages to her brother and as such this has improved the moral of many on board who have begun to compose their own messages. Naturally we have to screen them as we don't want anything to badly reflect on the StarVista corporation.

On to more serious matters. We can't launch shuttles or escape pods and several of my wonderful but stressed-out crew have attempted to go outside the ship manually via the maintenance hatches.

They've had to be hauled back inside as they encountered what several have called a form of jellified space around us. It has to be completely transparent as we can still see the views of the planet Tianca and its rings along with the stars of our galactic arm, but few now are interested in anything but trying to find out why we can't move the ship.

We are puzzled as to why no ships have arrived looking for us. With all our comms blocked that should at least have alerted someone that there was a problem, but so far we can see nothing extra outside. Chief Coaraskk has noted that what we see is almost a static view as if we were stuck in a recording and someone has hit the pause button. We've not told our passengers or the majority of the crew what he said, for fear of panic.

However, last week we had a small riot amongst the passengers as several Scorrons propounded a wild theory that the GAA itself had caused this to happen to the ship and for almost a week I had to enforce a form of martial law. I have never in all my years had to do such a thing or even know of it happening in the company's history. It is all so very disturbing and distressing.

I can add with pride however that one little person has really stood out in how well she is coping and indeed has begun to inspire everyone to hold out hope that someone should be on the way to find and rescue us.

Young Cherice Richmond has become the unofficial mascot and morale spokesperson for the ship, both passengers and crew. With her parents consent, every other night she does a little song and dance routine that she learns from the ship's library.

Each appearance is a different song or dance she has learned and along with help from Lariq and Trionice-pkci; the rest of the ship's official entertainers she has brought hope and solidarity to the ship.

There is no doubt in my mind that my career is over if we ever get rescued as I did instruct the crew to investigate the strange ripples that we could fully explain and that have somehow entrapped us. We have to accept tha…" The chimes from her comms interrupted Xaoping's train of dictation and she called out to the intercom. "Yes?"

The strained voice of Security Officer Zaclin had an urgency about it that snapped her attention into sharp focus.

"Captain, please come down to deck seven starboard side, docking port three. We have a situation."

"I expect that last ripple effect and passengers getting out of hand Zaclin?"

"Err, no, we have found an unusual stowaway…" he replied.

The captain stopped her musings in shock and shook her head. "Please repeat?"

"We have a stowaway sir and he appears to be in a critical condition."

"On my way, seal off that section."

"Already done sir."

On a big ship it did take time and almost six minutes later Xaoping approached docking port three to find a small team of three security crew, Security Chief Zaclin and Dr Sreisse in attendance with a medical team.

"Report."

The Last Voyage of the StarVista 4

"I'm not sure where to start captain." answered Zaclin. "Crew person Pralon was walking along this deck when… well, tell the captain yourself, Pralon."

She hesitantly stepped or rather slid forward, she was a member of the Crinlon culture who had three legs but rather than feet they appeared to glide along without having to lift their legs.

"I was just coming along here captain, doing extra checks on the structure as per your orders after the strange anomaly when, when…" She looked down then regained her composure before the Captain could say anything.

"Just as another ripple took place this person simply appeared out of the docking port and fell into the arrivals section. He was writhing in agony then went still, but I could see that he was still breathing. But the docking port was sealed with no sign of it being opened. From either side."

Xaoping acknowledged her report then turned to the medical team.

"Doctor, your report?"

"He looks Alteran, however, I can't seem to get a fix on his life signs but something is seriously wrong, so we need him in the central medical bay. I will seal it off once there and only my team and I will continue to examine him to determine his condition."

"Very well, any possible danger to us or the passengers?"

"I can't say but based on my observations and these strange scans over the last few minutes, I think we may be OK as they appear to be only associated with the 'guest'.

The Last Voyage of the StarVista 4

I don't know if it is related to the ongoing ripple effects we are having, but so far none of the passengers or crew have come forward with any strange illnesses or symptoms except for this person."

"So do we know who he is? Indenti-chip?"

"Well, apart from obviously being an Alteran, he has one, but for some reason I can't read it and the design is not a current one." answered Zaclin.

"How can it not be a current one?"

"I honestly don't have an answer Captain." replied Zaclin. "It is a design and software that I haven't come across before. One more thing if you will." Zaclin motioned to Crew Person Pralon and together they walked a few paces back down the corridor to the windows lining the rest of the corridor.

"Show the captain, Pralon."

Pralon indicated for Xaoping to look out, then she dimmed the section lights to a quarter intensity. Xaoping looked out but apart from stars there was only flotsam of a fine nature within a metre of the ship's hull, seemingly held within the liquefied space surrounding the ship.

Lots of it, however.

Zaclin spoke. "Something tried to dock with us, but it would appear to have been destroyed when the ripples struck."

"A rescue mission?" Xaoping asked hopefully.

"Possibly, but whatever happened I don't think the other ship survived based on that debris field." Zaclin replied.

The Last Voyage of the StarVista 4

"I concur." Xaoping looked thoughtful then came to a decision. "Carry out a full surface status check to ensure we haven't lost integrity."

"Aye Sir." Zaclin and Pralon responded. Captain Xaoping turned to Dr Sreisse.

"Have your team take this person to the medical bay, try to stabilise him and see if you can get him to talk. I want answers, understood?"

"Yes Captain."

"And another thing. Not a word to anyone else about our unexpected visitor."

Xaoping knew it was a lot to ask of them and left them to head for the command centre bridge with a heavy burden weighing upon her.

#

Three hours later Graylor entered Xaopings briefing room and the weary captain indicated for her to sit and report.

"Dr Sreisse has given me a preliminary report on our stowaway. He cannot explain it, but one moment the person is fine, next he is convulsing in agony and the medical bay instruments cannot detect him."

"You mean detect what's wrong with him."

"No, I really do mean they cannot detect his body or him at all for a few short minutes. It is unheard of. However, there is something that is equally strange. In the rare lucid moments when he can speak, he seems to suggest we are *missing*."

"Missing for five weeks, then yes. But it is he who is missing a spaceship."

The Last Voyage of the StarVista 4

"We have no idea what he means as he does seem delirious.

Of course, we are missing in one sense, we cannot leave so have not arrived back at Viliak StarPort Shalaiq so it is natural to assume they know we are in trouble.

But the authorities knew we were heading here so how hard can it be to find us?"

"True Graylor, my dear friend and colleague. What I can't fathom is how our 'guest' managed to find us and indeed attempt entry without us knowing or detecting his approach. Clearly it is very dangerous otherwise his ship would still be out there docked with us.

How did he dock with that liquefied space around us if we can't get out through it? I understand from Chief Coaraskk he has made no progress with either the engine fault or understanding what the 'liquified space' is that surrounds us. It is all very worrying, and I don't like not having answers."

"I agree, however there is one possible outcome that does not seem to have transpired."

"I don't follow you."

"Officer Carson's comments when we first encountered the ripples. He rather nervously postulated that the ripples reminded him of the strange custom his species had of catching the aquatic creatures of his planet using a line and hook. The ripples reminded him of us perhaps being caught on such a hook."

"Oh yes, I remember it now. Well, if there was someone or something doing this to us, I would have thought they would have reeled us in by now, don't you think?"

Graylor just stood for a few moments looking thoughtful.

"Probably, unless they have some strange plan for us. However, this is speculation… we've had no other indication of any other ship nearby as best we can tell, although the liquefied space is affecting all our readings."

Xaoping nodded and using a right second tentacle, gently prodded Graylor on her arm. "Make sure officer Carson doesn't remind anyone other than us of his original thoughts. I won't have rumours flying around or any more trouble on this ship if I can help it."

Graylor smiled grimly as she tried not to think of the possibilities of either mutiny or another riot by some passengers breaking out. She bowed her head and left Xaoping to her own thoughts.

The Last Voyage of the StarVista 4

A sudden emergence...

Captain's Report: Cantrara system extended stay: two months.

It has now been two Terran months since we found ourselves trapped in orbit around Tianca. Many passengers and indeed some crew have become restless and I have had to ask Chief Security Officer Zaclin to maintain strict order and prevent any riots. Chief Coaraskk and his team remain unable to explain our predicament which does not help with calming the fears and anxieties of everyone on board.

We have made no progress with our unexpected guest and he is confined to medical, but appears in no fit state to talk or explain who he is and how he managed to get on board. We have not been able to access his identi chip and Chief Coaraskk is becoming convinced the Alteran is from the future, of all things.

I can't have wild speculation at a time like this. In the occasional moments of clarity, the stowaway appears to be saying the StarVista 4 has been missing for decades but he rarely stays conscious for more than a few seconds, so it is extremely frustrating for Dr Sriesse to make headway in understanding what the problem is with the Alteran.

So for now his presence has been kept from the passengers and the majority of the crew until we can discover more about our unwanted guest.

We have tried again to push through the strange, liquefied space that surrounds but to no avail.

I do fear for our future and worry that we may reach a point where the passengers finally take things into their own hands.

What is so very strange is that no other ship has come to our aid despite us being missing for such a long time. Our extra visit to Tianca was supposed to have only lasted a maximum of two Terran days and with a return trip to Viliack, Spaceport Shalaiq of up to eight days, even adding a few extra days leeway, I would have expected rescue ships to have been dispatched once contact was lost. At the shortest interval they would have been here within two Terran weeks. It doesn't make sense."

The chimes sounded and she clicked to receive the call from Graylor.

"Captain, Astrophysicist Crayt and Geophysicist Raskaert wish to see you as soon as convenient?"

"Very well but I doubt they can solve the problem that has vexed Chief Coaraskk and his team all this time, trying to get us free. Send them in now and join us too."

A few moments later both specialists and Graylor stood before Xaoping Shoo who motioned for someone to speak up as the two specialists appeared a little reticent now, they had their audience with the captain.

Crayt was the first to speak up.

"Captain, as you are aware, we were tasked with studying the planet and rings in order to see if we could find anything out that may assist Chief Coaraskk in helping the ship break free.

The Last Voyage of the StarVista 4

There was nothing in our data outwardly to help so after a while, in agreement with the chief, we stopped our studies."

"What?" Xaoping was a little annoyed as she had not ordered them to stop and that neither the chief nor the two now before her had asked for permission to do so.

She waved a tentacle roughly to indicate displeasure and to continue.

Raskaert now spoke up.

"We didn't officially stop but decided to allow our various instruments to continue their scans and it was only an hour ago that I had to call Plep, apologies, Astrophysicist Crayt to say that something had changed."

"It was right in front of us all. But we'd all become bored with it since our entrapment. You see, some of the rings have vanished and in rapid time too."

"And...?" Xaoping didn't like being strung along as if it were a game.

"Well, we can't explain where or what has happened to the rings that have vanished. But the speed of them doing so gives us cause for concern and may explain why we can't communicate or receive anything from the GAA." continued Crayt. Raskaert saw the frustration building on the captain's face and butted in.

"Time for us is moving slower than outside the jellified space. Hence, we see things speeded up. Another thing that is now blindingly obvious is the few subtle storms we detected on approach and initial orbit, they don't exist either."

"Or rather, if we are slow then outside will appear fast to us and the planet's rotation, not just on its axis, but its orbit around Cantrara is so speeded up it has blurred any features." added Crayt before continuing, now with more enthusiasm. "Plus, the time effect must be linked to the orbital period of the planet which is why to us the stars have not changed."

"Barely," chimed in Raskaert.

"Well, yes, there is a very small shift. Captain we've possibly been out here for... years..." Crayt trailed off letting it sink in.

"Now look, I have utmost respect for your professions, but this is preposterous. I can't tell everyone we may have stuck out here for years! We've got growing unease as it is, can you imagine what would happen if the passengers, and indeed some of the crew would do if they thought we'd been out here for such a long time? Think of the effect on them and the implications, family members outside could have passed away."

Captain Xaoping Shoo then did something that neither of the specialists had ever witnessed before, she rolled each eye and fixed them both with an eye each in a disconcerting stare. "Does this help us to escape or not?"

"Crayt and Raskaert looked at her and shook their heads slowly.

"I thought so. Continue your studies but only report to myself or Graylor and not a word to anyone else at all. Understood? Dismissed. Graylor stay with me for a debrief."

The two scientists departed and as the door closed Xaoping looked at Graylor.

"What do you think?"

"Seems far fetched but both are experts in their fields and, well now they have mentioned it I can't remember how many rings the planet was supposed to have. There were several main broad rings at slightly different tilt to each other and tens of thousands of ringlets and small-scale structures. If such features are no longer visible, then at some point someone less qualified may well make the discovery if it is true and then we will be in serious trouble."

"My thoughts too, Graylor. My thoughts too."

#

Captain's live Report: Cantrara system extended stay: five months.

"This is the captain speaking. This is to advise that there is no concern about our provisions. StarVista fleet ships can all stay in space for over a Terran year and we have provisions to last longer than that as we always restock at all our primary stop-off starports during our voyage.

I emphasise that we can out last anything that this planetary system can hit us with, as the last five Terran months have shown.

Our specialist teams monitor the ripples but have detected a lessening of their strength which we may be able to take as a good sign that the effect holding the ship will also decrease and so allow us to escape.

The Last Voyage of the StarVista 4

We continue to broadcast distress beacons and messages and have no power problems, so will continue to honour requests to send messages back to our loved ones.

We still have no indication that any of the messages have escaped from the strange form of space that we are trapped in and have no explanation as to why no one has come to our rescue. We must hope that nothing has happened to the Galactic Arm Association whilst we have been entrapped here at Tianca.

We have not been able to find an explanation of why four of Tianca's larger rings have vanished and I urge you to keep a vigilant eye on the remaining rings. Please inform our newly formed science teams if you see anything out of the ordinary, especially if it appears connected with either the ship or the ring system. They will liaise with Astrophysicist Crayt, Geophysicist Raskeart and Chief Engineer Coaraskk.

I have good news about our little 'star' Cherice. As many of you are aware she was taken poorly a week ago after one of her lovely singsongs, but she is now back on her feet and determined to give another performance in a few days' time if her parents approve. I'm sure you will all wish her good health, and you will agree with me that she is a shining example of her species. Her parents can be very proud of her.

I will give another update either in a few days' time or if our circumstances change I will immediately inform you.

Captain Xaoping Shoo, out."

The Last Voyage of the StarVista 4

Xaoping looked tired and Graylor had to admit that they were all feeling the strain. The captain and she were in engineering with Chief Coaraskk when Ambassador Richmond had sought them out due to a large number of passengers beginning to question if the food supplies would hold out.

Food supplies, she mused. They were the last thing to worry about as they were almost totally self-sufficient. Indeed, the resupply stops were only for some of the more exotic items to ensure they could cater for everyone's and every species particular tastes, but the vast majority of food stuffs were grown and processed in the bowels of the ship with the various hydroponics labs.

Graylor quietly spoke to her.

"Captain, I'm getting very odd reports that some passengers and crew have experienced, well, how to put this, they seem to be having paranormal experiences…"

"Graylor, this is no time for silly pranks, surely the situation is bad enough without this form of hysteria creeping in."

"Agreed, but the ones reporting the events are quite sober and all describe the same thing. It is as if there are other people on board who can only occasionally be seen, heard or in one case felt. Chief Coaraskk here has a theory.

"Well, get to the point Coaraskk."

The captain's tone was a clear sign the strain was getting to her.

The Last Voyage of the StarVista 4

"It is a long shot, but what if, what if we are stranded, caught between our normal space time and some other space time and the ripples indicate we are in flux?"

"You've been talking to Crayt haven't you. Mentioned something similar a few days ago but I wouldn't hear of it. GAA science has never broken that barrier so why would it happen here of all places?"

"I don't have an answer but if we are slipping between different universes then perhaps the feelings of ghostly occurrences may actually be other people who happen to be in the same place of intersection between them. They may actually be looking for us…"

The intercom chimed and Xaoping shook her head and clicked to receive.

"Captain, we have another possible ripple starting in the remaining rings." Delieezas stated over the intercom.

"We'll be right there." Xaoping shot a glance at Graylor and they quickly exited and headed back to the command centre bridge. Graylor took up position next to Delieezas and they all braced themselves as Xaoping went over to the comms station and opened a ship wide universal channel.

"Ripple alert, everyone stay safe and keep still, that's the advice from our medical team, same as all previous events."

Everything shimmered for the umpteenth time, but something was different.

It was Officer Calsohn who seemed to sum it up.

"Anybody feel as though things are not real?"

Delieezas turned and nodded.

"My skin is prickling as if everything around us is charged with static."

"No, I just feel cold but the tips of my tentacles feel a little numb." commented Xaoping.

"I will scan the ship to see if there is anything different in our circumstances at the moment." Calsohn said and began to operate the console. Then he lifted his hands and, frowning, turned to them. "I. I can't seem to operate anything. Nothing is responding and I can't feel the surface and controls, or at least they don't feel 'real'. My fingers touch the surfaces but nothing happens."

Captain Xaoping went to open up the ship wide comms again but likewise could not get anything to work.

"Same here, anybody get anything to work?"

After a few moments of frantic activity the crew had to give up as nothing seemed to function. "I don't understand it. If we can't touch the controls then how can we be still standing? Let alone breathe the air?"

Graylor shook her head and motioned Delieezas to join her but as he stood up, another more violent ripple passed across them and, as they struggled to cope with the pain, five shapes appeared on the bridge out of nowhere accompanied by the most awful screams anyone could imagine…

Coming from the helm station…

To be continued…

The Last Voyage of the StarVista 4

Diary entry supplemental

The Last Voyage of the StarVista 4

Return transmissions from Daniel Richmond since final entry from Cherice Richmond, StarVista 4.
Note none have been acknowledged as received.

Day 197

Hi Cherice, little sis! I thought you would be in touch by now? How was that extra place they added to your voyage? I bet it was exciting? You will all be pleased to hear that I have decided not to get back with Carrie as she is apparently *still* seeing someone else, so she can't miss me that much can she! I'm so done with her now!

Looking forward to hearing about your extra stop. Love you, and to Mum and Dad. Bye Sis!

Love Danny.

Day 201

Little sis, my sweet little sister. The authorities are saying something has happened to the communications on the ship and that you will be in touch soon.

I am puzzled though as my Ziancan roommate also has family on the ship and she hasn't received any messages from her folks either, so I'm a bit worried. How does a big ship like that lose contact with anyone? Call soon won't you? Love you, tell Mum and Dad I love them too as well!

Bye.
Danny.

The Last Voyage of the StarVista 4

Day 211

Oh Cherice, Mum and Dad! Please don't let it be true. They are saying the StarVista 4 crashed into an unknown icy moon and everyone is lost. Please, please prove them wrong and call me.
    I love you all with all my heart so please, please send me a message. I can't bear the thought of losing you all …

Day 391

I am now sure you will never hear this but I felt I had to send one last message. They held the inquest yesterday and confirmed the loss with all hands of the StarVista 4. On Earth they are calling it the *Titanic affair* and many member worlds of the GAA are demanding to know why your ship was given permission to go to a relatively unexplored and un-vetted destination.
    As you know, I am not a superstitious person but for once in my life I lit a candle for you, Mum and Dad and everyone lost on the StarVista 4.
    This is my last transmission and I hope that you, Mum, Dad and all who sailed on the StarVista 4 are at peace with the universe.
    Bye my loving sister. I will never ever forget any of you.

Year: 2415 AC
    Dear Mum, Dad and Cherice. It is the tenth anniversary since we lost you and I felt the need to send another message.

The Last Voyage of the StarVista 4

We held a memorial service at Viliak, Spaceport Shalaiq and for those who could not attend directly, it was beamed across the whole of the GAA. We have been pressing for a full inquiry into the disaster since the news broke a decade ago, but we feel we are being stonewalled by bureaucracy and red tape.

The Cantrara system is permanently off limits since the accident and no ship is allowed to visit. They say it is to respect all the lives lost on the SV4, but that is hogwash. Very little evidence has been presented that the SV4 was completely destroyed. A few hull fragments and general debris of items that could be personal effects have been shown, but there is nothing to conclusively say they are from the SV4 or anybody on the ship.

The StarVista Corporation has collapsed as an investigation showed that the change to the voyage itinerary was confirmed by the CEO, Crylliac Zelt who committed suicide after receiving so many threats on his life. I don't really know whether to feel sorry for him or good riddance. The corporation saw huge losses as the people of the GAA shunned the company after the disaster and so the remaining five ships have been sold off and now belong to several different companies and given new names.

Anyhow, we will continue to fight for the truth and to ensure you are all never forgotten.

Your loving son and brother.
Daniel Richmond.

Year 2425 AC
Dear Cherice, Mom and Dad.

The Last Voyage of the StarVista 4

Is it really twenty years now? It feels like a life sentence and there is no day that goes by when I don't think of you all. Well, despite all our efforts, I don't think we will ever get to the truth of what happened to the ship and all of you.

The official report states that the strange multi-inclined ring system created an unusual interference that affected the StarVista 4's navigation sensors, which is why it crashed headlong into an uncharted icy moon, destroying both and leaving no survivors.

They say it happened so fast that not a single lifepod was launched and that is also the reason there was no mayday call. Although at your distance no one could have got there fast, the nearest star port was the Spaceport Shalaiq at Viliak. It would have taken several days at high speed to get to the Cantrara system from there for a possible rescue crew, even if they had received a mayday.

The captain and command crew have been vilified by the authorities as it was assumed they did not carry out due diligence on arrival at the Cantrara system. The vast majority of the surviving relatives take that with a large dose of salt I can tell you. I remember you having nothing but praise for them and I have made sure everyone else knows that too.

I married seven years ago, guess what? To Carrie. Her first marriage failed, and they had no children but we accidentally met up and had a long chat about our time together when I was at university and we just hit it off again. I guess we're more mature now.

We have a son and daughter, Carl and Natalie, yes, I know, your names, Mum and Dad.

The Last Voyage of the StarVista 4

We wanted to honour you, so we also gave Natalie a middle name, after you Cherice. At first, I wasn't sure about doing that but now it feels a fitting way to remember you all.

Life is OK, we live on Alteran but have a home on Earth as well, so we spend a year on each at a time as I can work via hyperbeam for my company. Carrie also works locally at the GAA interspecies medical facility, and we both look after the kids in turns, so life is very flexible.

Well, guess that's it for now. Not sure if I'll send another message but then again I said that many years ago and here I am, so we shall see.

Love and miss you all forever.
Daniel.

Year 2435 AC

Hello again. I didn't think I would do this but hey ho here I am again. Three decades! Carl is dating a Scorron, who would have thought it! Natalie Cherice is just finishing school and deciding on university, either at Zianca or Nissallia, as she is hooked on ancient history of the early species that formed the GAA. Carrie and I are just happy we have two well balanced offspring but it's only now I realise what you had to put up with, Mum and Dad, when I decided to go to the Alteran University. You have my sympathies, how did you put up with me?

Carrie looks back at the last time she saw you all via holocam when you were first on the StarVista 4 and cries when she sees the recording. She didn't appreciate back then how she was and constantly regrets how indifferent she was at the time.

She's a totally different person now and I think you all would have grown to love her as I have.

On a different note, we keep getting strange reports that an Alteran scout ship managed to get in to the Cantrara system and to the last known location of the StarVista 4 back in 2430. Word on the astro highways is that somehow it was destroyed but that it apparently found the StarVista 4.

All I can say is that some Alteran Astrophysicist, called Armandan Zolic, claims that the StarVista 4 is not destroyed but is trapped in some form of special space and that there is a possibility you may all still be alive.

Many of us think it is not right to get our hopes up after all this time. Too many families across many species from the GAA lost loved ones and it has brought up bad feelings. Some, including myself and Carrie, say that we should let sleeping dogs lie so to speak, not meaning you are dogs of course or that we wish to forget you!

We gather that Zolic of the Alteran Science Foundation is in hiding after receiving death threats from some of the families and that he has now been discredited and his theory debunked. Serves him right for stirring things up again. Well, must go now.

Perhaps send you a message in another ten years?

Danny.

Twenty five years later ...
Year 2460 AC
Hi, well, er, I'm not sure what to really say or how to actually start this. It feels odd but somehow, I think I should continue as they would have wanted it.

The Last Voyage of the StarVista 4

I'm sorry it has been so long, but things haven't been easy. My name is Natalie Cherice Richmond, daughter of Daniel and Carrie and I am forty.

The only surviving member of the Richmond clan as it happens. Mom, Dad, Carl and his wife, Xsriee -bl-fallr were killed by a freak accident whilst on holiday touring the towering waterfalls of Marlt on the planet Plckendar. That was one of your original destinations as I have been reading your diary, Cherice. It seems that you didn't actually get to see it due to a mix up in understanding seasonal variations of the local climate.

My family were taking a similar voyage to the one the ill-fated StarVista 4 was on. It was a ship originally called the StarVista 5 but had been renamed Calixzar. I gather that is the Alteran equivalent of the Earth's mythical Phoenix, I guess, thinking about it, it was appropriate. They visited the towering waterfalls of Marlt which now have a giant elevator that takes sightseers up and down it. Or rather it did …

I think I remember someone saying the Plckendar authorities were in the early planning stage for the elevator proposal when you were visiting. They completed it twelve of our years after you disappeared, and it's never failed.

But three years ago, on our family's voyage something broke away near the top of the falls and rocks fell down and struck the elevator so hard that part of it sheared off and fell almost eighty miles.

The Last Voyage of the StarVista 4

Out of the sixty sightseers on it, only one survived, she's known as the miracle of Marlt now. I lost all my family and so it took me until now to really take stock and try to move on.

Remember from Dad's last message that I was hoping to study ancient civilisations? I eventually went to Nissallia University and I passed my doctorate. On the downside, I was halfway across the GAA from Mum and Dad and I hardly ever saw them, which did cause us some friction.

We were going to meet up after their holiday voyage, but I guess history does repeat itself as Dad never got to meet up with you either. I received the news of the tragedy whilst I was en route to meet up with them at Igrocl, another of your original stopovers.

However, recently things have been a bit strange. I have been recruited by the Security Ministry of the GAA and I am breaking protocol by making this message. We have just spent a few weeks at the Cantrara system, indeed in orbit around Tianca. Someone followed up and 'improved on' Armandan Zolic's theory and they felt the StarVista 4 was indeed trapped in some sort of suspended version of space and that every so many years it reappears for a few hours. We waited but the ship never appeared, so it was considered a failure.

The theory is yet again a false promise, so we have now left the system and are heading back. It's all very secret, so the other surviving families don't know and probably never will.

The Last Voyage of the StarVista 4

I'm still not sure why I was asked to be on the mission, perhaps it is my family connection to the ship, I don't know. I did feel a certain 'connection' whilst at Tianca but, well that is just plain silly of me, isn't it?

So, the official version of events still stands but I have to admit that I felt odd out there. It was as if I was being watched by someone close by. I know, silly me, right? So that's it. I doubt I will leave another message as I don't really know what else to say.

Well, just to add, I look over the family albums now and then but with the loss of my family I find it hard, so forgive me if I don't send any more messages.

I wish I had known you all. It would have been great to have had grandparents and an aunty on Dad's side.

I'm sorry, I knew I would cry whilst doing this but now I understand how Dad felt when he received the news about the loss of the StarVista 4.

I'm going now. Rest in peace all of you, at least I guess you could say you all passed away doing something amazing whilst on holiday and I will remember you all like that.

Cherice, you used to finish many of your messages to my Dad in a special way so here goes...

Byeee..."

The Last Voyage of the StarVista 4

Natalie Cherice broke down and sobbed as her partner and lover, Lariq Siliq, put his arms around her for comfort. He briefly remembered his own uncle Lariq, lost as a crew member on the StarVista 4, whom he was named after, and he remembered the message his uncle had sent about a little girl called Cherice and how much fun she had been on the voyage.

He sighed, took Natalie Cherice by the hand and they headed back to their cabin as the GAA security ship Zal set course and sped out of the Cantrara system, never to return.

The Last Voyage of the StarVista 4

Epilogue
2481 AC
The Hansone family home

Andrew was captivated. Sir Harley Ryker-Smyth certainly had a way of keeping you entranced with the story, even if there was a chance he would end up agreeing with the official report. Most of these types of programmes led you in one direction building up expectation that something new had emerged and there really was a conspiracy, then they let you down by agreeing with the official line.

Andrew continued watching and was part way through the third segment when there was a light tapping on the door before his step mother entered.

"Hey young man, it's past eleven so come on, stop watching that drivel, turn it off and get to sleep."

"Aww, Mom, it was getting interesting, sounds like there is more to that missing ship than anyone knew."

"Yes, and if that chappie is right then I am a Ziancan Gnat's behind, so enough talk, bedtime. No arguments!"

Andrew slunk down on his bed and reluctantly switched the holoscreen off as his stepmother kissed him lightly on the forehead. She shook her head again then left, turning his light off as she went.

Darkness.

That didn't matter as he had his holo-tablet hidden, so under the bedclothes he set up with his earpiece and dived back into the docudrama.

The Last Voyage of the StarVista 4

"Welcome back fellow space enthusiasts." Sir Harley intoned, "What makes this voyage especially tragic is the unusual presence on board of eight-year-old Cherice Richmond, daughter of, at the time, recently appointed ambassadors of Terra to the Ziancan home world, Carl and Natalie Richmond. Unusual, in that at the time such long duration space cruises for fun were not considered healthy for youngsters. Clearly, strings had been pulled as the new ambassadors would be spending the next ten years of their lives on the Ziancan home planet and Cherice would grow up on an alien world.

To mitigate such a long ambassadorial role the family embarked on a luxury star cruise on what we now know as the ill-fated StarVista 4. But not all the family, for their eldest, Daniel, was in his final year at university and was not given leave to be on the voyage.

How this tragic turn of events would play out is well known to many due to young Cherice sending back regular holo messages to her brother who she idolised. He in turn was heartbroken when fate took a terrible hand and the StarVista 4 was lost."

Images of Cherice Richmond and her family cascaded across the screen and AJ paused several as he looked at the pretty young girl, and instantly fell in love with her, despite knowing they would never meet.

An hour later, his head was swimming with ideas as he fell asleep and despite Sir Harley Ryker-Smyth concluding that indeed the authorities were right all along, something kept bugging him about the facts as he drifted into a deep, star, planet and Cherice filled sleep.

The presence receded, knowing everything was now in place. Andrew James Hansone's fate had been decided that night...

Coming next in:
The Fate of the StarVista 4
Book 2 of the StarVista 4 saga

Andrew James Hansone was by all accounts obsessed.
Widely renowned in the Galactic Arm Association as an exceptional engineer and star ship designer, he had built many fine ships and had become extremely wealthy by GAA standards. Along with it he was also divorced three times. Many said it was his obsession that always got in the way of his relationships, and privately he agreed with the public speculation.

Since a young boy he'd been obsessed with one thing: What *really* happened to the StarVista 4 interstellar cruise ship, lost with all hands in July 2405.

It was now coming up to the 100th anniversary of that fateful final voyage and after years of research and planning, AJ, as he preferred to be called, was going to find it, no matter the cost…

Little does he or the crew of the EXSSV Erebus know, but their 'rescue mission' will have long lasting repercussions on the Galactic Arm Association civilisation as they discover signs of a growing threat against it.

With history between himself and the captain of the Erebus along with a chief engineer who has stalked him without his knowing, AJ will have his hands full as he embarks on his quest…

…to discover *the fate of the StarVista 4.*

Authors Note

The author has always had a love of Science Fiction be it via books by Arthur C Clarke, Edmund Cooper or Ian Banks and Greg Bear amongst many others. Since a child, stories have formed in his head, but he always struggled to get them down or complete any of them which was naturally frustrating.

Having a vague sceptical interest in ghostly goings on, he surprised himself by writing and completing his first full novel: 'A Ghostly Diversion' which for a month was an Amazon teen and young adult bestseller to his surprise and delight. Even more of a delight was the fact that at last he'd broken through a barrier and actually completed a full-scale novel and tied up its loose ends, before long a sequel was produced 'Secrets of Grasceby Manor'. Three more Ghost novels now form the five book 'James Hansone Ghost Mysteries' with more books on the way in the series.

However, this also spurred on the revival of interest in writing science fiction and work began on the StarVista 4 novel which originally encompassed what will now be books 1 & 2 of the 3-part StarVista 4 Saga.

In the meantime, a short novel: 'The Fragility of Existence' was published in early 2019 and is more of an apocalyptic style novel along the lines of H.G. Wells famous classic: The War of the Worlds. Originally a single standalone novel, this now will be a 4-book series with the overall title of 'Fragility of...'

These and future titles now form 'Astrospace Fiction' with all the books published to date having 4- and 5-star reviews (and of course the usual poor ratings from Trolls!).

So do check out the Astrospace web site for more details!

www.astrospace.co.uk

The Last Voyage of the StarVista 4

Astrospace Fiction Newsletter

To keep up to date with the novels written by Paul Money under the Astrospace Fiction banner, then why not sign up to the newsletter.

Those signing up will be the first to receive a *free* mini novel: "Lord Shabernackles of Grasceby Manor".

So, if you want to know more about the James Hansone Ghost Mysteries or the science fiction novels from Astrospace Fiction, such as how to purchase them and where, or when the next book in each series will be released, then simply sign up and you'll be the first to informed. There will also be occasional competitions or a give-away so worth subscribing to see what may be on offer soon. Note your information will not be passed on to third parties.

Just head on over to the following link where you can enter your email to be added to the newsletter list.

Note I will not share your email with anybody, and it is only for keeping up to date with Astrospace Fiction books.

https://mailchi.mp/1c69765ddf7a/jameshansonegm-signup

Best wishes and see you soon: Paul M

The Last Voyage of the StarVista 4

The Fragility of Existence
A Sci-Fi/Apocalyptic tale

The extermination of our species was probably inevitable when you look back with hindsight.
Every advanced civilisation has almost always wiped out the resident less advanced occupants whenever they came into contact.
So it was the same for us, Homo Sapiens.
But it wasn't supposed to have happened.

We were not to know that though.
Perhaps that is a good thing.
For the Universe...

Matt and Simone stared out at the devastation and knew it could only mean one thing... Humanity was about to become extinct.
Could they escape the fate they had seen befall others in their small village of 'Woldsfield'?
They were not going to wait around to find out...

Available on Amazon UK as Kindle, POD and Kindle Unlimited.
First of the 'Fragility of...' series

The James Hansone Ghost Mysteries

It all started with a simple unplanned diversion, *'A Ghostly Diversion'*.

James Hansone is a computer and IT specialist and a complete sceptic when it came to all things paranormal. Until *that* diversion. It changes everything once he becomes intrigued with a ghostly face at a broken window of a rundown cottage, deep in the Lincolnshire countryside. Little did he know that he would go on to uncover the mystery of a missing girl that would change his life forever.

Now with four sequels, James Hansone unwittingly becomes a ghost hunter roped in to explore further mysteries with more books planned in the series.

A Ghostly Diversion
Secrets of Grasceby Manor
Return to De Grasceby Manor
James and the Air of Tragedy
The Haunting of Grasceby Rectory
All available as kindle, print on demand and Kindle Unlimited from Amazon.

Check out Paul's Amazon author page: https://www.amazon.co.uk/Paul-L.-Money/e/B003VNGE1M

<u>Coming soon:</u>
The Fragility of Survival
Book 2 of the 'Fragility of..' series

Holidaying in the Algarve region of Portugal was the norm for Scott, Katrina, Danny and Robyn.

Sun, Sea, Sand and well, yes, Sex, all played a part in their plans, but not necessarily in that order.

And all was going well until the world ended and two of the foursome became trapped in a local cave system, unaware of what was happening to their friends and indeed the world at large.

As they emerge into a desolate landscape, the fight for survival begins…

Coming soon to Amazon as Kindle, POD and Kindle Unlimited.

Coming soon:

Nightscenes: Guide to Simple Astrophotography 2nd edition.

This book fills a space left by many astrophotography books by concentrating on only the astrophotography anyone can achieve with just a camera, set of lenses and a tripod. No telescope or complicated tracking mount required!
Topics covered include capturing: constellations, planets amongst the stars, lunar phases and eclipses, capturing the wonder that is the Northern Lights or Aurora plus lots more that can be achieved with just a basic set up of equipment.

This updated 2nd edition is larger format than its predecessor and includes many new images and new sections covering processing and smartphone astrophotography.

The Last Voyage of the StarVista 4

Coming soon to Kindle and Print on Demand via Amazon UK.

About the Author

Paul L Money is an astronomy, writer, public speaker, publisher and occasional broadcaster. He is also the Reviews Editor for the BBC Sky at Night magazine and for eight years until 2013 he was one of three Astronomers on the Omega Holidays Northern Lights Flights.

He is married to Lorraine whose hobby/interest is genealogy/ family history. As an astronomer Paul has been giving talks across the UK for over thirty years and was awarded the Eric Zuker award for services to astronomy in 2002 by the Federation of Astronomical Societies. In October 2012 he was awarded the 'Sir Arthur Clarke Lifetime Achievement Award, 2012' for his 'tireless promotion of astronomy and space to the public'.

His first novels were ghost stories: 'A Ghostly Diversion' followed by the sequel, 'Secrets of Grasceby Manor', then 'Return to De Grasceby Manor' followed in 2019 with 'James and the Air of Tragedy' in 2020 and 'The Haunting of Grasceby Rectory in 2022 with at least two more planned in the series.

The Last Voyage of the StarVista 4

A first foray into the realms of Sci Fi saw the publication of a shorter novel, 'The Fragility of Existence' in early 2019, a version of the 'end of the world' stories that seem popular. 'Fragility of Survival' is coming soon and is a standalone novel with 2 more in the 'Fragility' series in development.

'The *Last* Voyage of the StarVista 4' is the first novel to take place in the Galactic Arm Association (GAA) Universe and several more are planned, one ('The Fate of the StarVista 4') will be a sequel to this book whilst a third (The Legacy of the StarVista 4) will follow in due course. Another novel almost fully written (*'This New Horizon'*) will be the first of another trilogy whose story will eventually link up with the saga begun with 'The *Last* Voyage of StarVista 4'.

More info can be found at the Astrospace web site:
Astrospace/ Astrospace publications
http://www.astrospace.co.uk

November 2021/March 2023

Printed in Great Britain
by Amazon